A

Dark

Harvest

By
Stephen C. Bibler

First Paperback Edition

10987654321

Library of Congress Control Number: 2021903842

ISBN: 978-1-7367490-0-5

Acknowledgments

Errol Lincoln Uys, whose work, *Riding the Rails: Teenagers on the Move During the Great Depression*, Routledge, Taylor and Francis Group, N. Y., N. Y., 2003, is fat with history and imagery and inspired how I visualized the Great Depression. For that I am grateful.

I would also like to acknowledge the people who assisted in the production of this book, the readers who gave feedback, proofread, and edited. I am indebted to all of you. Any errors that remain—historical, creative, and grammatical—are mine.

For my children;
Emerald, Madison, and Dashiell.
The only thing that gives my life meaning.

A Dark Harvest

1

He was a small man with black round glasses that stood out against his small-boned face. Two vertical creases cut through his cheeks, as if the skin had been clawed, or stretched abnormally over his jaw. Dark blue canvas pants hung large upon his lean frame. He wore brown work boots with thick studded soles, smeared with goose grease to keep out the elements.

A gush of cold autumnal air filled his heavy canvas coat. A chill exploded across his taut lower back, cramping his shivering muscles. From his left coat pocket, he grabbed a bootlace and tied it around his middle.

"One might think I should have learned that lesson," he said to himself as he tied.

The wind, as old and cold as time, whispered down from the farthest reaches of the universe and brushed his cheek. He scratched his chin whiskers and thought on the breeze and what it must have witnessed.

The man pulled up on his pack then tugged at the loose collar ends of his heavy, canvas coat and pulled them together under his chin. Over his left shoulder he spied the eastern sky pooled in misery and black and bruised memories.

The dark path upon which he trod was enveloped in a quiet stillness, like the quiet in the aftermath of a brutal battle, when one is left with his soul scorched, the smell of cordite, and ringing ears.

The terrain rolled west beneath the hardscrabble road. The Sierra Nevada Mountains and infamous Donner party finally at his back, he trod more lightly, as though intruding on something sacred. He stopped and listened to the quiet all around.

He pulled the front of his dusty fedora and reached into his right coat pocket for the last of the dried squirrel meat. He tore off a chunk and stuck it in his right cheek, like chewing tobacco.

He accepted his plight; just one of a multitude of displaced souls who made up the armies of the night perpetually patrolling America's rural rub board roads, continually pulled forward by churning, bitching stomachs.

He walked head down and took notice of the rough road upon which his life was unraveling. He jerked the pack and bedroll that hung loosely over his right shoulder, then grasped his hat and palmed it firmly on the crown of his unkempt head. He sighed.

No lights shone as welcoming beckons on this moonless night. He stopped, held his breath, and listened.

"Finally," he said, tired of jumping off the side of the road every time a carload of damned drunks or vigilante gangs happened by.

A tired-sounding, overloaded, rattletrap of a truck limped up from behind on something less than a full complement of cylinders. Our walking man was sure a piston would shoot through the engine block and hood any second.

He straightened his shoulders and tossed his knapsack and bedroll higher up on his skinny shoulder. His canvas trousers and coat were slick with the filth that time on the road had wrought. His heart quickened.

The veteran pushed his dirty fedora far back on his head to reveal just another good citizen out walking in the middle of God knew where, in the middle of the night. His grimy face was smeared with beard stubble. Creases and facial scars were indistinguishable beneath the road grime. The good citizen smiled, like a used car salesman.

A black oxidized jalopy pulled alongside. The thump of the right, rear wheel slowed against the gravel road. The jalopy and all life disappeared within the truck's blue-grey smoke that engulfed them.

The truck was loaded down with all the junk the family owned. A goat, in a narrow slatted pen, was lashed to the passenger side door. On top of the truck's burden, the bodies of four weary children slept under sheets of canvas and green wool army blankets. On the tailgate of the jaded jalopy, three empty five-gallon tin cans, as empty as the travelers' stomachs, awaited something—anything.

Old rubber tires had been sliced and laid one on top of the other with care, then wired together around the circumference of the truck's wheel.

For two days the driver had stopped every few miles to rewire the strips of rubber to the vehicle's rim from a partial roll of baling wire he and his family had earned a month earlier from a day's labor on a dairy farm.

"Sweet Jesus! Do ya think someone should pull the fire alarm?" the walking man said with a smile, wanting to appear as affable as possible.

"Where ya headed, friend?" the man's tired voice asked across the sleeping corpses of his wife and newborn child.

"Anywhere that isn't here," our man said, waving the smoke away with a grin that showed remarkably white teeth.

"I ain't got any room on top. Kids is sleepin'. You got any money?"

"Not much, but if we can find work, I'll be happy to pay you your due, sir." The walking man held his smile an inordinately long time while the driver thought that through.

"Good enough, partner," the man reckoned, scratching the side of his noggin. "Ya can ride the front fender and hood there." A half-extended finger pointed from the end of a half-extended right arm. "As long as she stays on." And he meant that.

The walking man looked askance at the fender.

"Thanks! Much obliged. Name's George."

George placed his bindle above the area of the hood through which he suspected the piston would blow. He tipped his hat and eased his cold, tired body onto the warm hood of the faded black truck. He lifted his left leg onto the hood of the old heap. His right leg rested where the too-loose running board met the right fender, just in front of the goat pen. He grabbed hold of the back edge of the truck's hood with his left hand and felt the warmth billowing from under the hood. His other hand grasped the topmost forward board of the goat's pen.

Leaning back, he asked, "Say, what are you charging me for this buggy ride?"

"Half of whatever you make the first day," the driver said dryly. "Name's Otis. A pleasure."

George slowly turned to face the dark road ahead and pulled his fedora off against the chilling wind, then stuffed it inside his coat without care. Within a moment the chill pinched his cheeks. Tears welled up in his eyes. His primitively cut hair blew behind him in the cold air. Nothing was clear.

Fat was scarce on George, always had been. He had the flexibility and stamina of a marathon runner. Riding the truck's fender was easier than expected, but the chill, even at this reduced speed, was harsh. He tried not to think about it. Tears ran down his cheeks. Everything ahead, within the lights of the old heap, was a blur.

In his pack, George carried an envelope with identifying documents and a few photographs from his youth. An old daguerreotype, with silver plating worn thin, exposing the copper plate beneath, showed his parents in austere pioneer poses.

His mother and father were positioned on a Victorian stage. George's mother looked nervous as it was her first time in front of one of those new cameras. His father looked impatient and was unsociable with the effeminate photographer. George's big-breasted mother, with long dark hair pulled into a tight bun on top of her head, was sitting ramrod straight and held her son, George, swaddled in a blanket of mink pelts. Her thin lips revealed a chiseled sternness associated, by women of large cities, with a hard-as-nails prairie woman. White ruffles blossomed around her masculine face and above her black dress.

His father wore a brand-new tie, his first. One mud-covered boot stuck out from behind the velveteen chair on which his wife sat with the baby. George suspected the photo was taken in the late winter or early spring.

His father's nervous fingers, like sausages, fumbled with his wolf-skin cap. In the crook of his arm he held a long rifle used for taking down big game with one shot. He wore a cape of bearskin. His face was covered in full beard streaked with white. His hair was ponytailed, Indian style. Three long scars ran from his forehead, across his left eye to his ear. A bear mauling few had the privilege of recounting. The couple's eyes had been colored in with black ink.

Another photograph, a modern sepia on thick cardboard, with a dirty, white embossed border showed George with two pals on the deck of a U. S. Navy transport ship docked at some indistinguishable Philippine port.

A German photographer hitching a ride aboard the ship snapped the photo just as they had boarded and after spending the previous four months in the jungle hunting their prey; bandits and Spanish Marxists in what would become known as the Banana Wars. When not in the jungle fighting, or on-board ship headed to some other jungle to murder their enemies, these warriors were mostly shit-faced drunk.

The three young men in the photo were stripped to their waists. The soldier on the viewer's right, Joseph, wore a campaign hat and was easily the largest of the three and commanded the attention of the viewer. The short, stocky young man in the middle, Bert, sported a tattoo of an eagle with wings spread wide on his chest and down his arms. George, the smallest soldier, on the left, had eyes like two black holes reflecting the pitch of the universe.

Their tanned, youthful stomachs sported braided knots of muscle that became long and sinewy as they began to cover rib. Their biceps were hard as green apples. They wore summer-weight wool trousers wrapped in khaki leggings below the knee and covered the top of their muddy, brown boots. Their bodies, the color of walnuts, had a sweaty sheen under the tropical sun. Star-shaped shrapnel scars, scratches, and knife cuts were barely visible in the photograph.

Colt .45 revolvers hung low from their hips, the handles worn smooth.

George rested the butt of his lever action rifle on his right hip, the muzzle pointing skyward. He carried a straight razor, with celluloid scales, tucked into his right legging. A three-foot long machete with a brown cloth-covered handle was slung over his left shoulder and awaited use. Around his neck he wore a necklace with the ears of his enemy. They would not be hearing the heavens calling them home.

Bert, the bulldog with the eagle tattooed across his chest, rested his repeating rifle in the crook of his arm. A long menacing knife, sheathed in a scabbard, was tied with leather straps and strung across his chest. A fresh wound crusted over on the left side of his mouth giving one the impression of a perpetual smile.

Joseph wedged a double-barreled, side-by-side shotgun, sawed off at about nineteen inches under his right shoulder and over his right forearm. Another shotgun was slung across his back. A long hunting knife, with a bone handle and brass knuckles attached, was strapped to his right calf muscle. No one asked what kind of bone. Stuffed under the belt of his trousers were two trophy scalps.

Atop these youthful Greek-like figures were the expressions of much older, harder men. They were not cocky youths in showy poses, or dandies from the city, but professional fighters—scary Americans with flat, lethal, expressions of salt-crusted veterans just returned from battle, having murdered their enemy deep in a jungle where their parents would never find them.

Otis limped his broken vehicle slowly down the dark road. George looked into the darkness ahead, lost in the reverie of youthful, military adventures.

Baling wire exploded. Strips of rubber and wire slammed against the inside of the wheel well of the old heap of junk. At the sound of gunshot George instinctively ducked his head and searched for the direction of fire.

The truck slowed within seconds of the explosion sending rubber strips flying, spiraling into the night. George climbed off the fender and flexed his cold, stiff hands while Otis limped his weary truck on its hub into the campsite. George followed gathering the rubber strips along the muddy entrance to the migrant camp.

"This might be a blessing, I don't know. Lucky she held out till we got here," Otis said, pushing his hat up and onto the crown of his noggin. He placed both hands over his bony ass.

"Any who, this is as fur as a we're a goin' tonight, I reckon." He looked at the strips of rubber George had recovered. "Damnit!"

"Suits me just fine. Appreciate the ride this far. Where are we?" George asked, not really caring.

"Sacramento, I believe." Otis pointed to the brown haze hanging over the industrial night lights in the distance.

George surveyed the shantytown crafted from scrap wood, cardboard, flattened tin cans, and canvas sheeting.

"Jesus. I thought Sacramento would be nicer than this." The two shared nods and chuckled.

An okra-colored smoke bloomed upward from a brick stack. Acrid rust-colored smoke blossomed from other long-stemmed stacks of nearby factories then blew low across the squatters' camp.

Well-worn, muddy footpaths wound in and out of the migrant camp in all directions. Soiled diapers, wet, yellowed newspapers, and rags were strewn about the camp.

Partially filled pit toilets pocked the level, muddy ground. The corner of a page from *Life* magazine protruded from the edge of a shallow pit. The stink of rot and decay, even during the wet California autumn, was thick and palpable.

The acrid stench of animals marking territory wafted throughout the camp. Feral dogs cowered on the dark fringe of the camp, circling, sniffing, and eyeing perceived danger.

Dogfights broke out over spoiled scraps of food and were settled only when one mangy bitch ran yelping over the mountains of garbage and into the night, tail between her legs.

Vehicles were parked helter-skelter throughout the camp. Small, yellow cook fires licked at the night sky and illuminated the shanties, black automobiles, and tarpaulins stretched from their backs and sides. Dark, splintered shadows showed broken men and shattered women hunched over their menial work. They moved slowly across the canvas and cardboard walls of the Hooverville.

The scene reminded George of the villages in South America and the Philippines where garbage and shit were thoughtlessly dumped in the mud paths in front of huts.

Children cried. It did not matter the reason.

"Where ya from?" Otis asked.

"Originally from Oswego, New York, then Illinois; just south of Chicago. I had a little truck farm."

The two found a place to camp for the night on the darker fringe of the hobo jungle. George made ready his bedroll and watched the couple set up home.

In the truck's headlights rats, with ruby-red eyes, crawled in and out of the garbage of their human neighbors and were not afraid. The driver untied the canvas cover attached to a rail just above the back window of the truck. He staked the two opposite corners, then pulled another canvas sheet off the passenger side rail of the truck. In this fashion the household goods were covered with a little extra canvas off the end and passenger side of the truck for a kitchen, living room, and bedroom.

Otis's wife, like all the rest of the wives George had come across in his travels, was younger than she looked. She was skinny with sagging breasts; oily hair hung loose and sticky around her face. She set up her kitchen and spoke not a word as they went about their business.

There was a system to setting up the campsite that had been repeated day after day, over and over, dozens of times on their odyssey to and from only God knew where, zig-zagging their way across America chasing harvests, trying to put food in their mouths.

First, the fire and a pot of water to boil, then food for the four older children who had been riding atop the family's belongings in the back of the truck. George set a dark blue enamel coffee pot full of water for himself and the family in the young fire. A few tablespoons of this morning's coffee grounds, wrapped in cheesecloth, was all George had left.

The mother held the smallest child in a cloth cradle slung across her breasts and fried flour biscuits in bacon grease in a deep iron skillet. George tried not to stare, but his churning stomach started to howl. The smell! He reluctantly turned away from the aroma of the rue and sausage bits coming to a small boil. He could smell the pinch of pepper and his mouth watered.

"My God!" he thought. "If I could just lick the pan!"

George wondered when he might grab up a handful of dirt and shove it in his own starving pie-hole, like that fellow up in Canada a couple of years back.

Otis looked too old to be father to such young children. He appeared tired. He walked with a slight stoop and there was something amiss with his left leg, George thought. Their travail had lasted many years now. The man was wearing down. The children were anemic with sallow cheeks and straggly hair. They had not attended school in years. The baby was fussy. The family seemed to be continually whipped down life's rough road by hunger.

George had seen starvation before with its continual diarrhea and lethargy. Old, worn-out clothing hung on all. They would not admit defeat, but they were starving.

The town's people did not want these filthy road urchins near their own children.

The people in the cities and towns were tired of the sickness the migrants brought, of the continual want on their faces, and of their own guilt for not caring enough to want to help.

"Their filthy little hands always wanting more; it's just depressing having to look at them."

"God only knows what kinds of diseases they carry. The little gypsies."

Supper was served up for the skinny children. The adults had two biscuits each, with gravy. George savored every bite.

Otis talked of their home and the circuitous route which had landed them in this dark port tonight.

"Dry farmed oats and wheat back in Kansas, Nebraska, finally Eastern Colorado," he said. "Seems, every time we moved it was worse off than the place we just left. Eastern Colorado was like hell, man. I'm not kiddin'."

"Anyway, the gove'ment man say, 'grow more, earn more,' so we did."

George stoked the campfire to warm the children and listened to Otis's lament. George then sat and licked the gravy off his spoon and wiped the enamelware with his finger.

"Problem was, the topsoil blew away," Otis said. "No water, no rain. And the damned winds never stopped blowin'. Ya know what happened?" he asked rhetorically. "That damned gove'ment man come in and tol' me an' all my neighbors, the ones I was growin' the oats for, and tol' us, 'Ya'll, we gotta kill all them aminals you a keepin',' he says. 'It'll drive the price of beef and pork up,' gove'ment man says."

"Well, of course the gove'ment came in and done what they said they was a goin' ta do. It was the craziest damned thing I ever saw," Otis said.

He rubbed his dirty hand on his beard and stared into the campfire reflecting on the day he saw starving men shooting beef cattle and burying them in pits. "Millions of them, man! People were starvin' too!"

"Then I couldn't get a loan, cause the banker already knowed there weren't gonna be no one to sell my goddamn oats to! They done killed all the damned cows and pigs!" Otis yelled.

"The bank took the farm?" George asked.

"Oh, hell yes! Sonsabitches couldn't wait to kick us off our land. The land they couldn't wait to sell us. The same damned land no one else wanted! What the hell were they gonna do with the land? Nothin'! The ignorant bastards!"

"Never saved a penny. Each year's profits went for the next year's guano and seed."

Otis staked the last tent pole with two angry blows from the handmade, wooden mallet. "Wanna know somethin' really crazy?" Otis asked.

George moved in.

"That banker that threw us off our land?"

"Yeah?"

"Killed hisself about a month later." Otis shook his head, slowly. "Seems even he couldn't make no sense out of all the new gove'ment regulations either. How 'bout you?"

"Same story," George said.

After biscuits and coffee George and Otis talked to other men in the camp about finding work. It became apparent to both men as they walked the muddy path that the Hooverville was sitting on the city's dump. They stopped at an intersection where three muddy paths merged and looked around.

"Funny thing is," Otis continued with his story from supper, "the banker kept sayin' 'you gotta get bigger. You gotta get bigger if you're gonna make it.'" "Sonofabitch!" Otis complained. His fists lashed out at his invisible demon.

"A feller needs to decide for himself what "makin'" it is before he sets out to make it, by God! We was happy before the banker and gove'ment men got us bigger. The gove'ment should never done that to us."

"Man gets a job with the gove'ment, all the sudden he's smarter than you. Makes decisions on your life and you don't get any say so. He's never affected by his own orders. He doesn't have to take responsibility if it all goes to hell."

"Seems to me country people are simple, maybe not big on book learn' and so the answers to their questions ought to be simple too. Killin' cattle and pigs to make them scarce just don't seem right, not in my pocketbook, not with my God. Maybe I'm not a smart man though. Gove'ment makes life so complicated a man can hardly breathe."

"Kind of like trying to breathe during one of those dust storms." George said. "Hey!" He stopped and held up his arm to halt Otis's rant, "Look at the wheels of these jalopies. They're all sinking into the mud."

"They ain't been moved in a while." Otis said.

The two came upon a man sitting alone, staring into his camp's small fire. The man was dirty from his greasy, sparse hair to his muddy boots. His overalls were slick from living out of doors. He had no coat to protect himself from the damp, night fog. He wore only a thick shirt missing all the buttons and worn through the left elbow. He sat on a large round river rock, but there was no river in sight.

Squealing rats fought a few feet away, confounding the man's wretched thoughts. He glanced up at the two strangers with tired, red eyes and a filthy face that had not seen a razor in weeks. His eyes returned to the fire in search of answers that would never come.

"Is this here Hooverville as good as the livin' gets in this here sunny California?" Otis asked.

The man's gaze never drifted from his small warming fire. "You just ain't never been to Marysville, is all. Have ya?"

"No, sir. I haven't." George interjected.

"Well, this here place ain't so fuckin' bad."

"What folks paying around here?" Otis asked.

"Christ sakes, man!" the man yelled. He looked up from his inward pain.

"Payin'? They ain't a payin' nothin' so's you can survive on. My boy took sick the other day in Marysville and they kicked us out of the camp where we was stayin'. Six years ol'! So, we brought our boy here, to Sacramento."

"Do ya know what them damn people in town said? 'We cain't hep ya. Y'all ain't from around here.' So, my boy dies while those sonsabitches in Sacramento go home to their nice warm homes, an' food, an' clean beds."

The man's glare returned to the little fire, lamenting, "It ain't damn fair!"

Then looking at Otis and George again, "Do they think we's animals? I'm a man, by God! Jus' like them! What could it possibly cost them to help my little boy?" The man returned to the flames and rubbed the heels of his palms together. "I was told, 'We won't have a truck out there 'til tomorrow morning,' the man says!"

"Motherfuckers!" He spat. "That was three damned days ago!"

The man pulled his scalp back with both hands and slicked down his oily, thinning hair. He clasped his hands behind his head and bent over to keep from blubbering, like a damn baby again, but began blubbering anyway. With red-rimmed eyes and snot running out of his nose, he looked to George as if possessed by the devil.

A painful, guttural sound rose from deep within the man's contorted face, "I wish I could jus' fuckin' die! Goddamn it all to hell!"

"I'm sorry for your troubles. I wish there was something I could do," George said, looking at the mud between his boots.

Wisps of fog and a dirty yellow smoke crept over the mountains of garbage and continued to settle in the camp.

In the distance a husband and wife argued about money. Pots and pans clanged together throughout the camp. Hungry babies continued to cry.

The man sitting on the river rock jerked his thumb back and forth, like a hitchhiker, "Ya wanna help?" he asked. Pointing toward the shanty tied to the back of his jalopy, "Help her, for Chris' sake! I cain't fuckin' do nothin' no more!"

George walked to the vehicle, no more than ten feet away. The heap of junk sat on flattened tires; the rims had disappeared into the mud. He looked back to Otis. George knelt down and pushed the canvas cover of the shelter aside.

The stench was overwhelming. He drew back from the opening to catch his breath and to let the foul tent air dissipate into the night. George looked to Otis again who frowned and lowered his shaking head. George covered his face with the crook of his elbow and took off his hat. He crawled into the shelter.

The man's wife appeared young. The weight of her difficult life and her suffering was apparent to George. He guessed she had aged many years within the past few months.

"Ma'am," George said, placing his hand on her shoulder. "Can I get you some water?"

She stared straight ahead. Her hair, rolled into a bun on the back of her head days before, had fallen. Long bangs hung below her dirty chin and framed her face. Something, maybe a cross on a chain, hung from her neck and was held between her lips.

George could see the young boy's body had stiffened. He was a mess of evacuated shit and urine within the overalls that would be his burial clothes. George felt a sharp pain in his chest and bit into the sleeve of his coat. He reached for the lady's arm. She stiffened against his touch. Her eyes remained fixed. George tried to imagine how this woman's life had culminated with her sitting in a shit-strewn city dump cradling her dead son.

"It's all right now." George finally said. "Your little man . . . he no longer exists in this little bit of clay. Your little boy is safe and warm with Jesus."

She paid the stranger no attention.

"He's warm and has a full stomach, now." George whispered to the lady. "Yes, praise the salvation that is my sweet Jesus. Let's lift him up together. Let's let him be happy. Yes, sweet Jesus. Let's let him go home warm and with a full stomach, okay?"

There was movement from neither the woman, nor George. They sat, each at their own end of the universe. George again touched the lady's arm. She still resisted. George tried to appeal to her again, speaking softly.

"How about we get you cleaned up, hmm? I'll bet you could use some hot food too."

"His pain is finally gone. Let's help you over your pain now, okay?"

After a moment she relaxed against George's hand and finally released the young boy's stiff corpse. "There you go. Let him go now. That's it. Let me help you," George whispered.

George brushed back the canvas tent opening on his knees; Abraham offering up Isaac. The mother burst into tears and fell to her side.

The boy's father jumped to his feet and approached George with outstretched arms. The man's face contorted and wrinkled and did not look like a face at all.

"My baby!" he cried in a high whine as his boney knees sank into the mud in front of George.

"Thank you, mister," the man sniveled. "She wouldn't let me have him! I'm tellin' ya, I tried! She just wouldn't let me have him," he whined.

"I'm tired of fightin' her and all of it." The man convulsed, then dropped his head to the ground and wept over his son's little body.

George and Otis stood by fumbling with their hats. Finally, the father rose and took his little boy to the back of the vehicle where the family's clothing, blankets, everything they owned was stored. The father placed the little boy's body on his green blanket.

"What's his name?" George asked.

"Paul."

The father carefully wrapped his boy in the blanket and tucked the blanket under his chin. He then kissed him on the forehead.

The two strangers silently disappeared into the evening's fog. They crossed the dump to their campsite and spoke not at all.

Otis went to his family and hugged each of his children hard, then made ready for bed. Under their tarp, the mother would sleep on one side, the father on the other. The children snuggled down between their parents. They slept in their clothes and covered themselves with the wool army blankets, then the sheet of canvas.

George unrolled his bedding atop a long piece of carpet and sat, rump down, on his blankets. He pulled his boots off and looked into the night fog and tried to imagine himself on his front porch, reading by the light of his lantern.

George tied his boots to a strap underneath his knapsack that would serve as his pillow and which held all his belongings. He pulled and tossed his wool blankets until they covered his stockinged feet. He laid back, hat pulled over his face, and within a breath or two, his face felt warm once again. He rolled over on his side and pulled the wool blankets up tight. George placed his hat on his left ear, and thrust his hands deep into the pockets of his coat. His right hand came to rest holding his straight razor.

Throughout the foggy night George was continually awakened by fighting dogs, rats, and the comings and goings of fruit tramps, hoboes, and Okies. He woke once and tossed a couple of pieces of wood on the smoldering campfire.

He heard voices arguing about something down the muddy path. "Must be something important," George thought.

His mind drifted to the poor family who had lost their only child in the city's dump. "My God," he said to no one. He shivered and tried to think happier thoughts, but none came. Finally, his pack became too soft.

There was a sensation of falling and yet nothing by which to judge his descent. George continued to fall and did not care.

Exhaustion cut his lifeline to this world and set his weary soul free. A deep sleep came over him, like the sleep of a tired and thoroughly worn army.

He was home once again, on his front porch. It was an early summer evening and was not yet humid. Various bugs flew in and out of the light of his lantern. George was reading a copy of *The Iliad*, translated by Alexander Pope.

A glass of amber bourbon was set on the small table beside his chair and glistened and sweated with chards of chunked ice from the block cradled in a bed of straw beneath his kitchen floor.

In the middle distance a lone coyote called, begging for a mate. A whisper of cherry blend from George's pipe hung in the air.

He drank in the bourbon and held the cool amber in his mouth, slowly releasing the liquid gold down his throat. He listened to the coyotes just beyond the porch light. *The Iliad* lay open on his lap.

"Any moment might be our last. Everything is more beautiful because we are doomed."

2

It was getting on toward nightfall, late in the sweltering summer of 1901. While serving with an expeditionary force, in some unnamed jungle, George and his fellow soldiers found themselves surrounded by Spanish Marxists, leftist guerrillas, and their native guides.

The American soldiers laid still and listened to the hidden and well-fortified enemy that occupied the high ground on the soldiers' three sides. The ocean was to their rear. The boats that had brought them were long gone. Shrill war cries from the jungle coupled with threats of dismemberment and decapitation of the American expeditionary force.

"We gone cut you head off and use your skull for a bowl, gringo!"

"We gone cut you sack off and use it for tobacco!"

A warning in broken, accented English promised a slow death. The hectoring continued throughout the hot and humid night. Bugs ate at the soldiers' exposed flesh.

George, along with the rest of the small force, said nothing, and did not eat or sleep. Men curled up at the base of banana trees and rocks. Some soldiers lay sprawled on the dark jungle floor concealed by large tropical leaves, or beneath the cover of a fallen tree.

Now and again a shot was fired into their location. Rounds thumped into the fecund soil inches away and all around the soldiers. Sweat soaked uniforms crawled with every kind of insect. Moist, fertile soil stuck to their clothing, skin, and weapons.

Adrenaline coursed through their veins. The intensity of the situation grated against their sense of reason.

A few worried that thin thread of sanity which held them in place might snap. One feared it might be he who would jump up and run screaming into the jungle, only to be hacked down by enemy machetes.

The sweltering night seemed to last forever beneath the jungle's canopy. Men aged years in those horror-filled nights they would relive in their sleep for the rest of their lives.

A primal clarity came to the minds of those fighting for their survival. Senses were stripped raw; smells intensified, vision sharpened, hearing piqued to the single drop of dew as it splashed on a broad banana leaf somewhere in the dank, black jungle. One's heart idled at a much greater rate, as an athlete before a competition. A soldier's body shook uncontrollably.

Was it his primal urge to flee when we saw the boxer's knees shake when he first entered the ring? Or was it the man's primal urge, as predator, to leap upon his prey that made his knees shake uncontrollably in anticipation of the impending bout?

Blessed be the Lord, my rock,
Who trains my hands for war,
And my fingers for battle.

In the grey predawn light a highly choreographed chaos was unleashed on the leftist fighters.

The commander ordered, "Kill anything that moves!" And they did. Forty-two American soldiers set out after their prey.

The young, enthusiastic warriors ran, jumped, fired, and fell on their enemy in all directions. Now was the time for these soldiers to exact a maneuver, uphill, that would not be discussed outside that bloody jungle.

Blue-grey smoke rings emanated from the shotgun's muzzle. Joseph's side-by-side shredded foliage and tore gapping wounds in the jungle and those who stood veiled behind the large banana leaves thinking themselves untouchable.

George said to his sergeant. "See ya on the other side, sarge." He then jumped into the black hole. Bert scampered through the opening, followed by Joseph as he reloaded.

Into the rabbit hole, they called it, referencing Sherman's march on the South. Soldiers plowed through the jungle like tractors.

Close to mid-morning the American soldiers began to run out of ammunition. The fighting then became mixed in close, hand-to-hand combat. Blades were pulled and glinted in the hot sun. Within moments their long knives dripped with blood.

George pulled a straight razor from his legging, the blade running along the outside of his right fist. Others used bayonets to thrust into the bellies and ribs of their enemy or the backs of those who dared to escape.

A head was nearly severed from its body as Bert reached from behind, a handful of hair, then drew his long knife across his enemy's throat.

As ammunition ran out rifles became clubs, revolvers hammers to bash in the skulls of those who taunted them in the night.

There were no wasted moves. The soldiers reacted as charging lions. A soldier hacked away with his entrenching tool; the blade angled at ninety degrees. Another soldier leapt upon his enemy and with his rifle butt smashed the head of his adversary, as if breaking open a gourd back home in his garden for its seeds.

George sliced from left to right and did not wait to see the guerrilla's entrails fall to the jungle floor. George swiftly ducked and came up behind another Marxist and slit his throat from spine to Adam's apple.

Joseph rammed his knife into the belly of his enemy, driving his knife into the man's heart and lifting him off the ground. Joseph threw the body away and drove his knife through another man's neck and into his chest.

By noon, sweet enemy blood streamed down the mountainside. Quiet fell upon the jungle. The soldiers were left with only their thoughts and the familiar smell of battle coupled with their ever-present ringing ears. Fatigue had yet to set in. Like rainwater, sweat and blood spatter ran off chins and elbows, the adrenalin rush, the inner hum, still not satiated.

Soldiers congregated around their commander just off the top of the ridge they had won. The squad leaders reported no deaths and only a few lacerations from the close-in fighting.

"Scratches they can show their grandchildren." Joseph said, as he concentrated on sewing a few crude stitches into the forehead of one of his men.

"Sorry 'bout that nip on your noggin," he said, pulling the stitch tight, "It's not good to get too close to me when I'm workin'. I get so boiled up I swing on anything 'at moves."

The soldiers stood or knelt down on one knee in their sweaty, mud, and blood-soaked uniforms, waiting. A soldier straightened his uniform where the enemy had latched on, pleading in a last desperate act to survive.

With a blood-spattered face, the commander stood amongst his men, assessing the toll the battle had taken. The major raised the forward receiver group of his broken rifle by the barrel, the butt of which had been torn loose in a hellish clubbing. Blood and grey matter stuck to his neck, face, and uniform. He looked from one man to another. His nostrils flared and a snarl grew where his thin, closed mouth had been. His chest heaved in the humid air. Those not tending to others nodded. What words would suffice?

Men's souls were branded during those hot, sweltering days in the jungle by the actions that seared them to the very marrow of their essence. In that sweltering jungle, during the hand-to-hand combat, a few made promises to their God.

A veteran might jump with such a start as to awaken his wife's soft slumber. Asked what was the matter, the veteran would say it was just a bad or silly dream and not to worry. He would then lie still and watch the night turn to grey, unable to sleep, his skin clammy, brows furrowed beneath pained eyes in the twilight. Knotted and sweat-soaked sheets clenched, unconsciously, in his tightened fist.

The Spanish-American War, short as it was, with campaigns that extended from Cuba to the Philippines, ended America's first overseas military adventures. George and his fellow soldiers were discharged from the U. S. Army and went their separate ways.

The soldiers would, for the rest of their lives, remember their adventures hunting and finally capturing Aguinaldo, bringing the insurrection to an end. They would never forget their brave Macabebe Scouts.

Joseph and Bert were neighboring farmers back in California's San Joaquin Valley. George would return to Illinois for no particular reason other than that was where he had buried his parents after an outbreak of typhoid.

George planned to write of his experiences riding with Teddy Roosevelt and his hard-charging Rough Riders during the Spanish-American War. George, Joseph, and Bert were with the first American military unit to set foot on foreign soil; U.S. Army's murderous 22nd Infantry Regiment. Later, George would write about chasing Aguinaldo through the Philippines, the battles, and finally capturing him.

The American soldiers held images that could never be forgotten. When the soldiers reunited in the coming years, they would speak of their adventures with each other. With friends and family, the stories of their combat experiences within the dark and steamy jungles would be shared, never.

3

The U. S. government owed him no pension or further compensation for his military adventures. After George was discharged from the Army he put all his soldiering money into the down payment on a fallow, ten-acre parcel overgrown with weeds and brush.

The lay of the land, the way it sloped toward the south, the natural wood lot and windbreak on the north and west sides, suited him. The soil was mostly clay with a small patch of loam. That is where George decided the kitchen garden would go. The rest of the buildings, to include George's small home and pens, would be constructed within proximity of the garden.

"This is a damned nice little piece of land. I know you'll make a go of it," the banker said while shaking his hand upon signing the bank loan.

George nodded, ready to be rid of the man.

George planted his garden, then built a henhouse in which he lived until the barn was finished. He enjoyed a solitary life on the southern edge of Chicago, about three miles from the city. There was something about the quiet that made him happy. He loved to sit and listen to nothing.

He often made a pass by the library on his way home from selling produce and flowers in town. He would spend many hours watching the sun rise and set with a library book on his lap and quiet all around.

This small, unassuming man never spoke of his soldiering days. Who would have believed that George, the peaceful, gentleman farmer, had rolled up his sleeves, slit throats, and bashed in skulls with the butt of his revolver? He would continue to live and wrestle with his share of soldiers' nightmares, mostly on those steamy, hot Chicago nights that reminded him of the dark jungles of Cuba and the Philippines.

Once asleep, he might suddenly awaken, heart pounding, by the slightest noise, or by a giant brown face convulsing in the dark. Sweat would run down his face and neck.

George would then start a pot of coffee on the woodstove and light the lantern on his front porch. The veteran would read and drink coffee until the darkness faded into platinum dawn. The sun! Another night endured.

George led a self-sufficient life and had a little money left to put in his savings account at the bank for things he could not manufacture himself or for things for which he could not barter.

His tastes were simple. Popular books, like *The Maltese Falcon*, *Brave New World*, *The Metamorphosis,* and others filled a couple of shelves he had made from leftover barn wood. He sat at his writing table where he practiced writing short stories by his small fireplace.

After many years of laboring to create the life he had promised himself, he was finally content. He had a home with a barn and toolshed. Attached to one side of the barn George built a chicken coop. On the other side of the barn he built a lean-to and corral where he kept two horses. He enjoyed being busy, either growing or marketing his produce and meeting other people in the produce business.

The nightmares still came, just not as often.

4

The man scratched around in his garden that had been left unattended since the beginning of winter. The ground was still frozen and unable to be turned. Mostly, the long winter was wearing on him and he felt compelled to be outside working his farm, doing anything. He saw George approach from the south and moved to the garden fence to greet his neighbor.

"I guess people don't know what to make of this here crash, they callin' it," the neighbor said to George over his garden fence.

"No, sir. I been to three goat ropin's and four county fairs. I ain't never seen nothin' like this, ever!"

"Hoover said he don't see why this hiccough should last more 'an about six months or so." The man looked down the road in front of his garden, then back to George.

"I don't know, though. I'm jus' sayin' what I heard."

Shortly after those regretful comments by Hoover, there began an unprecedented run on the banks. People hoarded cash. Banks closed. Businesses shuddered. For most, there was money only for essentials. People no longer bought flowers as they once did. George saw his income cut in half the first year after the most devastating stock market crash in U. S. history.

For the next few years George managed as best he could. He still sold his produce, just not as much or for the prices that would sustain his farm. He hired himself out as a day laborer on some of the larger farms. Eventually, however, George was forced to sell his truck, but he kept one of his horses in an attempt to make enough money to keep his farm.

Five years into the correction that was to last only a few months, there was no work as a day laborer and work on his snow-covered farm was nonexistent. There was not enough money. People wanted to barter. Working for others left even less time to work his farm. Soon it was all he could do just to make the payments on the farm. He rode his horse to other farms and rode the outskirts of Chicago's south side for day jobs in the factories and mills that lined the city. He would do anything just to keep his farm. There just was not any work.

He talked with the bank's president and negotiated a longer mortgage on his farm with smaller payments. George and the banker rewrote the mortgage contract so the farm implements and other equipment George had purchased were written into the loan agreement. Eventually, George could not even make the smaller payments.

When the snow had finally melted and the spring root crops were coming in along with the lettuces, chards, and rhubarb, the city became infested with street vendors selling their wares, fruits, and vegetables.

A young boy sold used shoes on top of a box. Another young boy and his sister, both filthy, sold glass bottles they had found. The children slept on benches at the train station or curled up in Washington Park.

A few times a week George, having sold his horse, pulled his handcart three miles through the mud to town to sell his vegetables.

One evening, frustrated and weary, George pulled his nearly full produce cart home. He looked to the thin, orange marmalade horizon below a dove-grey sky. He watched the sun melt over the crusted, western edge of the earth as he pulled his cart.

From a darkened doorway a Rubenesque figure, with long curly hair, stood smoking a Turkish cigarette at the end of a long holder. She waved our man over to her porch. George approached slowly, leaving his cart of unsold produce at the curb. She leaned in and whispered in his ear.

"Lady!" George said incredulously. "Are you kidding me? The whole cart?"

5

Some larger farmers actually increased their acreage during the Great Depression, buying up foreclosed farms and equipment. They made a small profit from grain sales and the vendors they sent to the city's street corners to hock their fruits and vegetables.

George peddled his produce in the business district of Chicago and noted the faces of businessmen and bankers with whom he had dealt in the past. Now in direct competition with himself, the out-of-work businessmen peddled produce and dry goods on street corners. Some men, in three-piece suits, walked the city's streets wearing sandwich boards, begging for work.

Others waited in line for cups to be filled with thin soup, and day-old bread from the Salvation Army.

More businesses were shuttered. Homeless men and young people whose parents could no longer feed them set up camps in the doorways of shuttered businesses. Men started small, warming fires in barrels at the far ends of alleyways to warm their hands and soup cans of coffee.

"Six months my ass," George said, to no one in particular while pulling his cart.

"Three, four, five damned years and still no end in sight," a man complained.

Sadly, the produce and flower business George had built and nurtured from seed and sapling had finally gone back to the banker. For years to come that little parcel of land would sit fallow, south of Chicago.

It would be almost fifty years before George's farm would be used again. During the 1970's, high-density housing and low-end retail would overlay the farm, like a scab, as if George had never existed.

George's modest home and the outbuildings he had built would, in the meantime, fall like leaves, one board at a time, until eventually, all would be an indistinguishable mass of rubble in the fallow field where teenagers would gather to smoke cigarettes and drink pilfered alcohol to escape their parents.

"I've got nothing left to sell and no prospects for any money. I'm all in," George said.

"George, if there was anything we could do, you know we'd do it, don't ya?" his neighbor said.

"Sure I do, Clyde. Those big farmers will just come in here and outbid you all by a dollar. Nothing you can do about it," George said.

"You're a good man. There just isn't anything that can be done about this damned mess. Seems like the whole country's starving."

"What are ya gonna do, George?"

"I wish I knew, Clyde." George scratched the back of his neck. He removed his hat and wiped the inside sweatband of his fedora with his handkerchief. "I wish the hell I knew."

"You know you can stay in our barn, as long as you like," Clyde said.

"I appreciate that. I won't be a burden on anyone." George replaced his sweat-stained hat on his unkempt head. "Besides, you got enough to worry about with the new baby, your brother, and his family movin' in and all. I appreciate the offer, my friend."

George and his neighbor shook hands for the last time.

"I've got family out in California, Oakland," George said. "Why, who knows? I just might hitch my way out there and see if California's as nice as everyone says it is. I hear ya can grow anything out there. Maybe I'll become one of those movie stars. You suppose Hollywood could use another Clark Gable?"

For more years than George wanted to admit, he followed the harvests and rode the blinds of trains. He bummed rides on harvest trucks, and walked for days at a time. He, like many folks looking for work and food, slept in barns, under train trestles, bridges, empty ditches, parks, and just about every hobo jungle west of the Mississippi.

George would learn many first names of the people he came across, just never their last names. He would pick every fruit known to man and would harvest just about every type of vegetable known to North America. He just would not be allowed to keep any of it. During the late spring and early summer George joked he'd spent more time stooped over, pulling or cutting crops, than standing erect.

Sometimes just keeping food in one's stomach was a full-time job and seldom a great success. George found himself looking at other men's garbage more than once.

6

George looked up from the bottom of the hole just in time to see the first shovelful of dirt hit him in the face.

"What the hell!" he tried to exclaim, but the dirt was coming in too fast. Dirt was tossed in from both sides. He was unable to move his limbs. The dirt prevented him from rising or yelling for help. Another shovel of dirt hit him in the face. He could no longer breathe.

Finally, George jumped up, tearing at the tangle of blankets he had wrapped himself in during the night. He gasped for air. His hand found the blade in his coat pocket. His eyes darted all around seeking the threat.

Otis's children tickled George's face with long stalks of grass, giggling and bouncing at George's antics. George breathed deeply, smiled, and rubbed his damp head with his hat. He was happy to offer some respite from the lean and spartan existence led by le miserables.

Another foggy, California morning that offered the look and feel of cold, potato soup being poured down one's back. Jewels of water adorned George's blanket. His clothes were soaked through to his skin.

The same tired voices started anew, the argument from the previous evening. Pots and iron skillets clanged as the sojourners claimed one more victory over the darkness. A funk and steam rose off the mountains of garbage and blanketed the inhabitants of the Hooverville. The scent of putrefied slop stuck to the top of George's palate.

"Thirty-five cents an hour!" yelled the scarred, union man standing inside the circle of gathered men. "How the hell can a person live on that?" he asked, head bobbing like that of a prizefighter.

The road-weary men grumbled, listening to the latest word on the Great Depression and how this fellow was going to get the nation rolling again.

The speaker had a slightly foreign accent that gave his voice a sense of authority, perhaps even a little education. His shoes were spotless and his clothes were clean and pressed. George noticed his coat had every button. There were no holes in his clothing. A recent wound had lost its scab, but remained red on the side of his face.

With him was an entourage of men, drivers, strong-armed types, and a bare-knuckle fighter that George had seen before.

George listened and watched the orator. He had seen the same scenario played out before in parks, Hoovervilles, and hobo jungles. The union agitator's job was to enlighten the unenlightened listeners as to the abuses they were suffering at the hands of greedy businessmen and farmers, and how he and the union would represent and protect their rights in the new workplace.

"Look, today you work for twenty-five cents and tomorrow you'll be working for twenty!" prophesied the union man at the center of the group of tired, dirty men. He let his comment sink in for a moment.

"Look at the industrial might in Russia! While most of the damn factories here in America sit idle, they're starving you, your wife, and children! Look at yourselves! It's not your fault! What's been done to you is because of their greed!" the agitator complained.

"That one ain't idle," a man said, calmly pointing with his chin at the two, long-stemmed smokestacks of a factory in the distance.

"That ain't no factory, friend." Another man, from Kansas, said. "'less you call a renderin' plant a factory. You ain't been here too long, has ya?"

"I didn't think so. Well, when the wind changes direction, you gonna smell smells you ain't never smelled befo'e." Men in the crowd laughed.

"Yeah? Well, I'm not takin' it anymore!" said another fellow from somewhere within the crowd of tramps.

George knew the anonymous man was working with the union man. The speaker in the center of the ring did not look to acknowledge the only person in this group of men to support his position. George searched the crowd for other shills.

"And I don't blame you brother," said the union organizer. He waived a silencing hand above his shoulder.

"Unless we stand together against these corrupt factory farmers and corrupt businessmen," he said, as though offended, "it will be the ruination of our great country!"

"Can we afford to let them have their way and ruin our lives in the process? The system's broken, folks. Are we the ones who should have to pay for it? It's time we fundamentally change this broken system. Look at yourselves!" Some farmers took notice of the others, affirming their plight.

"Pay for it with what?" George wondered at the same time someone in the crowd yelled, "Change to what, Communism?"

"Asshole."

The men mumbled to themselves and those next to them.

A thin rail of a man in a snap-brim hat, with white whiskers spoke up. He wore blue denim overalls on top of long johns.

"I ain't got no problem with these farmers and businessmen. Hell, I'm a ff ff farmer myself. Least I was afore I lost everything." The old fellow looked down reflecting on his wrecked life.

"The problem is there's just too many of us tryin' to get too few jobs. Hell, if I still had my farm and two ol' boys showed up to do some work for me, I'd take the one who was gonna cost me ll ll less damned money. It just makes sense. Just as, back home, it just makes sense that a farmer can pay a tractor driver a buck and a quarter a day and replace a hundred sharecroppers." The farmers in the crowd of dirty men agreed. "We do what we have to, to survive."

"I don't know who is to blame and that's about the ss ss size of it. We all got ourselves into this mess by cc cc comin' here ta sunny California ta begin with. I mean, how many of you ff ff folks went to Arizona to pick cc cc cotton and saw four thousand folks applying for the same fifty pp pp pickin' jobs?" A number of hands raised, heads bobbled up and down.

"Then, tell me if I'm ll ll lying to ya all. All you folks decided, on your own now, to do the exact same thing each and every one of you other folks decided to do—come to cc cc California! Now, imagine these farmers who only need a hundred pp pp pickers or so and two thousand of you hungry folks ss ss show up and threaten to beat the shit out of him, his wife, and his horse if he don't hire you! Worse, his bb bb barn could get burned down if ya don't get to ww ww work, like this agitator fella says."

"Does that seem right? If it weren't right back home on our farms, why in hell is it okay nn nn now? How many of you had union pp pp pickets lined up on your road back home that wouldn't ll ll let no one in to work?"

The man in the center of the circle, coat opened now, hands on hips, hat pushed to the back of his head, turned his back to the farmer. "Ah!" The union agitator waved the farmer off with his hand.

"Come on, now! How many of you boys ever go see your boss for a raise, just to feed your family, and he up and fires you 'cause he can get cheaper help?"

"Hell, you been there longer, you know your way around the job better. Hell, you have all the experience. Why can't he pay you more? You're the one making him piles of money. It's labor that runs industry! Take back your power!"

A hum of grumbling, the voice of public opinion, and head nodding rose from the crowd.

"Let me help you with this. It's 'cause they wanna keep all the profits for themselves, that's why! Maybe you all didn't notice."

George noted the change in the speaker's cadence and his tone. "Hell, these damned farmers ain't nothin' but bankers with pitchforks! I say, let them run their businesses and farms, my friends. But the unions will run the labor that they need to make their filthy profits!" Cheers mixed with jeers and much muddy foot stomping issued from the crowd.

Then, before the crowd had quieted fully, the skinny beanpole, from Kansas, responded. "Well, a a ain't that their prerogative? I mean, what did they promise ya when you ss ss started? Maybe they don't need someone wit' all that experience. And if you're so damned good, why don't you just gg gg go find yourself a better payin' jj jj job? Or better yet, why don't you go start your own damn business, you're ss ss so ssmart?" Cheers and whistles drowned out the booing.

"Excuse me. Maybe you have enough to eat, but some of us don't! And it's because of them damned money-grubbers, we're going hungry and dying from starvation and living in the cold."

Oh, the mournful look. "What an actor," George thought.

"You ain't starving! Hell, you ain't even dirty!" a man yelled.

"Wadda ya mean, it's their ff ff fault? Don't they have the right to pay what they want to pay? It's their damned business. If they want to run it into the ground, let 'em, more for you and your new business venture. Th th they took the risk to start it. They tt tt took out the loans, worked day in aa aa and day out to grow the thing. I mean if you dd dd don't wanna work for the man dd dd don't. If he don't get his fruit or whatnot picked, it's his fault, ya ss ss see?"

"I'm as hungry as the next man—and that's a sight more hungry than you, friend. But damn it, there's just ss ss something wrong attackin' a mm mm man because he won't give you what is his to give or not!"

The old fellow scratched his dome and his voice fell to an almost unintelligible level. "There's just ss ss somethin' wrong with all this union business stirring people up, causing all this strife. People need to think for they ss ss selves."

"Easy for you to say, friend."

The union agitator, loosened his tie and removed his coat. He handed his coat to the large man standing behind him, the barn-fighter. The big man gently draped the agitator's coat over his left forearm. He picked small balls of wool from the coat and then gently, with care, smoothed the agitator's coat of any wrinkles.

7

Late in the summer, the same day the Ringling Brother's Circus hit town, George had been cutting hops and picking pears outside Yakima. He soon realized if one had cut hops and picked pears in Yakima, one had done all there was to do in Yakima. While talking to a couple of hop cutters, one fellow mentioned a barn fight taking place that evening.

Since his time in the infantry, George had been fascinated with the amount of pain an individual could endure and still keep going. He had been maimed in battle more than a few times. George had seen soldiers in much worse condition than he, and still they fought on. George had seen men without limbs crawl off the field of battle to die.

He witnessed a fellow soldier, without legs, pull himself to an upright position. Leaning his back against a palm tree, he cinched a tourniquet just above his right knee. There was nothing left of his other leg on which to secure a tourniquet. With bloody hands, knowing he would soon bleed out, the man attempted to light a cigarette. The poor soul's hands shook and were so wet with blood the matches became soaked. George wondered what that boy's mama would think if she could have seen him.

"Here, let me light that for you," George said to the man.

George shook himself from his reverie and recognized the union man's bodyguard as the brawler he had watched from high in the bleachers in the big white barn in Yakima.

The sun was setting below a red Bartlett pear orchard. The barn filled slowly as the preliminary bouts began with cockfighting. After four bouts of cockfighting, the dogs were brought in. Dogfights bothered George, who reached into his pocket for the pear he had pilfered earlier in the day. He could hear the dogs fight and the people cheer. George observed the people in the barn witnessing the dogs attack and tear at one another.

A couple of lightweight fighters entered the dirt floor of the makeshift arena after the last dog had been dragged out by his hind legs.

George looked down from the top of the makeshift bleachers and sliced the fruit with his knife and watched the fights below.

Men, like animals from the wild, beat the hell out of each other, amazing the crowd with their ferocity coupled with their chess-like movements. Elbows and knees flew. Heads butted together. Noses were mashed and sprayed blood down their chests in an inverted "V".

The big man, with the agitator, was the main event. George did not bet. He knew firsthand too often the unsuspecting littler man was the better fighter.

George remembered the big fighter looked intimidating. Scars littered his face and arms. He was muscular, scary to the average Joe anyway. George thought he looked spent. His hands were heavy. George was reminded of the soldiers' faces he had seen after coming out of battle.

The man's lack of speed explained the scars over both eyes and his lack of teeth. His nose was a mess.

This night was no different for the slow man who, as a boy, had been sold by his destitute father to a traveling sado-masochist.

"His life must have been something," George thought, "like stumbling around a tool shed blindfolded."

Tonight saw the big oaf fighting a young cattleman from Nevada. Some, witnessing the beating, groaned. Others turned their heads, or walked out of the barn with a sick feeling weighing in the bottom of their stomachs.

There was always a threat of mayhem in the air when unpopular union agitators, or organizers, as they liked to refer to themselves, spoke, as evidenced by the fresh scar on the side of the agitator's head that necessitated he buy some muscle to protect himself from getting his melon kicked in again.

It was after the fight in Yakima that the agitator paid that horrible and cruel man for the rights to the big fighter.

The handler knew the flaws in Roy's fighting style. After setting up fights, his handler had a shill bet against the idiot, Roy.

Roy's fighting career had run its course. He had been beaten senseless over the course of his bare-knuckle fighting career so many times his handler deemed him worthless for future fights, no longer a good investment. He needed someone younger.

Bare-knuckle venues were drying up. People took a dim view of men beating each other unconscious, sometimes to death. Getting rid of the bodies of dead fighters was a chore in which few wished to participate.

"Now, Roy, you go with this fella here," his handler told him. "He's your manager now. He bought you. You work for him now. You have to do what he tells you, see?"

"I like this work. I can do better. I don't want you to sell me. I just need some rest," Roy said.

He wiped his bleeding nose along his left arm, leaving a red streak. "Maybe some more training. Maybe we could go back to Cincinnati."

The agitator noticed the pock-marked skin of Roy. He had been burned with what looked like cigars his whole life. Some of the round scars were still fresh.

"Do better?" the man exclaimed. "Why, it's because you've been doing so good that we're going to give you some rest now. It's gonna be a vacation for you!" The man jabbed the red-hot end of his La Prosa, Clear Havana cigar at Roy and laughed. The union agitator felt uneasy.

"I'm gonna take care of you now," the agitator interjected. He held his breath then, "You won't have to fight so much, Roy." The agitator patted Roy on the back. "Your job will be simple. I just want you to protect me from people who might want to hurt me."

"Do you like to travel? I do a lot of traveling and talking with folks and help those folks that are down on their luck, like you. You can come with me and I'll take care of you. How would that be?"

"You help people, like me?"

"Sure I do. Ask your manager," the union agitator said as though he and Roy's handler had known each other for some time.

"But I still like to fight. It feels good," Roy explained. "I like it."

The man looked up from counting his bills. "You'll do what you're told, see?" He poked his cigar at Roy.

"We'll find you some fights, no doubt about that." The agitator remembered getting kicked in the head by a potato grower in Idaho. "Hopefully just none that involve me. That's where you come in."

The big man was spent. His reputation as a fighter to bet against became a liability for his manager. With the sport of bare-knuckle fighting beginning to wane, Roy's handler needed to make as much money as he could. Roy was no longer the answer.

Though lacking as a bare-knuckle fighter, Roy would serve and protect the union agitator from the likes of men that made up the skinny crowds that now surrounded them.

8

The agitator waved his arms about, limp at the wrists, as if swatting at flies. "You sound like one of those damned pigs who is locking us out, and starving us out, and kicking us out of town! You sound like one of those damned capitalist pigs that don't want to share. You sure you ain't one of those rich corporate farmers just coming in here to stir things up? Confuse the people while you confuse the issue?"

The old fella looked up sharply and pointed a stubby index finger, the tip of which had been lost when pinched between the horn of an angry bull and a six-inch steel corner post. "And you, ya ya ya sonofabitch," his face wrinkled along the fault lines of his life's labors, "sound like one of them damned, atheist Bolsheviks come over here to cause trouble in America! We don't need your bullshit, Bolshevik Revolution here, ya ya ya mmelon humpin' mmoron! We're Americans!"

George was struck by the clarity of the old fellow's argument as the crowd howled; easily the largest cheers of the meeting.

"And if I was younger, I'd rip ya a nn nn new asshole right here and now! And you, standing here ba ba bullshitting these people all the while speaking with that damned foreign accent as if it's somehow superior to American. Tell me, ss, ss son, which country kk kk kicked your dumb ass out?" The crowd went wild. A few hats were tossed in the air.

The agitator, pacing the center of the circle of men, threw his hands up, exposing thin white forearms.

"Look," the union man smiled, "I don't care about me. Ya see?"

"Christ all mighty and a crock of shit too," a man said walking away.

"If I did, I wouldn't be here talking to you boys right now." He raised his hands towards the sky, "If I cared just about me, I would be long gone from here. Brother, I care about you. I want to feed all of you. I want to help you!" He bit his lower lip and furrowed his sympathetic brow. Two men in suits started passing out fliers announcing the next meeting of the Agricultural Workers' Union.

"Haven't they made enough off us? Do more people have to get hurt in the rioting in the cities and on the farms? We just want what's our right. And Franklin Delano Roosevelt upholds that right through the establishment of the National Labor Relations Board! Yes, a place for labor at the bargaining table, finally! A voice for every man in the workplace."

"Oh, brother. My achin' ass." More folks faded into the fog.

The pitch of his voice increased, he walked around the center of the dissipating ring like the announcer at a cockfight. He looked to see how many would stay and listen to his gospel.

"But I can't help you without your help! Join me in righting the wrong which has been committed by those greedy business bastards," the martyr thrust his finger into the air toward Sacramento, "and we'll all eat! Why in hell can't they share what they've got too much of already?"

The few remaining stragglers, hands thrust deep into coat pockets, or the bibs of their overalls, nodded collectively at their self-anointed leader.

The old farmer was halfway back to his camp when George and Otis overtook him. Union fliers littered the muddy path.

The tall, old farmer walked head down, thumbs hitched in the sides of his overalls that, at some point, had clearly belonged to a much shorter man.

"Excuse me, sir," George said, "but could you tell us if there might be any work around here?"

The old man stopped and turned at the edge of his camp on the muddy footpath. "Only enough work ta, ta, ta starve you to death ss ss slowly, son," he stammered.

"Twenty cents if you pp pp pick cotton, but there ain't much of that left, if any. Sixteen hours a day seven days a week. If you're lucky you mm mm might be able to pick some row crops for two or three cents a bb bb box . . . might be some apples, pears left, here and there. After pickin' all day you might have enough mm mm money to buy yourself a meal. But son, your family gonna ss ss starve."

"It's like I was tryin' to tell them nn nn knot-heads over there. The damned Bolsheviks is happy just to ss ss stir the stew of hate, anything to muck up the American pond. We're in trouble, nn nn no doubt, but we don't need no damned 'change' like he's a sayin'. Why he's talkin' Socialism! It'll be the death of this cc cc country, just ww ww wait and see. Look what Lenin ...."

"I'm not married." George said.

"Huh? Oh, yeah. You're ss ss still gonna sstarve." He seemed to be looking for something he lost in the mud. Then, as if startled and looking directly into George's eyes, "Just not as soon."

A broken man sat on a cooking pot across the muddy path from where the men were talking and chimed in.

"We figured t' other day that of the two or three hundred people here, maybe fifty, sixty men will find work, temporary. The rest will leave, or starve, or die of some sickness. The county comes and hauls away one or two bodies a week, when they have to." The hungry man pointed to Sacramento with his head, too tired to rise. "Just stay out of town. City folks don't want to see the problem and you're the reminder. Farmers ain't so bad."

George studied the two men. Their hands were chapped and nails broken. Black grime embedded every crack and wrinkle of their hands and faces. Neither man had shaved in a long time. Each sprouted haircuts that were uneven and gouged. Spots of dried blood appeared here and there on their pale domes. Their boots were cracked and caked with mud. Their clothes were faded and well-worn, thin at the elbows and knees. They were proud, hardworking men, beaten down trying to stay alive.

"Most of us ran out of gas weeks ago, mister. No gas, no job. We can't go anywhere and there's not much food left. They don't want us in town; run us off. It's like we're just idling here and the gas is about to run out. Hell, for some of these folks, it already has."

"We're stuck here to starve to death. I'm so damned hungry I could eat cardboard. Ya see, every time a job comes open there's one of those damned union agitators yapping about how earning a little money is somehow worse than earning no money at all and letting your family starve."

"Thanks fellas. Good luck to you. I'll be on my way."

George whispered to his driver on the way back to their camp, "How much gas do you have?"

"Only what's in the gas tank. Whatta ya think's gonna happen to these folks?" Otis asked.

"Looks like they're gonna starve to death, or die from sickness," George said.

He reached into his trouser pocket and came out with two Standing Liberty quarters. "It's all I have. I wish I had more. Take care of your family."

"Don't we all? Much obliged." The driver handed one of the quarters back to George and tipped his hat. "Good luck."

Otis's wife was cleaning their new home. The children were cleaning cooking utensils and packing them in a black footlocker.

George doffed his hat to the woman and children then looked at the man knowingly. "I imagine you folks will want to be getting back on the road as soon as you can. Good luck!" Over his shoulder, he waved to the small, hungry children.

After pulling the collar of his coat up around his ears, George pulled his hat down low across his brow. About a quarter of a mile down the road, George looked back over his shoulder, edgy, like one who just walked away from a wreck he realizes should have killed him.

9

Thick, soupy fog hung in the air. A man, unable to even find a doorway in which to sleep, was soaked through to his skin. He had slept the previous night in the cold, damp fog balled up on a park bench. The skin on his fingers was shriveled and white. His hair was wet. Dew dripped down his face. The toe of each shoe had been torn away from being dragged across gravel and tie hopping freights.

The fool had been dragged by the ever-gaining trains until he could finally pull himself into a moving train car. His stark, wet, white feet were etched with the grime of the roads he had walked and the rail yards through which he had been dragged. There had been many.

"Say Mac, ya got a coat somewhere?" George asked the man.

The man leaned forward with his left shoulder as he walked and reminded George of a warped plank. He did not speak. His right hand slapped and pawed at his infected right ear.

"Excuse me. Have ya had any food lately?" George asked.

The plank twisted awkwardly to the right and could not quite turn his head enough to eyeball the man who was following him and who now intruded on his deranged world.

"Lea'e me alone!" he shouted and shuffled ahead at a faster pace. He looked back to measure the distance between himself and the stranger wearing round glasses.

George discerned a horse face with protruding, crooked yellow teeth surrounded by sparse, beard stubble. His eyebrows formed daggers above bulging brown eyes. He turned back to the road and leaned into his life's misfortune.

"Want some food, fella?" George asked.

The plank stopped suddenly, spun on his left foot and stood directly in front of George. The man's warm breath smelled of sour milk.

"Wa' ya got?"

George then realized the man was a half-wit and pulled a handful of crumbs from his coat pocket; the remainder of the biscuits Otis's wife had given him.

"You got a name, young man?"

George wondered if this fellow had run away from his parent's home, or if he had been kicked out for being the financial burden a near full-grown man placed on his destitute family.

George squeezed the crumbs into a ball and dropped the wad into the man's outstretched hand, then stepped back to get a better view of this sack of flesh propped up with sticks and bones.

No answer.

"Where ya headed?"

No answer.

Most of the crumbs fell between his fingers in his agitated attempt to eat. George's mouth watered as he watched the fallen crumbs melt into the wet road.

George stepped aside and continued walking. The half-wit followed, licking crumbs from the palm of his filthy hand. Crumbs stuck to his lips. He watched George closely.

"I'm thirsty. Get me water." the man commanded.

George turned back to the simpleton.

"I don't have any water. How 'bout we find some? I'm headed to Oakland; family there. Well, sort of extended family. At least, we're overdue for a visit. What's your name? Where you headed?"

Nothing.

"Aw, Jesus. Let's just find us a jungle and hang today; get you some food and water. I wouldn't kick out a fire today neither." George turned back to the road. "Don't you have a coat or something?"

"I know da jungle is," the man said. Crumbs were trapped in the stubble of his chin and upper lip.

George asked the fool the whereabouts of the jungle.

"Don't know, cain't see."

"You can't . . . oh. Is it close?" George asked. "I'm hoping to hop a freighter to Oakland, see? Make contact with my Uncle Jiggy. Maybe give me some time to dry out, do some laundry, and figure where to go next."

George continued. "Sweet Jesus, just to wrap these cracked hands around a steaming hot cup of black coffee would make me feel like one of the Rockefellers."

"Sweet Jesus! Hot coffee! Amen!"

George smiled, "That's right, brother. Amen."

Suddenly a steam engine's whistle screamed in the fog. They were close, and the sound so full, George had trouble discerning the exact location. Another whistle and George's ears and head pricked toward the sound.

"There it is," he said. "C'mon partner! That can't be more than a block or so away."

"C'mon padner," aped the idiot.

George noticed the difference of the crushed rock beneath their feet as they approached the switchyard. He was on guard for any bulls milling about in the fog. The tracks came into view just a few feet ahead and ran east to west. George crossed the tracks wanting to skirt the switchyard to his left.

"The jungle ought to be just outside of the yard and down the tracks a bit," George said. To give the switchyard a wide berth, George turned west again.

"Come on." The fool was close on his heels. George turned to the fool. "Do ya know where you are, now?"

"Home."

"Home, huh?"

Then more quietly, "Come on, my poor, ignorant friend. I'll get you some food and water, somehow."

The fool grabbed George by the coat sleeve and leaning into his walk, pulled George back towards the tracks. The switchyard and tracks appeared as the warmth of the engines helped burn away the surrounding fog. The train tracks separated into many more tracks where the train cars were jockeyed into position then connected to other trains.

"Hey! Come on. Let's go around. I don't need any trouble with the railroad."

A lone caboose sat on a set of tracks that was not connected to any other line, like a train car displayed in a park. On another set of tracks a few cars were connected, waiting to be hooked up to another engine. Up ahead an engine idled and waited for the engineer to back into other boxcars, gondolas, and flatbeds.

The fool headed toward the rust-colored caboose from the Union Pacific line. Just as they approached the steps at the back of the caboose, George ran into a bull coming around from the other side.

He was a fat man in a black, wool, watch coat and black felt bowler. His mustache required more time to groom each morning than George thought a man ought to give such considerations. It was the blue-black .38-caliber with the barrel that looked like a nine-inch gun off a navy destroyer that received George's immediate attention.

"Where the hell do you think you're goin', bub? Climb your ass down from there, now! Hands up!" the fat man ordered.

"I was just tryin' to help this fella here get something to eat," George said as he stepped away from the caboose. George wanted to put as much distance between him and the "nine incher" as he could. Grimy hands reached skyward.

"He was insistent we come to this old caboose. He was pulling on me. We were just . . . ."

"Where the hell have you been? I been lookin' all over for you."

"Huh? What do you . . . ?" George was cut off again.

"Shut up, you," the gun ordered.

"Yes, sir."

The fool spoke up, "Los' in da smoke. Thirsty."

"Well," the bull told the fool while eyeing George, "Come on, let's get you cleaned up. Then we'll get you somethin' to eat. How 'bout some hot coffee, huh? Maybe a ham sandwich?"

"Hot coffee! Okay!" said the idiot. "I like ham."

"You been travelin' with Charlie here, mister?"

Hesitantly, "Well, no, not exactly. I came on him this morning," George said, still holding his skinny white arms high above his head. "I don't have any water."

"Oh, ya did, huh?"

"Yes, sir."

The bull poked the barrel of the .38 on the tip of George's nose. "Put 'em down. Don't do nothin' stupid, see?"

"No, sir. I wouldn't think o' doin' nothin' stupid," said the gentle George. He slowly lowered his hands to his sides.

Charlie led, then George, then the .38-caliber. All were followed by the bull swinging a blackjack with his free hand.

"You two know each other?" George asked as the platform of the loading dock and pale yellow offices appeared through the fog.

"Yeah, Charlie's been hangin' around this yard since he could crawl. Loves trains. We look out for him when he's around. Sometimes ol' Charlie takes off and we don't see him for a spell. He likes to ride the rails with the 'boes and tramps. He likes to ride in the rain for some reason."

"We leave that old, broke down caboose, parked over there, for him when he doesn't want to go home. Just a bed with some blankets. We stuck a washbasin and dresser in there for him."

"His pa beats him somethin' awful. His old man's a good for nothin' drunk who don't care a lick what happens to ol' Charlie. Just beats the hell out of him, ya know? Just fuckin' awful. Every now and again, Charlie goes home. Comes back all beat to hell. I don't get it."

The three climbed the steps of the platform. Charlie opened the second door they came to. As they entered the bull's office a blast of warm air bellowed out from the office doorway. The little potbelly was kicked up to high and shortly began to roar. George thought how nice it was to just be warm once again.

The office smelled of sweat, old coffee, and cigar smoke. Pale yellow walls held nothing except one grey window, without curtains, that had not been washed in years. A round black-framed clock hung on a nail above the door. The floor had long ago lost its finish. A small oak desk, varnished to a light umber, was centered in the tiny room. The stove was set between the desk and window. On top of the desk sat a coffee pot and green blotter with brown triangles at each corner. Old newspapers covered the desktop and the floor behind the oak chair. A wastebasket sat empty beside the desk.

"Here ya go Charlie, nice, hot, cup of coffee." The bull handed a filthy, stained coffee cup to Charlie who took it eagerly and slurped with his large, horse lips.

The railroad cop reached into his lunch bag and pulled out two ham sandwiches and gave them to Charlie, who devoured them and allowed all to watch it happen.

George looked on incredulously.

The bull turned to George and asked glumly, "What's your story, citizen?"

George looked from the ham, cheese, and mayonnaise on white bread sloshing around in Charlie's mouth to the bull.

"Same as most. I lost everything I'd worked my whole life for." George reflected on his past. "The bank came and took my farm. That was back in Illinois. I'm headed to Oakland, now. I have family there. I have money. I'm not a vagrant."

"Well, dry off a bit. You got a cup?"

George relaxed, "Yes, sir, I do."

"Get yourself some mud there. You fed Charlie here, did ya?"

"Yes, sir, I did." George reached into the middle of his bindle and retrieved his tin cup. The enamel was chipped in a few places and had begun to rust.

"After you grab that cup, how 'bout spillin' all your pockets on the desk here, boots too."

George slowed his reach for the pot of coffee. He knew some of these bulls were the biggest thieves one could ever have the misfortune to run across. George wondered how far he could get after smashing the bull over the head with the full coffee pot.

He set the coffee cup on the dusty, wooden floor next to the wall and began emptying his pockets on the desk. From his coat pocket George pulled out a pinch of biscuit dust and made a neat pile on the bull's desk.

The bull's eyes looked from the small pile of crumbs to the skinny man's face. From his trousers, George pulled a kind of pocketknife the bull had never seen.

"Odd. What kind of knife is this?"

"Oh, that's a butterfly knife. I picked it up in the Philippines."

George placed his Standing Liberty quarter, a small sewing kit, a wallet, and an address book on the desk blotter. George stood barefooted. His wet socks left an imprint of his feet on the wood floor.

"Go ahead and put your socks and shoes by the stove," the bull said. "Give them a chance to dry out a bit."

The bull tore into George's wallet pulling cards, pictures and scraps of paper from inside. He tossed the well-worn and empty wallet on the desk. The bull then grabbed the address book and thumbed the pages. The addresses were from Illinois except a couple that were in California.

George's socks and boots became warm. Water evaporated as steam rose from his socks.

"Where'd you say you were headed, Mister?"

"Oakland."

"Who lives there?"

"My uncle and aunt. I haven't kept in touch with anyone much, lately."

"Well, seems to check out. Go ahead and put it back. What ya got in the bedroll?"

"Nothin' much, some clothes, change of socks, a few odds and ends from home, a razor."

"Let's have a little lookie, lookie. Spill it," the bull ordered.

George unrolled his bindle and stood by with his back against the wall, ready for inspection.

"Go ahead and pull that bindle apart." The railroad detective saw the razor, soap, and a rag.

He said, "Hand me that envelope, there," pointing from his chair.

Thumbing through the envelope, the bull realized it contained personal papers of identification, old photos and addresses.

The bull pointed to the soldier staring into the universe and asked, "That you?"

"Yes, sir, me and a couple of my buddies."

"How long you in?"

"'bout eight years."

"What made ya get out?"

George smiled. "Life expectancy isn't very long. I just wanted to settle down, I guess."

"I was in for a few years; damned rough life. Make an old man outta ya real fast."

George nodded.

"I was in the Marines, in China," the bull bragged. "Damned rough life."

"Army," George said

"A doggie," the Marine said, displaying an age-old inter-service competitiveness.

The idiot continued to slurp his coffee and gnaw at the sandwich while he looked at pictures in the newspaper.

"Hand me your boots."

George did as he was told. The left boot sported a hole clear through the sole. The bull pulled the insoles out of the boots. There was no money.

"That quarter it?"

"That's it."

Throwing the boot down and stuffing the insole into the top of the boot, the bull said, "After you two have a chance to warm up, and you get your stuff together, we'll take a little ride."

"Am I going to jail?" George quickly remembered his manners. "Sir?"

No answer. George set about making plans to make a run for it and getting lost in the fog.

"Excuse me. Do ya mind?" George pointed at the newspaper on the floor and then to his boot with the hole.

"Help yerself."

"Much obliged for the coffee. And thanks for the newspaper."

George folded a thick section of news and slid it into his canvas coat pocket for later. His socks were not yet dry, but were warmer than before.

Charlie scraped the biscuit crumbs off the desktop, tossed them into his mouth, and headed for the door. George looked on hungrily and pulled his bindle over his shoulder, then grabbed his coffee from the floor and swallowed the rest quickly.

The bull walked the two men down the steps and over to the black Ford sedan with the Southern Pacific Railroad Company emblem on the driver's door.

Ten minutes later, the bull pulled into a parking spot in front of the police station. George shook his head and remained silent.

"Is there any way we can work this out between us? We're veterans, for God's sake!" he finally blurted out.

"No," the bull said, concealing his smile. "Get out!"

George opened the door and got out. Charlie and the bull stayed in the car. "You gotta be kidding if you think I'm turning myself in," George thought.

"Go on," the bull commanded.

"Ten, fifteen feet, opposite side of the car from the cop is when I'll make my jump. Make him shoot through or around Charlie. Dodge. Zig-zag. Get lost in the fog and get out of town." George planned his escape.

He took a few steps toward the police station to feign his resignation to turn himself in. The bull admonished him.

"No! Not there! The waffle house!" The bull jacked his thumb, "Across the street!"

He then flipped a Mercury dime to George and said, "Grab yourself somethin' to eat. The next train headin' west'll get you to

Oakland by tonight. Should be headin' out about two o'clock."
George stood, mouth agape.

"Catch it just outside the switchyard and we won't have a
problem. There's a jungle out there. Tell them Mike sent ya."

"Thank you." George felt pinpricks across his chest realizing
he just about ran out on a dime.

"Us vets gotta stick together." The bull laughed and waved to
George as he backed out of the parking place. "I love doin' that to
people!" he shouted to George as he drove away.

George stood in the street, dumbfounded. "I must never try to
make sense of this world again."

The sign above the large restaurant's windows read, "Fried
Chicken and Waffles." George meekly entered the diner door, not
knowing if that was the name of the restaurant or the menu.

The cook looked up from his griddle at the vagrant in filthy
clothes.

George cared not at all what people thought of him. He was
met by the aroma of sizzling sausages, fried eggs, toast, and fried
potatoes with chunks of bell pepper and red onion. The smell of
coffee, as it sloshed around in thick coffee mugs, was strong.

His stomach began its impatient and terrible bitching. George
pulled up to the counter where the previous patron's plate awaited
removal. He looked up at the cook and slammed the Standing
Liberty and the Mercury dime on the counter to prove he had money.

The cook slowly returned his attention to the meat cooking on
the grill.

There was a piece of wheat toast with butter on the plate in
front of George when he sat down. It disappeared along with a swipe
of yolk before the waitress could take the plate away.

The waitress turned to the cook and whispered, "Pile on another scoop of taters, Paulie. He's hungry." She slid George an extra plate of toast. George began to purr, like one of those new V16 Caddys.

"My sweet Jesus!" he thought. "It's been so long."

After wiping his plate clean with a slice of toast George asked if there was any work he could do instead of having to use his quarter and new dime. The capitalist.

10

The fog was thick and hung in the air, like dense smoke from a forest fire. Men had been standing in the wet line since before sunup. They stamped their feet, collars turned up, one wide lapel folded in on top of the other. Fedoras and snap-brims, pulled low across foreheads, forbade eye contact. The shaved and bathed were the exception.

Tobacco smoke ballooned upward from the line of bleak-looking men with creased faces and whose clothes smelled of sweat and wet wool. The line inched forward in wet leather shoes.

"Sunny California? This here's the most miserable damned place I've ever been! Do ya ever get to see this here fuckin' state more than five feet at a time?"

Laughter rose from the line of shabby, skinny men.

A ship's horn exploded in the thick fog and echoed down the peninsula.

"Son of a bitch! How can a man stand to live with that kind of damned noise scare'n hell out'n 'im every damned day? Jesus Christ!"

Ladies, in the dark mourning colors of the Salvation Army passed out pamphlets and offered encouragement or admonishment, whichever they deemed necessary.

"You men need to mind your language," a "Sally" scolded.

"Taking the good Lord's name in vain will *not* help you find salvation!" She turned and scolded the other end of the line. "And it certainly will not help this line move any more efficiently! Now, *behave*!" Embarrassed, she blushed at her own strength as she strode away.

Men leaned against the front of empty offices that lined the deserted street. Here and there a foot was raised against the wet brick wall. Hands dug deep into empty pockets, fiddling with holes at the bottom. Others leaned on their shoulders as if to brace up the wall. A head rested against the wall and looked skyward as though awaiting salvation. Here and there a tin cup dinged against the bricks. A man dropped a mason jar that shattered on the wet sidewalk. Broken glass crunched beneath the men's feet. The wet line inched forward.

Men took the Salvation Army's pamphlets and read to themselves. One old fellow stuffed the sheets into the sole of his shoe. Steam spiraled upward from the sewers. On a long table stood steaming pots of thin soup, baskets of rolls, and a large stewpot of black coffee.

"One ladle per man, one bread per man, one cup of coffee per man. Praise Jesus! Keep it movin' gents, keep it movin'. One ladle per man, one bread per man, one cup of coffee per man. Praise Jesus! Keep it movin' gents, keep it movin'," the captain repeated in a bored monotone.

"God bless the Salvation Army and you, sister," one old codger said with his crumpled hat in hand, his cup filled to the brim with steaming chicken broth. It was his first hot food in over a week. His infirm hand shook and spilled much of his cup of soup as he walked away.

The old man had been surviving on food from the trash cans behind the restaurant two blocks away, but with the large influx of homeless men moving into the San Francisco bay area from up north and back east due to the change of seasons, he'd been pushed out by the hungrier men just coming in off the road. The old man was relegated to the shit-and-piss stained doorway of a vacant, brick building.

A faded, dark, green one-ton truck with side racks and a green canvas cover over the back pulled up to the long line of men at the East Bay Salvation Army soup line. The brakes squeaked as the truck came to a stop. The engine idling, the tailgate swung down and two men in fedoras and baseball jackets jumped out of the back of the truck. Another truck pulled up behind the first.

"Okay, okay!" yelled the short guy. "Hang on, hang on. We can only take some of ya. How many trucks do y'all see, huh? Nice and orderly, now, see?"

"What kind of work is it?" a voice asked from the line.

The factory man chomped down and spoke around the wet cigar stuck in the corner of his mouth. "The kind 'at pays . . . ya knucklehead. If ya got some special qualification, say so!" the little bulldog barked.

"I can operate a crane," said George without moving from the soup line. "Never dropped a load in my life," he lied.

11

George had just turned twenty-two years old and was hungover from celebrating the fact he had survived another jaunt into the dark and dangerous jungle with his pals, Joseph and Bert. More accurately all three young men were still stinking drunk at 0730 hours. They had spent the past few days drinking and whoring after coming out of the jungle alive.

George's head spun. There had been nothing approaching sleep since leaving the torn and bloody jungle and its screams. Sure, a nodding off here and there, but nothing resembling sweet sleep between two cool, clean, crisp, bedsheets. Their condition, after what they had endured the last few weeks, was a constant physical and mental numbness. Faces back home were vague, names forgotten.

If one stiff swig of Jack Daniel's would get one pleasantly numbed, then four or five shots of ol' number 7 would become a runaway train on one's path to Wellville.

Sweat poured into his eyes. Just as he stepped through the barrack's doors, he and his merrymaking buddies were accosted by a lieutenant and ordered to assist with the loading of equipment onboard the ship that would carry them home, to San Francisco, via the canal. It had been over two years since they had set foot on American soil.

Arriving at the dock as ordered, George was told by a tall, barrel-chested staff sergeant, "Climb aboard there, ol' son. I'm gonna make an expert of ya in about three minutes, got it?"

"Shut up and listen!"

He could hardly focus on the large sergeant before him. George wiped his smeared glasses with his dirty shirttail. "Hey, sarge, I don't think . . . I'm not feeling . . . ." The smoke from the crane's exhaust punched his head and gut, pushing him over the edge. His head spun. George thought he might pass out.

"Shad up and listen, will ya? I ain't got no time for your bullshit, corporal. When the man over there whistles," the sergeant pointed to a man standing in front of a little shack on the dock, "you pull this lever to make the hook go up, see? You push or pull this lever here an' it makes the hook on the crane go up or down. See? Up, down, up, down."

"You move the lever left or right and the load moves left or right, see?" The crane's hook moved up, right, then left, down.

Below, sailors attached the hook to a large cargo net. The signal was given and the staff sergeant pulled the lever raising the cargo. "See? That's easy right?" He moved another lever and the cargo net moved to a position above the deck of the ship. "See? Push this lever slowly and you lower the cargo to the deck of the ship. Okay?" He looked at his clipboard. "Any questions?"

"I'm'not feel . . . ."

"No? Good. Here, you do it."

The smell of the two soiled, sweating men filled the small, enclosed cab of the crane. The humidity was stifling. The whistle sounded and George pulled the lever that lifted the gear contained in the jute netting.

"There ya go! You're an expert!" The sergeant slapped George on the back. Little yellow stars shot out from the back of his eyeballs. Acid billowed up from his stomach into his mouth. The staff sergeant jumped down from the crane and headed back to his office with the fan.

It was 110 degrees and nearly 83 percent humidity. The sun blinded George. He moved the other lever left, the load moved left and then slammed into the side of the ship about twenty feet short of the ship's deck. Men on the dock chuckled. George moved the load up and to the left, over the deck. Rather than easing off the lever, George let go the lever and the load came to an abrupt stop and swung dangerously to and fro.

Men scattered in all directions on the deck of the ship. One sailor jumped onto the cargo netting to keep from being shoved overboard. After the cargo landed with a loud thud, the deck hands were all too eager to let George know how they felt about his use of the crane. They yelled and cussed. They shook their fists at the wretch stuck in Phalaris's brazen bull that was the crane's cab.

Another whistle and George lifted the hook and swung it low, over the side of the ship, scattering the men on the dock below. George moved the crane to the right and lowered it to where more gear was waiting on a flatbed truck.

A whistle and the crane lifted the gear off the bed of the truck and over the deck of the ship. The load swayed back and forth. George tried not to look at it. He pushed the lever forward to lower the load onto the deck of the ship. He realized too late that the load was moving too fast towards the deck. George let loose the lever. The load came to an abrupt stop and pulled the whole crane forward on its front wheels. The back two wheels of the crane came off the dock and then bounced back down. More laughs from the dockhands and plenty of cussing. Joseph and Bert enjoyed the spectacle, guffawing and backslapping one another, both still drunk.

Fumes from the crane's engine filled the small hot and humid cab. George threw up yellow bile that splashed atop the dock next to the crane. Joe and Bert could hardly keep from wetting themselves with laughter.

A whistle, and the crane moved up, then over to the ship's deck. A whistle, and he lowered the hooked gear. The officer on the ship's deck, starboard side, shook his head and yelled at George who was head down, gagging on more yellow bile.

Another whistle and George looked up to the man standing directly in front of the sun. George shielded his tearing eyes. Midgets banged their way out of the galvanized garbage can that was his head. He could not see through his filthy, smeared glasses. The sun's heat beat through the grey streaked windshield of the crane. He moved the crane laterally and threw up again. Vomit splashed atop the controls of the crane. Joe and Bert laughed hysterically.

George leaned his dizzy head on the control lever of the crane to rest his pounding head. The seventy-pound hook free-fell from the height of the ship's deck. The massive hook punched a hole through the dock and into the bay. Joe and Bert, along with other soldiers and sailors moving around on the dock jumped to safety.

The two soldiers, eyes as large as Peace Dollars, stood amazed and unmoving for the split second it took them to realize no one was hurt. They continued their carefree laughter. After all they had been through, that they should end up being killed by the cargo hook of a crane was hilarious.

"Holy shit! Did you see that! George damned near killed us."

George shook his head to relieve himself of the memory of his Veracruz adventure.

Hungry men squeezed into the funnel of humanity at the back of the two trucks. George smiled, grimly, remembering his youthful antics. The soldiers of salvation looked on; their bread line greatly reduced.

"Climb in four-eyes! Hey, move forward there comrade! Let this one in," the taller man yelled. "He's got skills!"

George declined. "Hey, you know what? No, thanks anyway. I'm not feeln' so good just now. But thank you, kindly."

George watched the starving men loaded like cattle into the trucks. The two men in baseball jackets slammed the doors of the trucks and drove off with their fresh batch of scabs.

Up the Embarcadero the welcoming committee from the fish cannery's local union awaited them with clubs and Molotov cocktails.

12

"Hey, Mac! Get your ass up. Ya can't sleep here. Com' on, move you!" The beat cop said. He tapped on our sojourner's shoulder with his nightstick.

George pulled his hat back, head full of sand, and looked up at the officer. "But I don't have anywhere to go."

"Oh, so you're a vag, are ya?" the flatfoot said with a slight Irish brogue.

George shot from the bus bench and grabbed his bedroll and began walking away from the officer. "No, sir. I'm, I mean, I was just waitin' and fell asleep. I'm on my way now. I've got an uncle I need to find. Sorry to be a bother to you."

"Ya don't say? Come here, you. And where might your kin be a livin'?" the officer asked with a hint of ennui.

George stopped. "I don't really know, I'm new here."

"Aren't ya all? Every time the train arrives with all you 'boes aboard, the city's population doubles! Come on, now. Let's go!" the officer said. He took off his hat and wiped the sweat off his bald head and the sweatband inside his hat. He did not look at George.

George swallowed. "Well, my uncle told me to visit if I had a chance. I guess this is my chance. I lost my farm and I'm trying to find my uncle's house. I fell asleep. I have money."

"Where's your uncle livin'?"

"I was told by a neighbor of his to check Pipe City, at the end of 19th Street."

"No." The officer now reminded George of a priest, rather than a cop. "Your uncle doesn't live there anymore. Might of lived there, but don't no more. The place is all gone now. When did you last contact your uncle?"

George was more than a little embarrassed. "Longer than I'd like to have to tell, to be honest."

"Well, he ain't there no more, I'll tell you that. But see for yourself. 19th Street is about six blocks that a way. Turn right and then head toward the bay, about a block this side of the bay, by the tracks. Right at the end of 19th, there. You'll see."

"Thank you, officer. I'll be on my way."

"Don't let me catch ya sleeping on my benches no more! Understand? If the ladies complain to my captain about you vagrants sleeping on the bus benches beneath their apartment windows . . . , well we just can't have none of that, now, can we?" the cop said, continuing to walk the beat he had walked for years.

The officer twirled the baton that dangled from a leather strap wound around his right wrist and whistled an Irish tune of love lost. Long steps, with feet splayed far apart, carried him confidently uphill into the fog.

The sticky fog clung to George's heavy coat, weighing it down like a shell across his shoulders and back as he descended the hill.

He realized that if he splayed his arms to either side and walked carefully, the inside front and back of his coat did not touch his chest, stomach, or back.

"I need to eat," he told the wet sidewalk.

Ahead, somewhere in the fog, George heard the sound of heavy equipment. "Jesus! If I ever land another job, so help me . . . ." His pace quickened as he headed toward the sound.

"Excuse me," George said to a passerby on the street. "Is Pipe City around here? A police officer told me it was around here. I'm looking for my uncle."

"Nope. You got it all wrong, pal. Pipe City is where people were living a year or so ago when they lost their homes. They lived in the big sewer pipes while the sewer was being dug, see? When the workers needed the pipe, the people was told to shove off."

George was momentarily lost.

"Hear them over there? The same sewer systems goin' in, just further up the bay."

George continued to head in the direction of the work.

Large sewer pipes were stacked on their sides, one atop the other, the length of a city block. He could see people sitting in the sewer pipes reading newspapers, smoking cigarettes, legs dangling from the ends of the large pipes. Some people slept. Another block and George found working men hoisting large sections of concrete sewer pipes into a trench. Other men worked at digging and cleaning out the ditch with pickaxes and shovels to assist in placing the pipe.

"Who's in charge here?" George asked the man shoveling clay in the bottom of the ditch. The grey clay stunk of sulfur.

"Up yonder, in the truck," the worker said.

George noted the heavy country accent; Arkansas, maybe Oklahoma, and guessed the man was just another nomad from the bowels of the country who hoped to find California his mecca.

"How's the work? Worked here long?" George quizzed.

"Oh, 'bout a week or two, I guess." The Okie spied the crew boss headed their way and turned back to his shovel and continued digging the wet clay.

"Thanks, kindly." George said.

The crew boss eyed George as they passed one another. It took all George had to make a conscious effort to keep from mirroring the crew boss's stare. George continued up the street without giving the man any notice, other than a tip of the hat.

American Concrete and Steel Pipe Company was painted on the side of the idling truck the foreman drove. Few men stood in line ahead of George to be interviewed.

"Hey! Get the hell outta here. Ya drunk!" the foreman said. The drunk stumbled aside. The next man approached the truck window. "You too! Get the hell outta here you two. Damned drunks. Where the hell do ya all find the money to stay drunk?"

"What the hell do you want?" the man yelled from behind the driver's window of his truck. He shook his head and ash fell off his cigarette.

"No! I tol' you yesterday. You're too fuckin' old. Get outta here, would ya? Civil War vets. Vets from the Great War! Jesus Christ!"

George doffed his cap to the Civil War veteran and then it was his turn at the truck window. The foreman looked at George's size and told him there was not much work left. "'bout done here. Besides, you're kinda small. We need men with a few more rocks in their pockets. Know what I mean, Mac?" The foreman turned back to the blueprints outlining where the new sewer pipes were to be buried along the edge of the bay.

"I had a farm in Illinois. I know what work is." George said.

"You drink?"

"No, sir."

The foreman looked George over.

"Well, you know what I mean, hardly ever. I would rather eat and don't mind working for it neither," George said.

"'s that right?" The foreman knew the best workers were gobbling up work in the shipyards and canneries as soon as an opening became available.

"I can do anything you ask and don't complain a bit."

"You one of them union boys?"

"No, sir. Never wanted anything I didn't earn myself."

"You a red?"

"No, sir."

The foreman pulled the cigarette from his mouth and blew out a diesel-engine's worth of smoke.

"A'right. Okay. I'll give ya a try. Twenty-five cents an hour. Grab yourself a pick out o' the back there. And I want it back at the end of the day! You lose my tools and you lose your job, got it?"

"Yes, sir." George grabbed a broad-bladed pickaxe from the bed of the truck.

"Run on back there and see the fella in the red shirt, he's the crew boss. He'll put you to work. Tell him I said to give ya a go. We work from can-to-can't see. We stop at noon for lunch, thirty minutes. Payday is every Friday, cash. Any questions?"

"Thanks for givin' me a go, mister. I won't let you down."

The foreman noted the time and took George's name and marked him present for work.

"Go on. Get goin'. You're on my time now!" the foreman yelled.

George trotted off to meet his new crew boss.

"I don't care who you are or where you came from. You know how to use that thing?" The crew boss pointed to the pickaxe and spit tobacco juice, in a long brown stream, between his boots.

"Yes, sir."

"Well, climb your skinny ass down in there and get to yanking up some of that clay, boy! I ain't payin' you to stand around holding that pickaxe up." He kicked George in the seat of the pants as he bent over, about ready to jump into the ditch.

"See them two ol' boys over yonder, again the wall?"

George recognized the two skinny drunks that the foreman dismissed earlier.

"Yes, sir."

The crew boss spit another stream of brown tobacco juice between his boots. "They want your job. Some days the line for these jobs reaches clean to the end of the block. Likely go straight into Frisco if not for the bay. Anyway, please screw this up so as I can give it 'em."

Setting his bedroll aside, George climbed into the ditch and started busting up clay for the workers with the shovels. The foreman hadrealized George was not tall enough to throw the wet clay out of the ditch with a shovel. The pickaxe was the better tool for him. Those with the shovels were the taller men who could look up and over the sides of the ditch. The top edge of the ditch was a few inches above George's head.

George stabbed at the wet, grey clay which came away from the earth in clumps as large as a loaf of round bread. Within minutes George's boots were laden with slick, wet clay. It was difficult to move or maintain a solid footing. On and on, throughout the morning, George chopped at the clay without a break or looking up. He allowed his mind to wander to relieve the ache in his muscles and his boredom.

A seasoned working man knew not to give consideration to each and every laborious stroke; the weight of the pickaxe on his back and shoulders, the blisters that burned as the skin tore away then flapped against the wood handle. The continual drip, drip, drip of salty sweat into his eyes made matters worse, but did nothing to deter the working man. On and on, hour-by-hour, the exhausting labor continued as the sun warmed.

Passersby watched the choreography; the rise and fall of the heavy pickaxes mingled with the rise and fall of the shovels ridding the ditch of the heavy clay. Foot-by-foot, one shovel load at a time, mounds of clay paralleled the ditch. The smell of sulfur hung in the air. The crew boss walked the length of the work crew, scrutinizing their work.

A glob of earthen clay the size of a baseball slammed into George's left ear. Only by bracing himself against the right side of the ditch did he keep himself from pitching over completely. His ear rang with a dull pain. He momentarily lost his balance.

"Hey, wake the fuck up, asshole! Are you deaf? I said, break for lunch!" Then, as the crew boss walked away, he finished with, "Dumbass."

George was still groggy from the cheap shot. He looked hard at the crew boss, who had turned and was yelling at the other ditch diggers to be back on the job in thirty minutes, or else.

George climbed out at the end of the ditch and scraped clay from the side of his reddening face and neck.

"Don't mind him, he jus' misses being tit-fed. Name's Ernie." the Okie said.

The two shook hands. Ernie noticed George's bindle and asked if he had eaten recently.

"I have a couple of hard rolls from the Sally," George said, wiping clay off his shoulder and chest. "Would you like one?"

"He's got a couple of hard rolls . . ." the Okie said and turned to no one in particular, then continued, ". . . from the Sally." Ernie shook his head. "Oh, man! Com' on. There's a deli 'round the corner." He grabbed George's left arm. Ernie pulled George. "Let's get us sump'n to eat. You gonna love 'em." Ernie winked at George who continued to dig wet clay out of his ear.

Embarrassed at his monetary straits, George thanked the Okie and raised his hand as if to pass on the offer. George looked up from his muddy shirt and searched the street for the crew boss who was leaning on the foreman's truck bed, sipping coffee.

He pulled at George's elbow. "Come on. Forget him. Sammie's on me." The Okie slapped George on the back. "You kin pay me back at the end of the week," he said.

No happier ditch diggers were on the face of the earth, sitting there dangling their feet into the open trench. Roast beef with all the trimmings and extra onion and yellow peppers.

"Sweet Jesus! Eat, you bitch." George commanded his stomach.

"What?" Ernie asked.

"Nothing," George said.

Between bites there was only time for the Okie to tell of his plight and what had brought him to this place in his life.

It was the same for most all the folks George had come across in his travels. Lost farms, dust storms, inept government regulations, unions blocked workers in favor of others, it was all the same.

Ernie told George of his family that had come with him to California for the promise of opportunity. He spoke of his mother and father who might be joining him and his wife, and of a brother who was married with two children and another on the way.

"They're headed to California as we speak," he said.

The crew boss began hollering and intimidating the work crew back into action.

"Come on, ya lazy bastards! Move your asses or lose your job!" he yelled.

The ditch diggers begrudgingly climbed back into the ditch and continued stabbing at the heavy, stinking clay.

At dusk the foreman returned in his truck to collect the digging tools and to check on the crew's progress before telling the crew boss to cut the men loose for the day. The sun had set and he wanted to get home to his dinner.

"All right you lousy bums, knock off for the rest of the day. Be back at 5:30, or you lose your job," the crew boss threatened.

George and Ernie were too tired to be offended by their boss's castigation. Both were just happy to have had a good day's work. Being useful made a man proud and gave him a sense of worth. George looked forward to receiving a full day's wages and imagined what the few dollars could buy and all he could do with the cash.

George watched the crew boss pull the pint of whisky from his hip pocket and raise it to his lips taking a long pull from the bottle.

"Com'n George. Staring that man down isn't gonna get you fed and into bed. Now, let's get some distance on this hole in the ground. Where you headed?"

George continued to stare at the crew boss. "I don't know." George then turned to the Okie. "I thought I'd try to find a doorway or something. I got an uncle who lives around here somewhere." He continued walking and cleaning his scratched eyeglasses on his dirty shirt.

"Now hang on there, George. We got us a little place. Jus' my wife an' baby an' me. It ain't much, truly, but you can stay with us 'til you find sump'n better. It'll keep the damned fog off n ya."

"Thanks, just the same."

"Suit yourself. See ya tomorrow, friend."

George plodded in heavy, mud-laden boots toward the row of flophouses on the water's edge, the sun just set.

Men huddled in front of the flea-infested rooms for rent along 7th Street, talking, while they warmed themselves over a fire that had been built in a rusty, fifty-gallon drum. Jazz, along with the stink from the canneries, blew along the east bay. Neon lights reflected the names of flophouses, bars, and hop joints in the wet streets.

George pushed past all the derelicts and nonsense. He asked the desk clerk if he had heard of Pipe City.

"That place? It doesn't exist anymore, not like it used to. When they were laying the sewer pipes for the Embarcadero, they stored those big six-foot pipes up the street there. People started living in them, but when the concrete pipes were needed, the people had to move."

"Where'd they all go?" George asked.

"Hell knows. Here, there, out with the tide, I guess. A few live there and get run off every day or so. No families."

"You want a room, or not?" the clerk asked.

For fifteen cents George rented the bridal suit, an open bay on the top floor of the flophouse strewn with sawdust and stinking men. There were no beds. Strange, dirty men who stunk from a life lived out of doors were sprawled on the floor, in no particular order, and snored heavily. Some lie in their own vomit having drunk themselves stupid trying to forget the pain of their bad decisions.

When told of the vomit in the bridal suit, the clerk said, "I know. I know. I clean it once a day. That's it. Unless you wanna clean it for a nickel. Uh huh. I'll be up in a couple of hours. Meanwhile, throw some sawdust on it, would ya? It'll help keep the flies down. Won't stink so bad."

In front of the flophouse, huddled around the burning metal drum, philosophers continued their discussion on politics and dust storms. Only recently had they taken up the debate on Hitler attacking Poland and about how far he might go.

Lonely men talked about the prospects of a real job in one of the factories, canneries, other food-processing plants, or even the California Cotton Mill down in Jingletown. Some men talked of work in the shipyards that were ramping up to support Britain in their war against Germany.

The men passed around a bottle of muscatel and talked of the unions and the beatings they delivered to the scabs. Another pull or two on the bottle and the talk turned to socialists, government corruption, Roosevelt, and the democrats giving the country to the far-left progressives with the creation of government programs, or alphabet soup as they were called, of agencies and requisite regulations that governed how businesses would be allowed to operate and people to live.

"Yeah! Well, you're a damned, filthy capitalist!" one drunk yelled at another.

An old drunk squatted on his haunches, his back against the wet, brick wall of the alleyway. His whiskers covered the collar of his dirty shirt and charity sports coat and gave one the impression of Walt Whitman. His eyes were closed as he seemed to strain trying to remember the verse to a poem fading from his old man's memory. Tobacco stained his beard.

The clerk leaned over the counter and yelled to the drunks to get out of the doorway. George climbed the dark stairwell that smelled from the ammonia of urine and the sweet, sickly, stink of vomit to the bridal suite.

13

Seagulls with black-tipped wings dipped and screeched. They rode the air current along the water's edge, snatching up crumbs dropped by indifferent city dwellers and shitting on pedestrians walking the Embarcadero.

The gulls hovered just out of reach of the fishermen on the wharf and dove into the bay for the entrails of the freshly gutted fish. Wooden rails and pilings were painted with thick coats of black and white gull shit. The air stunk with the smell of bait and large pots filled with boiling crabs and fish. The air was filled with a strong scent of death.

"If it ain't the damned bums and hoboes stealing food and shitting in the doorways, it's the damned gulls makin' a menace," said the angry flatfoot. He wiped black and white shit off the right side of his hat and shoulder. "Son of a bitch!"

Pedestrians pretended not to notice and averted their eyes as they passed by the angry officer.

The city's buildings, wet with fog, looked to be made of steel, lead, and coke. Dew dripped from the building's window ledges, street lamps, and signs.

"It's like the whole damned city's melting," a newly arrived migrant said standing in a soup line.

Under heavy, threatening, rain clouds George happily footed his way to his third day of honest work, bindle slung across his shoulder. He still had part of the 35 cents he'd been carrying since Sacramento. He'd made it to payday with an Indian Head nickel in his pocket.

He reached for the pickaxe as the crew boss grabbed the handle and slammed the tool down on the tailgate of the pick-up truck. "You're done."

"What's going on?" George was shaken into a higher state of consciousness, like an animal swatted for no apparent reason. He slid his bedroll from his shoulder.

"I don't answer to you," the crew boss said. "Scram 'fore I clock ya, see?" The crew boss waved a menacing fist at the smaller man.

"Well, I just want to know what I did to get fired," George said. "Maybe we can work this out. There has to be some sort of misunderstanding here."

The crew boss raised his clipboard as if to strike George on the top of his head. "I told you to scram, little man!"

The crew boss met George's fist with the center of his face. The clipboard and pencil stub he was holding darted in separate directions and bounced to the street. The crew boss's knees buckled while he grasped for George's sleeve as he went down. Like an explosion, George jerked his arm away.

The veteran's mind entered that dark place better left on the battlefield. The distinction between past war and present reality was no longer clear. Death and its location were relative.

His face cracked. His eyes were like torches. His teeth gnashed together. His fists tightened, like leather straps. As the bigger man stumbled to gain his feet, George plowed another fist into the man's face.

"I'm going to bust your face into little pieces. This little man's about to whip your big, fat ass like it's never been whipped before," George menaced.

Men stopped working to witness what they all had wanted to do, but for which none possessed the courage. The crew boss attempted to rise. A shot behind his ear sent him crashing back down. George's knee smashed into the side of the man's head. After a moment, the crew boss slowly raised his head, not knowing what was happening. The gristle in the dazed man's nose split with a right cross from George's elbow. Teeth slammed together, chipped, and fell from the man's broken mouth. White flakes stuck to the confused crew boss's blood-soaked lips. He limply tried to gain just his knees. All the weight of the little man's body came in behind his elbow as it smashed into the back of the dazed man's neck.

The spectators stood with dropped jaws and raised eyebrows. A rolled cigarette hung, smokeless, from the lower lip of one opened mouth. Others squinted; heads half turned at the beating the little man administered to the larger man. There was no let up, no reprieve, nowhere to hide. Some cringed and finally, sickened by the show, turned their heads. Today no quarter would be given, no prisoners taken.

"George! Stop! No more! You're gonna kill him!" Ernie stammered, visibly shaken. There was no pugilistic response on the part of the crew boss. For most, but not veterans, this fight would be over.

"If I cared about kissing another man's ass and abusing those that weren't as well off as me, I'd take your job from you today." George leaned in close to the man's ear. "Lucky for you, I'm in a good fuckin' mood, Mac . . . ," George looked up at the bystanders, some women, then knelt closer to the man's ear, pulling the butterfly knife from his hip pocket and flashing it against the crew boss's neck, ". . . or I'd stuff your fuckin' guts down your throat for you."

"George! For God's sake, stop!" Ernie yelled.

George's movement was a blur. People gasped and averted their eyes. The crew boss's ear lay on the wet street.

George shot another glance at the people gathered; the new hires brought in at a cheaper rate by the crew boss. Nobody moved. The crew boss gained his hands and knees. George kicked him in the ass and sent him into the ditch.

A flip of the wrist and the butterfly knife flashed, then disappeared into George's sleeve. He straightened up, pulled his jacket together, and grabbed his hat that had been lost while he beat the bigger man senseless.

The foreman opened his truck door. George approached.

"He had it comin' since he thought it smart to kick me and hit me on the side of the head with that clod of clay. He likes to hurt people." George looked, from the top of the trench where he had kicked the crew boss over the edge, to the foreman. "If you're a fair man I won't have a problem here. I'll take what pay I have comin' and be gone."

"That was quite a whoopin' you gave him. Think he's still alive down there?"

A nervous smile surrounded the foreman's cigarette. "What kind of work do you do, brother?"

"You're one of those prizefighters, ain't ya? Lightweight? A soldier? I bet you was a soldier."

George stepped closer to the foreman. "Man like that likes to inflict pain, ought never be allowed in a position over others. You should know that. These days are hard enough on a man." George looked to the trench. All work had stopped. A worker was helping the crew boss to his feet.

George turned back to the foreman. "One day it will be your turn. This city life, the bitches it breeds . . . just give me my money."

"Well, he's the police chief's cousin, so I kinda had to hire him. I owed him a favor. You kind of did what a lot of folks have been wanting to, but were too chicken to."

The foreman looked to his pad that contained the names of the work crew. "Hmm, seems some happy fool never wrote your name on the pad." He tore the page that contained George's name and handed it to him. "You may not want to stay around here too long. Know what I mean, friend?"

George took his pay in cash.

The crew boss climbed to the top edge of the ditch with the aid of one of the workers. On his knees he swayed to and fro. A steady stream of blood ran down his face and neck into a puddle on the street. He fell forward on his hands.

George walked over to where the crew boss tried to steady himself. George grabbed up a handful of wet clay that lined the trench and smashed the crew boss on the left side of his head and tumbled him back into the trench. The crew boss lay face up in a few inches of water. He did not move. Piss mixed with water and blood in the bottom of the trench.

"My money says you was a soldier. Am I right?"

"There's the man you need to be your crew boss. He's got a wife and a new baby. He's a fair man. Not like that piece of shit."

George stuffed the money into his pocket, not noticing the bonus and walked past Ernie, head down, filled with disgust.

"George?"

14

George checked in with the canning companies along the bay's shore. Union bullying had taken over most of the factories and canneries of the east bay and along California's golden coast. Those jobs went to family and friends of the union representatives or the company. The same was true of the Kaiser Steel plant that had recently opened. George even tried to land a job on some of the fishing trawlers. Nothing doing.

"You're just no good in the city. I can't explain it, exactly, George," Ernie said as his wife handed George a bag containing a couple of sandwiches.

"We can adapt to city life, but boy, you're still half wild." Ernie smiled. His perception was not lost on George.

"Thanks for letting me sleep on your couch the last few days. I appreciate the risk you took for me, my friend. Ma'am."

"Thank you for helping me get the new job. I think we might make it after all," Ernie said.

The bus came to a stop all in a huff. The driver pulled on the well-worn, metal handle that was attached to the two doors. The doors drew in the heat from the diesel engine with a gush of air.

"Best we get on back to the roost, Marlene, and see what's for supper. It's time. Now, you take care of yourself and write."

George shook hands with the new crew boss, tipped his hat to Ernie's wife and climbed aboard the bus. On either side of the glass, they waved.

"Anybody shows up with only one ear, don't hire him. Got it?"

Ernie shook his head at the veteran's dark humor.

The brakes hissed and the doors swung shut. George took a window seat up front and watched the road ahead disappear below the windshield, leaving nothing but blue sky as the bus made the ascent up the big, new Oakland Bay Bridge toward San Francisco. George stood to make sure the road was still there. After taking his seat he looked at his swollen hand and shook his head.

15

In San Francisco's Tenderloin District and Chinatown, the city's cops participated in graft much more than they subdued. They took bribes that allowed common pickpockets, second-story men, and common street thugs to work their turf without competition. The same deal was offered to prostitutes and pimps who, pushed out of the Barbary Coast District, were allowed to work without interference, but for a pinch. Wine dumps and hop joints, not as popular as they once were, operated without harassment, for the right price, just as on Oakland's 7th Street. Gambling was overlooked at the billiard halls and boxing gyms that sponsored Saturday night at the fights.

Politicians turned their heads at ballot fixing they instigated and other campaign fraud. Corruption at San Francisco's city hall insisted that the poor and hungry remain poor and hungry.

During his first days in San Francisco George explored the city's museum, library, wharf, produce district, and art galleries. He found a soup line and later, another infested flop house for fifteen cents a night.

In the room to George's left, a man preached hell and damnation out the window to the drunks and shooters in the alley below. On George's right, two drunks fought over the last few pulls on a bottle of cheap wine; across the hall, a crap game.

Through the newly constructed marvel everyone called the Golden Gate Bridge, the sun set in burnt orange and raspberry swirls across the darkening, azure Pacific Ocean.

Gulls, having painted the bay area black and white, quietly settled in for the night. Hoboes and bums wrapped the little clothing they had, even newspapers, around their bodies and balled up in the doorways of the derelict and dark buildings all around San Francisco.

The people on the street below were loud and argumentative. George listened to a man, somewhere down the foggy street, play a mournful jazz tune on his saxophone. A police car, siren screaming, sped toward another calamity as George closed the door to his room and stepped across the narrow hallway.

16

The bell above the door announced the big man's entrance. He stood at one end of the diner and took its measure. The bustling diner greeted him with the slap of heavy white dishes being stacked in the cook's station above the griddle. Cigarette smoke and conversation flowed from the full tables divided by high, wooden partitions.

Between each booth was a hat and coat hook. Waitresses yelled orders to the short-order cook, an unshaven Italian, named Gigio, who was dressed in a white V-neck t-shirt. A cigarette dangled from the left side of his mouth. Squinting through the smoke he looked out at the crowd over the counter.

"Hey, hey, Joe Mac, whatta ya say, huh?" The cook's arms danced a jig over the griddle with his hands out of site, below the cook's counter.

The clang of tin utensils beat time against coffee cups and dishes throughout the diner. The scene stirred Joseph McCracken with the wonder of how all this came together. He believed the thin veneer of civilization that held the lid on dark chaos was best exemplified in America's diners. The fire from Gigio's grill flashed with yellow and orange flames reaching three-feet high.

The diner was a symphony of wants and needs being satisfied by both the customers and owners. Has not the agrarian and fry cook filled the bellies of multitudes so America could pursue her highest ambitions?

Joseph removed his well-worn fedora. He placed it on a single peg by the restaurant's entrance. He wore brown work boots, gray utility trousers folded at the cuffs, and a blue, tartan-plaid, flannel shirt, unbuttoned and exposing his thermal undershirt. Dark, dry cracks covered his fingers and knuckles, stained black from long, arduous hours, most recently picking, pruning, digging, wrenching, prying, and pulling. His hair, grey at the temples, was short and uncombed.

He stepped behind the counter and took his coffee mug from the hook above the coffee pots. The mug disappeared in his left hand and gave one the impression Joseph poured coffee directly into his open fist.

"Morning, Joe Mac!" A couple of good old boys at the back of the diner spied and waved to Joseph, then continued with their conversation.

Joseph inhaled deeply, the smell of bacon, eggs, fried potatoes, and toast mixed with the aroma of hot coffee. It was not just the smell of food cooking, it meant they would not go hungry today. Breakfast was commerce, production, industry, liberty, and the freedom to enjoy it all at one's leisure, out of the harsh elements.

Joseph took a seat at the counter and watched his friend Gigio working like a madman trying to keep up with all the patrons' orders. "Damned dago, you look busier than a one-legged man in an ass kickin' contest!" Joseph said. "Did you save me any?"

Plates hit the stainless-steel counter separating the cook's kitchen from the waitresses' station. Gigio banged out a ditty on the ringer calling the waitresses' attention to the hot food ready to serve. Gigio flipped the toggle switch that lit the numbers; 2, 5, 7, 11, so the waitresses could see, from the length of the restaurant, to which table the orders were to be delivered.

"Let's go ladies! Hot food for hungry American citizens! I didn't come halfway around the world to serve cold food to my American friends!"

"Hardy, harr, harr," Gigio continued with Joseph. "Any later and you'd have to order lunch! Why are you so late, too much Glenfiddich last night, huh, too much haggis?" he yelled over the din of patrons. "The sun's near up!"

Joseph smiled. "Very funny. I was up late getting ready for the harvest."

"How do you like the new light system? Tells the waitresses which booth the order's for. They don't have to walk the whole length of the restaurant to check. Just look at the light!"

"Hey! Fancy!" Joseph said.

"Ain't technology great?" Gigio asked rhetorically. "Time is money, my friend!"

The sky changed from black and blue to dove grey. The Sierra Nevada Mountains were etched in a pre-dawn platinum that threatened to explode any second. The tubs overflowed with dirty dishes and napkins. The waitress attempted to balance yet one more saucer on top of the mountain of dirty dishes beneath the counter. The saucer slipped and shattered on the floor. Of course, that was followed by the nonsensical, yet obligatory, schadenfreude from a few goofs starved for enlightenment.

The lethargic busboy meandered from the kitchen to sweep up the pieces, but not to collect the tubs full of dirty dishes under the counter or on trollies throughout the diner.

"If you don't move your little butt and quit with that lazy attitude," Agnes said, shaking her finger at the young man and frowning, "I'm gonna kick your skinny little ass the hell out of this damned restaurant!"

"Now get this mess swept up and get those tubs emptied!" In a whirl Agnes strode, coffee pot in each hand, to the applause of the patrons. Gigio and Joseph shared a glance and smiled.

The sun broke from behind the mountains, casting shards of sunlight through the giant, yellowing ash trees. Long, purple shadows webbed down Yosemite Avenue. The large windows fronting the diner's southern exposure offered early customers a feast of light's triumph over darkness.

From one booth to another, a volley of conversation. "Hey, Cy'," as Cyril was called, "I hear you finally sold that alfalfa," a neighbor said.

"I thought I saw you out there waterin' them bails down last night," said another fellow, sitting across the table from Cyril. Laughter spilled, even from those not familiar with the parties involved.

"Now, that's a damn lie, Orville, and you know it," Cyril said. "I'd never do nothin' like that." He winked at his friends at the table across the aisle.

"Not if you didn't think you could get away with it," a buddy at the cash register interjected. More laughter from the patrons.

"Oh yeah? Well, wasn't it you got caught fillin' your hogs' bellies with lead pellets in their feed just 'fore weighing in for slaughter last year?"

All of a sudden patrons groaned and gasped. The sun's golden blaze slammed against the large, plate glass windows of the diner. Customers winced at the brightness; a few giggled at the explosion of light.

"Well. Get out there and unroll the damned awning!" Agnes shook her head. "I swear! That boy'd lose his pecker if it wasn't attached."

Agnes took off from the cook's window with two armloads of breakfast plates full of steaming food.

Bacon and sausage sizzled, along with a couple of steaks, four hot link sausages, and six pork chops on the grill. Chorizo and scrambled eggs mounded up on the cooler end of the griddle. The waffle iron oozed batter and steam. Homemade venison and wild boar chili simmered at the end of the cook's station. Rabbit stew or duck sausage with sauerkraut were the day's lunch specials. Bert supplied the rabbit and duck. Boar and venison steaks thawed in a pan by the griddle alongside the beef steaks. Coffee percolated in the waitresses' station.

Joseph's mouth watered from the aroma. The busboy slammed his cart between the counter and waitresses' station collecting tubs of dirty dishes, replacing them with empty tubs under the counter.

"Okay boys, take it easy or you're liable to end up with a pot of hot java in your lap." Gigio's wife, Mildred, slapped a plate of boar's sausage, fried potatoes with onions, and eggs over easy on the counter in front of Joseph then returned with a plate of sausage and gravy over two biscuits.

Bert, approached the cash register. He pointed to Joseph's massive back and said, "There's a couple of plates in under there somewhere, but don't go stickin' your hand in there just yet. Wait for 'im to fall asleep, first."

Without looking up, and between chewing food, Joseph asked, "What are you doing today, besides annoying paying customers?"

Gigio smiled, listening to his friends.

"Cleaning bunny cages and the delivery truck, staying out of Ethel's way," he said. "What's up with you folks?"

"Hey, Bertie bring me two dozen bunnies and a half dozen Canadian's."

Bert gave Gigio a thumbs up. "Gotcha! Tomorrow."

Joseph continued. "Apple harvest; checking boxes, conveyor belts. I'm gonna do a dry run. Maybe take a drive down to the river, see if any of those folks want to do some picking, earn a little money. I don't need that many. Maybe twenty or so."

An eavesdropping patron added, "I swear, if we're not having to deal with damned unions and picking crews, it's the damned wholesalers and buyers up in San Francisco. Sometimes, it's more work than it's worth. Let 'em grow their own damned food, boy! Wouldn't the price of produce go up then?"

"I can deal with the buyers. It's the trash hanging out all along the market district," Joseph returned, "the one's trying to relieve us of a season's wages. Know what I mean?"

"Yep, prostitutes, pick-pockets, dope fiends . . . the city's riddled with that shit."

"Well, that and gull shit."

"Yeah, well, you might want to keep an eye out for some of those organizers when you head down to the river."

"I was over at Floyd's gettin' a trim and a shave and this ol' boy was there. Had a scar on the left side of his melon, like someone knocked the hell out of him, and not that long ago from the look of it." The patron grabbed a toothpick from the shot glass by the register. "Anyway, he was talkin' of organizing against citrus."

"I'm pickin' apples," Joseph said.

He looked incredulously at Joseph. "Yeah? I hadn't heard."

Bert chuckled at the man's sarcasm. "Well, maybe apples, grapes, and cotton will give them knuckleheads something to warm up on until the citrus is ready. Why else is he here so early?"

When it's harvestin' time, it's organizin' time here in what used to be a great valley," Bert said.

"Say! What's so wrong about wantin' more money for doin' these lousy jobs, huh?" the busboy interjected.

Joseph held his coffee cup to his lips and eyed the busboy.

Agnes slapped him on the back of his head. "Nothing if you'd just do these lousy jobs!" She continued on through the bat doors to the kitchen in search of more napkins the busboy should have already put in the dispensers.

The patron was a big cattleman who lived southeast of Chowchilla. He approached the small crowd at the cash register. "Let those little red bastards come near my ranch and I'll cut 'em three ways; long, deep, and repeatedly."

"You wouldn't hurt someone just because they wanted a better life, would you?" asked the busboy.

"If they came on my property to make demands of me, I would. Who says I have to support their better life? Besides, they don't have a problem shittin' on the side of my road, in orchards, in alfalfa fields, row crops. No, they don't stop at that. They burn barns, packing sheds that don't belong to them, but for which they demand a say. Killing workers who just want to go back to work?"

"Hell! I've found dead cattle on my property cut up and boned. Just took the damned meat and ran!"

"Why work? Hell, just take what you want till you get what you consider to be your fair share. They all seem ready to give up a little freedom forever for a little food, shelter today."

"I could go on, but you get my drift. It's those union types think labor is the savior of American industry that are causin' the problems."

"I'm sayin' they aren't, mostly because they don't have a skill or any financial interest in the business. Anyone can see, because of all the trouble with unions, workers are just goin' to be replaced by machines. Wait and see."

"Without me and these waitresses, this place would close down," the busboy argued.

"Please, go on," Bert said. He winked at Joseph.

"Uh, huh, I thought so. You little asshole. Without Gigio and Maggie takin' the risk of starting this place, before you were born, there wouldn't be a diner for you to demand ownership of. I knew you was red," the rancher said. "You ever seen an organizer on my property, boy?"

"No."

"And you never will, neither." The rancher pulled his cowboy hat low, thumbing the edge of the hat's brim.

"That's the way with them. They want part, hell, half of what you have as long as you have it to take. But let one of us fall on hard times and see how many of them union bastards are camped in our orchards donating their union dues and time to getting our farms up and running again."

"It's us sticking our necks out, taking all the risks. It's us who should be getting the profits, least most of them, anyway. Hell, if a man doesn't want to work, he can jus' move his tired ass on down the road," Bert said directly to the busboy now. "But he doesn't have to stand out in the road so's no one else, who wants to work, can't get in."

"They ain't even from this area, anyway. Mostly San Francisco and Sacramento," said the rancher.

"Roosevelt's minimum-wage law says I don't pay a minimum amount to an employee per hour, it's against the law. Okay, we just won't hire. How smart was that? How many business owners won't hire just because they can't afford to pay what the government *considers* fair, then *demands* the rancher pay it? There's only so much money for labor costs. Gigio's just going to raise the price of waffles to pay the hourly rate Roosevelt demands he pay to the busboy. You and I are going to pay for it in the end."

"Trust me, they're gonna use this crisis we're in to take more control. You ever see a government give back power?"

"But they're so much smarter than us filthy farmers." Bert said. "They all have the answers on how you can be happier if you just listen to them. Would someone please tell our self-anointed betters, we pick the way we choose to live here in America? Not them? When was the last time one of them took responsibility for their bad decision? Ever see one of them politicians get fired?"

"The problem I have is that if you don't give them union people what they demand they're just as likely to incite the migrants to burn down your barn. Either way, they win. They get their money or they enrage people who then destroy fields and barns and factories. Either way, I lose," another man added.

Mildred worked her coffee pot like an oil derrick down the row of tables toward the cash register where the farmers and ranchers gathered.

"Say Milly, what if you had yourself a real cook, not that hash slingin' wop back there, but a real cook? And this cook says to you, 'Milly, I've been here for ten years. I can cook anything. I want more money.' What do you say to him?" the rancher asked.

"Yeah, like that little Bolsheveki you have working for you." Bert said, pointing at the busboy who cowered from the attention.

"I'd show him the door. I don't need a high-priced, gourmet chef. I need someone who can sling hash and fast too. We have a nice little business here and it doesn't require any great skill, just a lot of long, hard hours. If I had a gourmet restaurant I'd pay the going rate for a gourmet chef, but then I wouldn't have any of you boys as customers. I'm pretty sure about that."

"Now let's go! Move it! I got hungry customers who want to come in and eat and you all are blocking my door. Come on, now! Let's go!"

There was laughter and a shuffling of feet between the ringing of the cash register and the bell above the diner door.

The last in line to pay, Cyril, asked Millie and Joseph, "Think your dishwasher's red?"

"I know he's red!" said Agnes as she blew by with plates full of food.

"I think he wants to learn. He's curious." Millie said.

"Just to let you know, I seen him over at the park hanging out with those agitators that give their speeches on weekends. That fella with the scar he was talkin' about was there. Him and that teacher from the high school, what's his name? Scambray. That's it."

"What?" Millie said.

"Scambray, the teacher over at the high school. I saw him over there listening to speeches with ol' butt boy back there, the dishwasher," Cyril said. "And that fella with the scar."

"Say, Joe Mac, you got time to take an order before you leave?" Gigio called out from the cook's counter.

Cyril raised his hand to all around in salutation. Farmers paid their tabs and left a nickel or dime for Agnes or Millie.

Joseph, with a mouthful of food, waved.

"Whata ya got out there, Joe?" Millie asked.

Joseph swallowed. "Usual, later summer and the beginnings of early fall vegetables; carrots, beets, potatoes, summer squash. Winter squash isn't ready yet. Salad greens are coming on, pumpkins, garlic and onions, last of the corn."

"How about bring me eight boxes? I think I can make some minestrone soup, maybe a nice stew . . . slaw, cobblers. Hey, how about apples, got any left?"

"As a matter of fact, we're pickin' in a couple of days. Grapes are done," Joseph said after slurping his hot coffee. "Soon as I can get the shed up and running and get a crew together. Then," Joseph slapped his hands together, "off to San Francisco. Should be finished by the weekend." Joseph rubbed his chin and thought of the work ahead and the long drive.

"I can bring you a couple of boxes on my way out of town, or I can tell Dash to bring them with your order."

"Sure Joe, Dash can bring them. I can make some apple pies, cobbler, squash soup, sauce . . . we can always use apples. Make it five vegetables and three boxes of apples. Alright, what else you got?"

"A little dried meat. Hogs and calves are about ready. That's five vegetable and you say three apples?"

"Yeah. No, wait. If it's your last haul of the season let's make it eight and five. I'll get back to you on the meat. Let me see what I got," Millie said. She rang another customer through the register.

"I'll tell Dash." Joseph thanked Millie, whom he had known his entire life. Gigio raised a free hand while he worked a large pumice stone back and forth across the griddle.

"Hardest working man in town," Joseph said to Milly.

After sliding a Standing Liberty quarter under his plate, Joseph donned his hat and headed to the door.

"Say, Joe Mac, ya goin' huntin' anytime soon? I'm gonna need some meat," Gigio said. He wiped his greasy hands on his apron.

Joseph smiled and looked at Mildred, "How about when I get done with the apples? We can take a couple of days and either work the foothills or work both sides of the river for a couple of days."

"Swell. See you then."

The bell above the diner door announced Joseph's exit.

He enjoyed the first crisp, autumn wind licking down from off the coast of British Columbia. The scent of Western Cedar smoke drifted on the breeze.

The little town of Madera was coming alive with shop owners opening doors and pushing carts of wares and local produce to the sidewalk in front of their shops. Old man Saroyan unrolled the green and white canvas awning in front of his market and waved to Joseph.

Citizens leaving the diner headed to their offices and greeted each other along their walk.

17

In 1843, Joseph's grandfather, Ivor, jumped off the exploratory expedition charged with mapping the hinterland of California for the burgeoning United States government.

Ivor spoke the language of the Mariposa Indians. He trapped furs and sought gold in the valley known as Ahwahne. He hunted with them and took no meat. He even gathered wood, ground acorns, and helped the women of the tribe stake skins to dry in the sun.

The Mariposa warriors made fun of Ivor helping the women. One warrior jokingly asked for Ivor's hand in marriage.

Having garnered the trust of the Mariposa Indians, Ivor traded and translated between the tribe and thousands of the newly arrived gold prospectors to the magnificent valley.

To ensure the Mariposa tribe's relationship with the whites would grow stronger, the chief gave his daughter to Ivor. Her name was Ti'wa Umta and Ivor called her Ti. Ivor and his new bride settled down in Ahwahne and soon had a young son, Jack.

The quiet life Ivor and Ti had built in one of the most beautiful places on earth was disrupted, all at once, by three gold miners who arrived from San Francisco. They misunderstood the primitive state of the local tribe and attempted to take advantage of trading and the tribe's women. The three prospectors had little regard for that which Ivor pleaded on behalf of the Mariposas. The disrespect resulted in an attack that left the three intruders dead at the hands of the insulted Mariposas who did not deny their deed, justified by tribal law.

The Mariposa Battalion was ordered to dispatch the Mariposas from their homes. Only after the battalion's second attempt at removing the Indians did the Mariposa grudgingly depart. They traveled east, and eventually, those that did not attempt to return to Ahwahne, disappeared into the tribe of Mono Lake, Paiute Indians of eastern California. Some of the tribe, however, evaded the Mariposa Battalion and continued to live in Ahwahne as they had for thousands of years.

Rather than moving east toward the Paiute Indians Ivor McCracken, Ti, and their new son Jack, moved their small family to what later would become Eastern Madera County, after first separating from Fresno County in 1893.

On the Valley floor, Ivor busied himself with his farm and, along with a half dozen Mariposa Indians, herded hogs to feed the people of the fast-growing port town of San Francisco and her immigrants seeking gold. Ivor especially enjoyed taking the Mariposas for their first visit to San Francisco.

Ivor, his beautiful wife, and Jack worked their land together, often with the assistance of Ti's family. Slowly, they gained control of the available water. Then, a patch for grazing here, a patch for growing vegetables there, became a reality. First, an acre or two, then three, until the time when, in keeping with the tradition of the large Spanish haciendas, the U. S. government granted Ivor the land as it is presently occupied by his descendants.

Ivor turned the plow loose behind a couple of seventeen-hand, side-by-side, jack mules. The Mariposas came to watch Ivor work the giant mules and cut open the ground with the shiny metal plow shears. The Indians were employed to assist with the crops and their quality of life improved. Ivor taught them how to turn the earth into grain, how to capture the water, and feed their people.

In the previous millennium the natives had not the notion of putting a plow in the earth, nor were they inclined to raise cattle as had the Spanish a generation before Ivor scouted for Kit Carson.

Here, in this backwater to the gold rush of 1849, prehistoric stone tools met the iron plow for the first time. It was these early explorers and homesteaders such as Ivor, Henry Miller and Charles Lux, turned Californio farmer and rancher, who redirected the waters of the San Joaquin River for the irrigation of crops and grazing land for cattle that allowed the miners and the suppliers to the miners of the gold rush to eat.

Successively, generation upon generation labored at such tasks as digging wells and creating water supplies, creating ponding basins to capture natural run-off and spring water, constructing out buildings, fencing, and finally a barn. Gardens were grown and vegetables stored for winter. Fields were cleared of trees and granite boulders for plowing.

Jack, Joseph, Bert, and Gigio hunted wild boar and elk that roamed the valley foothills and river area, and black bears, deer, and mountain lions higher up. Jack instructed the young men in the art of skinning and staking hides as learned from his mother.

What was killed was eaten; skins and sinew were never wasted. The whole valley lay before them. In Joseph's youth, men were gone for days, surviving on the San Joaquin River and surrounding habitat. They followed the river west to where it turned north and would eventually empty into Suisun Bay.

The valley was an Elysian field where horses stood chest deep in wildflowers and wild grasses for grazing. Standing in the center of the Valley a person could look west and see the Pacific Coastal Range and east to the Sierra Nevada Mountains, sixty miles apart.

Gigio, Bert, and Joseph would ride their horses south from their farms and camp along the San Joaquin River's north bank. With the camp's fire started, Gigio prepared fresh fish and eggs. The boys would tear up a round loaf of bread amongst themselves and drink hot, black coffee with wild honey stolen from the large hives along the banks of the San Joaquin River. They fished the rapid waters for Chinook salmon and rainbow trout. Bass and catfish were taken from the deep, dark pools along the river's edge.

There were always rabbits, squirrels, foxes, raccoons, coyotes, and opossum. Ducks and geese, in the midst of their migratory descent into Central and South America were a delicacy for all. The birds' flight would block out the sun as they migrated.

Bert started a business supplying the local communities with fresh duck, goose, and rabbit. He hauled wagons, loaded with mounds of fowl from a day's shooting, to Fresno and Madera butchers.

Autumn was the time when the natives would come out of the snowy mountains and feast with the early McCracken family, when Joseph was still very young and his father, Jack, still in his prime.

Jack and Joseph were hunting in the foothills, east of their farm, when Jack's wife Elizabeth gave birth to their second child. Eliza, as Jack called her, gave birth alone in the cold house while her men were gone, then died. Their baby girl, without a chance for survival also died and went unnamed until years later, in horror, Florence found out her husband Joseph had a younger sister. Florence pleaded with Jack to name his daughter.

The older Joseph became, the farther his hunting adventures took him, until one day Joseph returned from the small railroad town of Fresno and told his father that he and Bert had joined the Army. Joseph said they wanted to see if the world had more to offer than the hot and dusty San Joaquin Valley.

Jack had lied about his age. At fourteen years old he left Ivor for the Civil War. Only when Joseph had told him of joining the Army did Jack understand how his own father must have felt when he spoke of his itch to leave the Valley and join the fighting on the side of the North.

When chores allowed, Joseph and his son, Dashiell, along with Bert and Gigio, rode horses down to the San Joaquin River and camped. Sometimes Jack would tag along, but mostly getting older and with his eyesight and memory fading, he felt a nuisance and came up with excuses not to go. Jack was now hunched over and required a cane to walk. He had quit riding and working horses when he turned eighty, over a decade ago.

Jack set a pitcher of lemonade on the table. He and his daughter-in-law, Florence, sat on the wrap around porch. He asked her questions just to hear her melodic voice.

Florence asked Jack of his childhood growing up with the Indians of Yosemite and the surrounding area. She asked about Jack's wife, who had come through Fresno with her family on their way to Sacramento, then decided to stay when her family continued north. She talked with Jack about Joseph's sister, Shannon.

Jack listened to Floe's voice float on the air above as they drank hot tea or lemonade and watched the purple-and-red sunset on the far side of the Pacific Coastal Range, through the yellowing leaves of the walnut trees.

"Hail to thee, blithe Spirit!
Bird thou never wert,
That from Heaven, or near it,
Pourest thy full heart
In profuse strains of unpremeditated art."

18

Years earlier migrants created a hobo jungle below the Southern Pacific Railway line, where it intersects the San Joaquin River.

Joseph suspected the Mariposas, or Yokuts as they were now called, had fishing camps, hunted, and had collected honey in this area for thousands of years. West of the intersection there was a gradual descent to the terrain that allowed cars and small trucks to drive to the river's edge.

Joseph noticed ramshackle cars and trucks on flattened tires along the river's edge. Piles of trash close to the river threatened to contaminate the water supply farther downstream.

"I wonder if people will ever quit wandering the earth and finally find peace and settle down."

"A man could know the world and never leave his front gate," Joseph thought, recalling the Chinese philosopher. He had not been interested in the world since he had come home from his hitch in the army. Joseph found peace with his family and within the boundaries of his farm.

East, under the railway trestle, camped single men, hoboes, bums, walking men, drifters, fruit tramps, and criminals on the lam.

They resided in the hobo jungle while looking for work or to take a short break in their travels.

In the early morning some men squatted and talked quietly while smoking rolled cigarettes and warming their backsides by smoky fires.

From high on the northern bank of the San Joaquin River, Joseph watched a man roll pipe tobacco with cigarette paper. A baby's cry came from the west camp. Joseph moved toward the crying child. He shuffled his way down the steep switchback used by hunting parties of the Yokut Indians and wild animals. He pulled a trail of dust behind himself rather than driving his truck farther down the river. Joseph grabbed and held tight to a large Manzanita bush to keep from sliding down the embankment. Finally, at the bottom, and after gaining everyone's attention, Joseph approached. He noted the dirty and tattered clothes of the people milling about their vehicles. The river's bank was alive with small fires.

Here and there lanterns hung from thin tree limbs or balanced on uneven boulders and lighted the river's pebbled shore. A few men shaved and washed their privates amongst the sycamore and cottonwood trees, away from the families camped at the river's edge. Every face was a shadow at this early, still hour. Men and women stopped, frozen in time.

Joseph came into full view and was not the county sheriff, or a thug looking to steal their change. Men from the eastern camp walked under the trestle bridge and stood or leaned against the railroad pilings to listen to what the stranger had to say.

"Mornin'," Joseph said as he raised his hand in salutation. "I have work for the next couple of days if any of you folks are interested." He scanned the western camp, maybe seven or eight families.

A dirty figure approached Joseph from behind. Roy reminded Joseph of a victim of a bombing. The large-boned man had primitively cut, filthy hair matted on the top of his head. Joseph noticed Roy's broken nose that had not been set properly and scars over both eyebrows. The man's arms were decorated with scars from knife cuts and cigar burns. His dark eyes seemed to have been pushed back into his head and were red around the edges. His dirty overalls, with a thick sheen of grime, covered dirty, red faded long johns. He stood still. His thick lower lip hung heavy. The man held an eating tin in one hand and a knife and fork in the other.

"I'll take it," the big man said.

"You a fightin' man?" Joseph asked.

"I scrap a bit. You gotta fight for me, you have to talk to my boss."

Joseph noticed the man's teeth had been knocked out leaving a black rectangle in his face. Small cauliflower bunches sprouted from either side of his melon.

Joseph turned so the majority of the folks gathered could hear.

"I can employ about thirty or so people for a day or two, is all."

"What's the work?"

"I have apples that need to be picked. No agitator types, got it? I'll put anyone causing trouble out on his ear."

"I said, I'd take the job," the fighter said.

"I heard you." Joseph looked the man in the eyes.

"You ain't afraid of them organizers, are you?"

"Not a bit, friend. There isn't a man walking the face of this earth I'm afraid of. I just want my trees picked, in good time, with no trouble."

Speaking to the crowd again, "I don't care about all that organizing nonsense and trouble that goes with it."

A voice from the bachelors' camp said, "Lots of folks here 'bouts don't take too kindly to the way all you farmers been treatin' 'em."

Joseph turned towards the speaker.

"Maybe, like you, they ought to find another line of work then. My neighbors don't take too kindly to strangers sleeping, shitting in their orchards, and stealing from them."

The fighter smiled stupidly, scratched his fat face with his fork, and said, "Maybe you got a point there." Then with his smile fading, "There ain't no work right now doin' nothin' else."

Joseph looked toward the families. "We have a small family operation. Break for lunch and an hour before dusk to put equipment away and clean up. You get back and forth to the orchard yourselves. You can't stay in the orchards and my neighbors won't have anyone squatting in their fields. Too much trash is left behind. I'm paying . . . ," Joseph raised his voice for all to hear so there would be no misunderstanding, ". . . five cents a five-gallon bucket, seven cents for a picking bag, and . . . ,"

"Jesus Christ! A man can't eat on five cents a bucket, let alone his family! Don't you hear that baby crying over yonder?" a voice said from the crowd of bachelors.

Joseph could not see the man behind the voice. Nor did he look. ". . . twenty-five cents an hour for the packing shed. Like I said, I've got work for about thirty or so people, for a couple of days.

I'm not a big farmer. But, considering the dire straits folks are in, I'm willing to hire you folks when I can, to help out a little."

"Guess ya can't hear that baby cryin' over yonder," another voice said.

Joe turned around to face the bachelor camp and continued, "I'm not lookin' for trouble. If you want a job and a hot meal, I have work for you. If your aim is to get people riled up and cause problems, my farm would not be the place for you."

"You want trouble, I'll answer to that."

"More babies are a goin' hungry tonight, I guess."

Joseph walked over to the fighting man, "What's your name?" he asked.

"Roy."

"Okay, Roy, I don't know if you know who that is, and I'm thinking you do. I don't want trouble, but you'll find plenty if they cause any problems at my place."

Joseph left directions to his farm and told the people to arrive at sunup if they wanted the work. He then headed west down the automobile path rather than attempting the switchback he first descended.

The fighter turned to the agitator and smiled. "Did I do a good job?"

"Just fine, big boy," the agitator rubbed the scar on his head. "Now, let's get some of these folks together; see what we got here."

19

Tired, solitary men who moved mostly in the dark and laid low during the day meandered in at all hours throughout the night and remained just beyond the camp's fires and lanterns, on the peripheral and darker edges of camp.

The quiet men were not fruit tramps nor migrants. About the union business, they cared not a whit. Some of these weary men had been in camp less than an hour or so. They said little and spoke of no direction in particular regarding where they had come from or their destination. Their pasts were a closed book. First names were used and those were a lie. They would not be picking fruit or working fields today.

As the morning sky turned from charcoal to grey, Roy and the agitator began kicking the sleeping men of the bachelor's camp and barking orders to fall in or get left behind. The men slowly began piecing together their day, while others tried to sleep and were annoyed by the commotion.

Those yawning, rubbing eyes, and scratching crotches, meandered one behind the other, farting, like farm animals, all along the gravel path that took them to the top where the union vehicles idled.

To the migrants down at the river's edge, Roy yelled from up top, "If you need a ride we got three cars! Climb in or climb on!"

"Wanna tell them when we're leaving?" the union man asked.

"Roy?"

"Yeah, boss?"

"Do you want to tell them when we're leaving?"

Roy took a deep breath. "And we're leaving in five minutes! We'll see the rest of you there!"

Never, on the face of the earth, had there been a more disheveled looking mob of nomads on their path to financial freedom and independence. The small caravan of six vehicles inched down the dusty gravel road. As though spirits draped in black, workers hung on the outside of each vehicle, coats, jackets, and hats flapping and popping in the breeze.

The dark, oxidized jalopies limped to the right side of the road, just before arriving at Joseph's long driveway. The quiet army-in-rags milled around their vehicles and stood huddled together toward the front of the column.

"You folks can leave your cars here and follow me up the drive to the packing shed and we'll get you going with equipment and instructions," Bert said.

At the packing shed Joseph addressed the crowd of pickers.

"Please be gentle with the fruit. It bruises easily. I know what it takes to pick this orchard. I've been picking it my whole life. My son here will be the pacer. Keep up with him, you'll be fine."

"Looks to me like that healthy young lad there can outwork any of us starving here."

"If you don't want the job, now's the time to leave. If you want to agitate, go somewhere else. I told you yesterday." Joseph said, noticing the mouth. "Give me an excuse to kick you out of here, along with your boys."

He then turned to Bert, "Looks like the one they've been talkin' about got in under the wire. See the scar on the side of his face?"

"Yep. Want me to throw his ass out?" Bert asked.

"Not yet."

Joseph spoke to the workers as Bert and Dashiell passed out picking bags, buckets, and ladders, "You get paid by the container. Like I said, five cents a bucket and seven cents a bag. Don't leave anything on the trees. Bert, Dashiell, anything to add?"

"Load up! Let's get to work! The day's wasting away here. Leave that agitatin' bullshit out of my orchard!" Jack commanded. The pickers loaded on the bin trailer that Jack drove to the apple orchard.

Picking began at the farthest tree row from the shed. Bert assigned four pickers to a tree. He knew the pickers, as with his horses headed to the barn, tended to walk and work faster the closer they got to the packing shed.

Jack drove the team of two Creams down the third row of trees and stopped at the sixth tree in. The horses snuffed the ground and shook in their harnesses and rings. Bert lifted two short ladders from one of the boxes on the bin trailer and propped them against the sides of the four-by-four foot square bins to assist the pickers unloading their buckets and bags of apples.

"And don't be breaking the tree limbs all to hell and gone, neither. Let's go. Time's wastin'!" Jack shouted.

The morning was cool under the canopy of shade provided by the apple trees. Dappled rays of sunlight broke through the limbs and leaves of the trees heavily laden with dark-red, Arkansas Black apples. Dust particles from workers, animals, and equipment danced in the beams of sunlight.

Dashiell started in on his row scampering up the ladder and into the big apple tree while other workers picked around the bottom edges of the tree.

The agitator looked up. "Hey, kid. How's it goin'?" he asked Dashiell and offered a pleasant smile.

Dashiell paid no attention to the man with the worm scar on his face, other than to acknowledge his greeting.

Joseph took the remaining workers into the packing shed and prepared to receive the apples.

Jack slowly climbed down from the wagon. His cane hung from his right forearm. Bert watched the bowlegged, old man slowly descend from the wagon and wondered how many more harvests old Jack had in him. Jack wiped the sweatband of his hat then gathered a few apples that had fallen to the ground and sliced them for the horses. He patted and talked to the Creams as he fed them. Foam dripped into puddles on the ground below the horses' chins.

Pickers began to descend the ladders with picking buckets and bags full of sweet, delicious apples. Jack took up his penny can. As each picker unloaded their basket or bag into the bin, Jack handed them their pennies. He also inspected the quality of the apples coming from the pickers.

"Hey, damn it! You bounce another bucket of apples into a bin like that and it'll be your last," Jack admonished all of the pickers.

"Jesus Christ! Use your heads! You bruise them, they're worthless. We didn't work on them since last fall's pruning just so you could come in here and ruin them in an afternoon. Now be careful! Goddamn it all to hell!"

20

Joseph finished giving the tour of the packing shed and assigned the migrants their jobs. The packing shed was white washed to reflect the sun's rays and had a corrugated tin roof. Without electricity, the migrants worked in shadow, except where the double shed doors were opened at either end. The people went to work preparing the shed to receive the fruit.

Driving another team of Creams, Bert pulled his bin trailer into the orchard a row over and just beyond Jack's crew. He moved the penny bucket to the empty wagon and helped Jack down.

Bert mounted the wagon with bins full of apples and drove the first of many loads to the west end of the packing shed to be unloaded and processed by the crew assembled in the shed to inspect, size, and pack the apples into boxes.

He drove the team as close to the edge of the platform of the packing shed as possible. The side rails of the bin trailer were taken off by a couple of dock workers. The bins were then pushed across the rollers on the bottom of the bin trailer onto the rollers of the shed's loading dock with minimal lifting, thus very little bruising of the fruit.

The day warmed. Joseph and his father walked the orchard to check the progress of the workers. The dark, rich, orchard floor reminded Joseph of the jungles he had fought in alongside Bert and George. Memories flashed across Joseph's consciousness.

A jungle. The rich, dark, fecund soil. The face of an enemy combatant in his last gasp for air. Memories haunted at the oddest times, day or night, without warning. Faces flashed before the mind's eye and of which would never be spoken. The memory Joseph held snapped and he was brought back to the present by the sound of Bert yelling at one of the pickers.

The weight of the picked apples worked against the muscles in the legs as hungry and sore laborers climbed up and down the ladders throughout the morning. Moving ladders, carrying nearly half their weight in apples, and always it seemed, reaching for apples and limbs just beyond one's safe reach, wore down the pickers.

The workers began their day weak with hunger. Others, inexperienced at picking anything, worked through their aches and pains. It was the reward of cash money they sought; money for food, supplies, maybe even a little respect.

Oh! Just for the sound of two silver bells ringing in one's pocket! They labored on throughout the morning in a quiet, monotonous drone, like bees gathering pollen.

At lunch break the pickers, shiny with sweat and head down, wiped themselves with rags or handkerchiefs, some of which had been cut down from old bedding. They arched and twisted to stretch tired and cramped bodies. They drove knotted fists into the small of their backs to loosen taut muscles. They gathered around their vehicles and ate on what they had available and drank coffee or water supplied by the McCrackens.

Workers shed their outer garments. Some folks napped on the ground under orchard trees, or curled in a fetal position with fedoras blocking the light. Some napped in their vehicles. Worn boots stuck out of the passenger-side window of one junker. A smelly pair of filthy socks, full of rent, stuck out of a window revealing grotesque white sweaty feet, toes etched in black.

People smiled and scratched their heads at the innovative packing process the McCracken's had created in the shed. Electricity had not found its way to this part of the county and it would be years before it would.

The whole operation was designed to lessen, to the greatest extent possible, the lifting and dumping of fruit. Their rationale was that they could work longer and more efficiently, and of course the fruit would incur less damage. Their method was crude and more reminiscent of the dawn of the industrial revolution. However, the operation was efficient, economical, and most importantly, simple.

An old, dilapidated, flatbed truck was the power source that ran the entire operation. The truck, minus its wheels, was raised and level with the gearbox inside the shed. Joseph used his Lincoln welder powered by a gas generator to weld the frame of the truck to metal posts set in the ground. The rear axle of the truck was fitted with two sprockets that drove two chains attached to sprockets in the corner of the shed. The sprockets drove a conveyor system which transported the produce around the shed in an oval pattern. It was the same type of engineering used when the men cut wood high up in the mountains.

The truck would be jacked up, the wheel taken off and replaced with a hub that drove a six-inch-wide belt that powered a saw blade.

Apple bins were pushed off the trailer and across the rollers of the dock to large galvanized horse troughs used as cooling and cleaning tanks.

Apples retrieved from the cooling tank were placed on the conveyor belt to be culled, sorted, polished, and packed. Bad or culled produce was tossed behind the sorters into bins to be used as feed for livestock.

Three cardboard boxes set on racks at a 45-degree angle next to the culler and packers. The finished produce was packed by size; large, medium, and small with boxes labeled accordingly. On each box was the packer's initials, for quality control. Boxes were inspected and tallied by Joseph. Packers were paid by the number of boxes packed. Full boxes were removed from their racks and put onto hand trucks, then wheeled to the opposite end of the packing shed from which the fruit entered.

Workers kept the full boxes of fruit moving out to the awaiting truck. Empty boxes replaced full boxes.

Joseph continued to conduct quality checks and stack apple boxes on his truck as the movers brought box after box of fruit to the awaiting flatbed truck.

This labor continued, uninterrupted, throughout the morning and only stopped at midday for the noon meal, then back at it until nearly thirty minutes before dark. Thus, the citizen his fresh apple.

The sun's light almost spent, the workers dragged their weary souls toward their vehicles parked along the road. Jack, Joseph, Dashiell, and Bert met the well-worn workers where the end of the gravel driveway met the hardscrabble road.

Bert sat in the front of the wagon eating his supper scooped from pots in the back of the wagon. Jack and Dashiell ladled hot chili beans and rice onto plates and into cups and tin cans. One fellow took his meal on a piece of tree bark, another on an old hubcap.

Earlier in the day, Florence had taken a few of the older women and those too young to work in the orchard or shed to her home. There she instructed them in preparing the evening's meal and other, more domesticated, chores. Some worked in the vegetable garden pulling vegetables and washing them for others to pickle. Some cleaned dishes while others prepared food for the picking and shed crews.

Florence had them thoroughly wash themselves and their children outside in a makeshift shower concealed within four large tarps strung from giant walnut trees. The difference a little respect added to the quality of their lives could not be measured. Florence's house and yard were filled with women enjoying each other's company.

Florence had discussed with Joseph the idea of hiring a woman to live with them and help with the gardening, cleaning, and various other chores on the farm. She adored the young ladies and she loved their little children. Surrounded by men and farm chores, Florence prized the opportunity to participate in women's talk. Joseph was, it seemed, perpetually distracted by the farm's management.

The McCracken family began the practice of feeding their workers years earlier when the Yokut tribe helped with the planting, harvesting, and construction on the farm. Some farmers feared feeding the migrants would be seen as a weakness to be exploited by the migrants traveling up and down the Golden State Highway. Not so the McCrackens.

Joseph's philosophy was to treat others as he would hope to be treated if he had lost his farm and was down on his luck. There were, however, those who could not be placated.

Dashiell ladled from two, large, steaming pots. From the first pot, a scoop of rice. From the second, a ladle of chili with wild bore's meat, tomatoes, onions, beans, and peppers was poured over the steaming rice. There was always a large pot of stewed in-season vegetables available for the workers.

"This all we get for sweatin' all day long picking your apples?" The agitator said.

Dashiell recognized the man from earlier that morning and understood, then, how the fellow might have received the scar on his face.

"No, sir. You got paid for the work you did. This is extra."

The union man took a quick step toward Dashiell. "You gettin' smart with me, boy?"

"No, sir. I was just . . . ."

Joseph slammed the lid on the pot of stewed vegetables. Bert laid his plate gently, quietly on the wooden seat of the wagon and slowly climbed down. Dashiell was the son that Bert and his wife, Ethel could never have. Bert's heart rate began to quicken, muscles became taut within his sweat-dried work clothes. He slowly walked to the other end of the wagon where Dashiell was serving.

Joseph's large frame blocked the view of the man with the worm scar on the side of his head.

"You seem not to appreciate the thought. You don't want the food, back away from the pots, mister," Joseph said.

Bert took note of the eerie, unemotional monotone of Joseph's voice. Bert had heard Joseph's quiet tone before. It never ended well for the other party. Joseph was the personification of quiet before the storm and Bert respected Joseph's lethality.

"I got no kick with these folks. You don't want the food? Move the hell away from them pots. I'll take his portion too," a fruit tramp said from the line.

"Well, I'll tell you one thing," the agitator said. He surveyed the man and the line of hungry folks. "You might fool some of these people with your cheap offer of kindness," he looked back at Joseph and Bert, "a little bit of beans and rice." His face wrinkled into a dried apple. He moved to the vicinity of his protectors and stood amongst them. "I'm not fooled. Tomorrow will be different."

"Boy! Why don't you take that agitatin' bullshit back to old Europe where it belongs?" Bert said.

He and Joseph were a combination of hardtack farmers who had butchered, worked large animals, and lived muscular lives out of doors and lethal veterans who had chased Marxists throughout the Philippines, Central, and South America. They could not be intimidated by what was standing in front of them now. The scent of musk filled the air as Bert and Joseph converged on the union man.

"You got your pay. You got your food. Now clear out, mister. Don't come back tomorrow!" Joseph commanded.

Joseph's eyes were lit. Looking at the bare-knuckle fighter Joseph said, "I told you I didn't want the likes of them on my property if they were gonna be a problem. You one of them?"

The fighter looked at Joseph innocently. "Not me. I like to eat too much."

"Don't come back tomorrow." Joseph commanded.

"You da boss. No sweat off my ass." Roy smiled.

"Who do you think you are, God? Telling a man when he can and can't work, when he can and can't eat. I could have you shut down tomorrow." The agitator snapped his fingers. "Like that!"

"Your fruit can rot along with you, for all I care. Labor rules industry! Without labor your factory farm dries up and blows away!"

"Ya ignorant little, Wobblie bastard," Bert said. "You think this is your land and you have a say? We ain't saying when you can and can't work. I'm saying you can't work here, ya fuckin' moron!" Bert was locked on his prey.

"Where were you when this land was being cleared, or planted, or the irrigation water was being brought to each tree by bucket? Back in Europe? Where the hell were you when we worked fourteen- and twenty-hour days putting all this together?" Bert was just coming to a boil.

"Our parents taught the Indians around here how to farm and feed themselves. Where were you then?"

On the hoods and in the seats of vehicles, with doors flung open, or sitting on the running boards, the migrants watched the action. A walking man held a lump of food motionless between jaw and cheek.

"We killed socialist bastards, like you, by the bushel basket!"

Jack's English mastiffs, Diesel, Kanga, and Axel were in the back of the wagon and growled a low, guttural warning. Joseph raised his hand and the giant beasts quieted down, but remained attentive.

"The man said clear out!" Bert made a move toward the agitator. Joseph grabbed his arm and held him back.

"Ya ungrateful sonofabitch!" Bert declared while being restrained. "This is the most food some of these people have had in days! *And it ain't enough*? I'm gonna eat your fuckin' eyeballs!"

A man sat on the running board of one of the vehicles eating, a large spoonful of food was suspended between his plate and mouth. One old man who could no longer hear gummed his food and chuckled at his good fortune.

"Hot Damn! These are high times, my friends! Hot damn!"

Joseph and Bert backed the agitator and his men, who had gathered during the conversation, toward their vehicles. A few workers mumbled to themselves. Others spoke to those within earshot.

"I'll be back. This here's a fine place to work." From another, "First time I ever got a meal."

Those who rode in with the agitator now watched while shoveling food.

"Oh, I'll be back, too. On that you can count, my friend!" The agitator looked at the farmers. "That road isn't yours!" the agitator roared.

His men scraped the last of their food into their mouths as they congregated more closely around the agitator. The barn-fighter moved between Bert and the union man. "Nope," he said to Bert. The union man stepped closer to his car and the protection of the fighter.

He turned to Joseph, "You better sleep with one eye open, mister. You will answer for your injustices." He then pointed a finger, as if it were a pistol, at Dashiell. He clicked his tongue and winked.

"Get rid of that shit! We don't need their goddamn food," he yelled at the fighter, still shoveling.

"Communist bastard!" Joseph said as he and Dashiell both headed for the agitator's car. Bert and Jack were successful only in restraining Dashiell, the younger version of his father. Joseph yanked his arm loose from Bert's grasp.

He smashed into Roy and sent him sprawling to the other side of the road with his plate and eating utensils. The veteran grabbed the agitator by the collar of his shirt. A meaty, right fist from on high slammed into the worm on the side of the agitator's face. Joseph slammed another right, emphasizing the first knuckles of his hand, into the side of the man's head. The agitator's men moved toward Joseph.

Joseph grabbed up the agitator and flung him into the road towards his men. Joseph was grabbed from behind by Bert as a couple of the agitator's men moved to pick their boss up off the road.

Roy gathered himself up, surprised at the farmer's strength. He flung down his tin of food and went after Joseph who was headed for him.

Jack unloaded one barrel from the Lefever shotgun into the air. The horses started but remained in place. The agitator's men stopped in their tracks. The mastiffs whined to be loosed.

"Next one will drop a few men I suspect." Jack pointed the gun at the fighter.

"Hold on Hoss! That piece of shit ain't worth it," Bert said

"You heard me. Out!" Joseph barked over Bert's struggling body. "Now!" His brow furrowed, as if a three-sheer plow had been pulled across his forehead. His teeth gnashed together.

"I'm goin', I'm goin'. You heard me too, plowboy," the union man said, rubbing the side of his swollen head. The union man's men gathered the agitator's plate, and fork from the road. Two other workers quietly tossed their food onto the ground and climbed into the agitator's car. Roy climbed onto the running board, shielding his boss from any attempted assault by the farmers.

"None of you all need come back tomorrow, neither." Jack said to the few men filing into the vehicles.

"No law against driving a vehicle down a country road, is there, old man?"

"Not so long as you keep your ass movin'," Jack responded.

"For those that are interested in work tomorrow, there will be work. Don't worry about that. Six o'clock, sharp. I'll be here with a shotgun."

The agitator's car passed the farmers.

"See you tomorrow, plowboys," the agitator said as the car turned around in Joseph's driveway.

"Up yours! Ya jackass!" Bert thrust the middle finger of his right hand into the air. Joseph said nothing, but only stared at the low head perched in the passenger window of the car as it moved slowly past. Joseph imagined the agitator's head exploding from a shotgun blast.

"Come on folks, let's get you finished up here. We still got lots more work tonight," Jack said.

"Any of you want the rest of this food? We're going to throw it out if you don't take it." It was not until Jack smiled that the tired and hungry pickers came closer.

A few vehicle headlights were turned on. People moved with long dark shadows attached to and from the pots of steaming food.

"If you can't work for what we're payin', then I hope you can find work worth the pay ya get. We don't have to be enemies," Jack explained.

The Creams shivered in their harnesses and stamped their feet. The migrants descended upon the wagon. The large mastiff, Diesel, yawned and lay back down in the wagon with Axel and Kanga. Within a few minutes the pots were wiped clean with chunks of bread and flour tortillas.

After the last vehicle turned around and headed back to the river, Joseph turned his team of two into the gravel drive that led back to the house. Bert rode shotgun. Jack and Dashiell sat with their legs dangling off the back end of the wagon.

A low, grey tulle fog appeared in large patches on the ground. The horses kicked up puffs of fog as they pulled the wagon down the driveway. Summer, once again, had made her turn toward autumn.

"Dash?"

"Yeah?"

"You don't need to tell your ma about any of that."

"Yep."

Dashiell jumped off the back of the wagon and held Jack's forearm as he scooted off the back. Dashiell took the shotgun from his grandfather and dragged the pots to be cleaned from the back of the wagon. He brought a basket of food from the kitchen and climbed back on the wagon. The three then continued on to the barn. Dashiell unharnessed the Creams, groomed, fed, watered and then turned the beasts out for the night. Their big rumps disappeared into the night that had descended, like a blanket on a cage, over the Valley.

Small lanterns burned in the packing shed and behind the McCracken home where Joseph and Bert's preparations for the next day continued late into the evening. Supplies were restocked, wheels were greased, conveyor belts and pulley wheels aligned and tightened. The barrel of water that served to cool the engine needed to be refilled. The dogs took up positions between the home and barn.

"I sure feel bad about going to San Francisco, considering."

"Nonsense. Those dumbasses? We've been through worse than this," Bert chuckled to himself. "You just get up there safely. Take a nap somewhere. Don't push it too hard. We can handle anything that comes up here. Trust me."

"I'll be over first thing in the morning. I imagine between your pa, Dash, and me, we can get a few apples off a few trees. You get those apples to market and we'll be waiting for you with another full load when you return," Bert said.

"Between the union agitators and those shits at the San Francisco market, it's damned difficult just to farm and sell produce any more."

"Boy! That's no lie."

Dashiell grabbed a chunk of bread from the basket and tore at it with his teeth.

"What else ya need help with?"

"Fill the water barrel, would ya Dash?"

"Fangio's always been a pain, but I get the best price, with a little work. The pimp at the diner and the jackasses that hang out with him are the bigger problem," Joseph said. "It seems every time I'm up there and they see my truck, boy here they come to steal produce, break a light, or pop a tire. Little bastards."

"I imagine it's like that for all of 'em up there. They're parasites. It's what they do."

Joseph drank from a large, dark, sticky coffee mug the color of root beer candy. "I better get going. I'll stop by Cy's and let him know what happened."

Joseph and Dashiell pulled a dark green and well-worn canvas sheet over the load and tightened up the corners. The covered boxes of apples were tied down with three-quarter inch, hemp ropes. Joseph pulled two trucker's knots taut and tucked the ends of the ropes into the sides of the truck.

"Go! We'll finish up here, then I gotta get the rabbits fed and watered!"

"Still goin' with the rabbits, huh?"

"Ah, hell! I don't know. Still trying to figure it out," Bert said.

Joseph patted Dashiell on the back and winked. "You're in charge."

"You got a good one there, Joe Mac." Bert said.

Joseph pulled on the headlights of his truck as he headed west down the gravel driveway with the first of two loads of fresh apples. He drove in the monotonous, high rpm, second gear.

In the grazing land across the road from the McCracken's farm a pack of coyotes yelped and nipped at each other as they fought themselves into a hierarchy for the night.

Joseph pulled onto the county road and began the long, dark drive toward San Francisco's market district.

21

A few muscle-sore and weary pickers left their cars and wandered into camp from the switchback leading to the water. Two cars took the longer route, allowing them to park and set up camp at the river's edge.

Once all the transients had returned, the agitator gathered his men. He spoke loudly of the injustice served up earlier by the greedy McCracken family. He spoke with the cadence of a southern preacher.

Small fires lit up the dirty faces of the camp's inhabitants. Shadow and light jumped amongst the old growth cottonwood and sycamore trees. Smoke slowly rose from the small fires. The acrid smell burned one's nostrils.

The agitator spoke of the future and how all would have a fair share in the profits now held by the greedy few. He stirred the fire with a limb from the nearest sycamore tree.

"Amen!" was even thrown in now and again by his cronies. He appealed to their hearts, their feelings, but never their sense of logic.

The agitator talked big and loud. His sympathetic words were all too familiar to the gathered men. They had heard other union organizers, mostly around the larger cities, saying the same thing.

Only in the last seven or eight years had the unions moved their ideology to America's farms.

He talked big and loud for the migrant families to hear on the other side of the camp. Some men wandered towards the bachelor's side and listened.

Life, though still wrought by poverty, ill-health, and malnutrition, was better than when they first awoke that morning. A meal had been saved for another day, a double bonus for many of the hungry migrants.

Those not involved in the labor-organizing-talk spent their time cleaning themselves at the river's edge or tended to their belongings. Two older women, past their prime, and a young lady in her mid-twenties, sewed patches on clothing by a smoky fire and talked quietly while another woman consoled her hungry children. Closer to the men talking, a fellow wired the sole of his shoe back together with a borrowed pair of pliers.

A couple of fathers approached the bachelors' camp with tobacco pipes and listened to the conversation as they warmed themselves over the campfire. One finally spoke up and asked what the rest of the larger group had wanted to know since arriving back at camp.

"What you boys got planned for them fellers tomorrow?"

"Well, didn't they just show you what I've been saying? Those plowboys want to control all of agriculture, and I say it is labor that should be king! Tomorrow we'll see."

"Tonight, I'm here to talk with you all. Maybe I can explain how things are . . . on the global level." The agitator rubbed the swollen wormlike scar with a dirty, scuffed hand that held his cigarette.

"They seemed like damned nice people to me," said the fellow wiring his shoe together. "I mean with the meal and the culls and all. I ain't got no truck with them. I'm goin' back tomorrow."

Other men agreed, they would also go back. More men joined the group until their numbers were close to two dozen and a few teenagers. Those close in sat or squatted by the fire. The rest of the men stood in close, shoulder to shoulder, as though a choir of the poor singing laments into the campfire. Firelight and shadows bounced among the tree tops and the dirty, contorted faces.

"Maybe you'll be a scab and I'll guarantee you'll not have a good day tomorrow," said the agitator. He pointed the smoking end of his stick at the migrant.

"You know he wants those damned apples picked. Another week and they'll be no good. It's no skin off my nose, one way or the other, if he sells them."

"But, if we don't stand up for ourselves, no one else will either," said one of the agitator's men to no one in particular.

"He don't want you to get organized so he don't have to pay no more money. That's why he kicked us out o' there today," said another union man.

"Who the hell are you?" a short, swarthy man asked. "Just causing a bunch of trouble over nothing."

"Look, mister, mind if I know your name? Fine then. It doesn't matter."

"If you work for that man tomorrow it's like telling him you ain't worth nothin'. He sets the pay, how long you'll work. Hell, he even tells you what's for supper. Don't you have any pride?" the agitator inquired gruffly, looking upon the tired, bearded faces of the pickers. "What are ya, a bunch of damned monkeys?"

"Can't you all stand up on your own two feet and tell them you want more, that you want your fair share? He has plenty. Look at those farmers! Do any of those men look like they were starving, like you and me?" The agitator did not wait for an answer.

"Hell no!"

"I say we go out there tomorrow and teach them and the rest of those dumb farmers up and down the Valley a thing or two about what it means to share. What's right! What it means to be a man! Can't they see! Can't they see the rags we are forced to wear because of them? Can't they see we just want what's fair? Our children are starving, dying of sickness. They don't even want your children in their schools. You have to stand together or you'll die. They can't treat us like animals." A few heads bobbed up and down.

Another in the crowd scratched his noggin, "Them McCrackens ain't bad people. Just wanna get their fruit picked and get on with it."

Another migrant said, "They ain't no big farmers. But I guess we gonna have to stick together."

The agitator rubbed the scar along his face and smiled.

"Far as I could see today, them McCrackens did us okay. And the food weren't bad neither," another man said.

"Ain't about a bunch of beans!"

"It is to me," the fellow smiled, pleased with himself.

"You think it is, but that's what McCracken wants you to think. You're all fat and happy now with your bellies full of their beans and rice, but what about tomorrow, or the next day, or next week for that matter? How many years does this have to go on? It has to stop. When will you make a stand and be heard? You've all been starving and now, because of a handful of beans and rice, you're willing to roll over and take what they decide you're worth?"

A short Basque with a large mustache warmed his rump against the campfire. "Mister McCracken could pay more if he wanted to, maybe." He pointed to the heavens. "What is true, God knows. Mr. McCracken knows what he can get away with as the owner. There are just too many of us who are willing to work for a little money and a little food rather than not work at all. He didn't have to feed us, but he did. He is doing what he can, same as you and me, or at least some of us, if the table was turned."

The man turned toward the fire and rubbed his hands together.

"I am going to work tomorrow, with my family. I like the way it feels. Troubles? We all have troubles. Hard times?" He shrugged his shoulders, twisted the ends of his mustache and stared into the camp's fire. "Are there any other times?"

Quickly he turned back to the crowd of men.

"Tomorrow when my family goes to work the Lord will know we're not looking for more trouble. It seems to find us easily enough on its own. But tomorrow I want to sleep with a full stomach, as tonight, not with bruised ribs and knots on my head."

The short man tugged at the ends of his mustache, brushed the ends aside and tipped his hat to the crowd of men around the fire. He sucked air through his teeth, as if dislodging a scrap from tonight's dinner. He twirled his mustache, head down, and walked to his camp.

"Are you people blind? Can't you see what they're doing here? He'll pay less tomorrow than he did today. And you're daft if you think that plow-handle won't be talking to the other farmers around here telling them what he paid so they can offer even less;

five cents today, four cents tomorrow. Mark my words, these people won't be happy till they've worked us all to death."

One of the younger men spoke up. "What that fella says is right. I seen it myself, over in Salinas."

"We was cuttin' lettuce a while back, and the next day the farmer come out and says he weren't a goin' to pay us as much as he did the day afo'. Well, let me tell ya somethin', we had us a damned riot right there."

"Workers started dumping boxes of lettuce. Others ran through the field and kicked the unpicked heads as far as they could."

With a smile that spoke to his self-congratulatory hedonism, he recounted how the farmer and his hired men just stood by and watched the field be destroyed by the angry mob.

"Hell, there were just too many of us for them to take on," the man chuckled.

"We had to hightail it out of there 'cause the sheriff and his deputies were a comin', sure enough, but we let them know they cain't keep us down!"

The organizer concealed his joy at the turn of events. "Amen, brother!"

"You're all hearing it here for yourselves. I know I won't stop until everyone of you has a decent wage. Look how many workers there are here. Those two damned farmers doling out pennies, as if we were grateful children, can't stand up to us if we stand together."

"Now, hang on a minute!" a man shouted. "You're makin' that sound like it was some kind of victory."

"We showed them!" the young man said.

"No! I say you became a criminal when you destroyed what wasn't yours. You're the ones who had to hightail it out of town.

And now, you can't go back for fear the sheriff or farmers will recognize you. You're the one who went without pay that day. You were poorer at the end of the day," he said, then lowered his voice shamefully, "and not just from lack of pay. You lost your honor." The man walked back toward the family side of the camp.

"A farm ain't no different than a railroad, a mining company, a logging company, or any other big, damned factory. They make money by not sharing with you. Without you, the work can't get done! Labor is the engine of the corporate, farming industry, not some damned man on his wagon, sitting there with a damned penny bucket between his feet."

Men mumbled to those next to them regarding the merits of the man's argument. Another man spoke to the group.

"I don't know if I believe what you're telling us, least ways some of it. A hell of a lot more work went into that farming operation than just sitting with a penny bucket between their feet. You oversimplify." The man paused to remember what he wanted to say.

"The problem I have is makin' up my mind whether you're a communist agitator or union agitator. Now, if you be a red bastard, you got problems a plenty, friend."

"If you be a union organizer, I can only tell you that you boys have been stirring up more mess than most of us want to deal with."

"Look at how stirred up folks are down in Bakersfield with burning up all those books by Steinbeck. You've upset most everyone in the Valley and half the migrants."

"We don't disagree with what you're sayin', least ways some of it, only how ya all are gettin' it done."

"Most all of us are farmers too. We can see both sides of this issue; we're not stupid. Maybe some of you can't 'cause maybe you aren't from farms. You come to the fields from the factories back East, Frisco, Detroit, or wherever the hell you say you're from."

"You said earlier, farms ain't no different than a big factory. We know that ain't so. Now, here you go messing with folks that just want to eat. Least ways, most people think you union men only want a higher wage for us so's you can get a piece of it. Now, how right is that?"

"Tomorrow I'm going to tell that farmer we ain't working unless he doubles our wages!" The organizer nodded to his men who started passing out flyers to folks in the crowd who would take them. The migrants looked from the sheets being passed around to the agitator.

A man asked, "How many of you are there?"

"We're everywhere," the agitator said with a grin. "Here. Lookin' forward to seeing you there, neighbor." The agitator stuck a flyer in the man's jacket and patted him on the chest.

MASS MEETING

OF

CAWIU
Cannery and Agricultural Workers' Industrial Union
A greater share in the profits!
Don't let them steal your dreams!
Lecture by Tom Collins
September 29, '40
7:00 pm

Little Church of Hope
Corner of East Main Street and South Sullivan Avenue
Stockton, Calif.
Hot meal will be provided!

"We're having a rally in Stockton in a few days. We're going to have a fine meeting and the church is putting on a music show after supper. Heck! Maybe even Steinbeck, himself, will show up!"

Then speaking to the crowd of men, the agitator lit a cigarette and continued with the union's mantra.

"If you'll stand with us tomorrow, I'll negotiate a higher wage for you." A few heads bobbed up and down, but most not at all.

"Now if you can't support us trying to help you make more money tomorrow, at least help us by staying away. There may be trouble, if that's what they want."

"We'll be there an hour before sun up to negotiate. Those that can support us can come along and those that can't ought to take the day off."

A fruit tramp spoke up. "Look, them folks don't mean none of us any harm. They just want them apples picked. They said they didn't want you back tomorrow. If you show up, there's gonna be trouble for sure. They ain't big farmers or a factory as you call it. They're just tryin' to make a livin'."

A union man walked over to the dissident. "If I see you tomorrow, we're gonna butt heads." He then poked the man in the shoulder, "Count on it."

"Now, we're gonna stand in the road, drive up and down . . . whatever we have to do, to disrupt their operation. They don't own the road."

"Let me see a show of hands. Who's with us tomorrow? Uh huh. Who's gonna work for whatever they're offering tomorrow?" The organizer counted.

"I guess we'll see where we all stand tomorrow." With that the union boss moved towards his tent. "What time is it? Anybody know? Night, folks." The crowd melted away from the dying campfire.

A man mumbled to himself, "Jesus! Here we go again. Can't a man just work where and when he wants to without being pulled from one side to the other?"

22

George reached into his trouser pocket and felt the handful of change; the winnings from the previous night's crap game. He was as rich as he'd been in more than a year. The bus, heading to San Francisco's Market District, stopped with a hiss and George climbed aboard.

George thought he might land a job in the produce business or maybe even find work with one of the farmers who were delivering fresh fruits and vegetables from farms all over California to be sold or shipped throughout the world.

Once delivered and within minutes of being purchased, wholesalers would turn around and sell the fruits, vegetables, eggs, and cheese to market owners and chefs from restaurants and hotels from around the San Francisco Bay area.

The bus came to a jolting halt. The light was green, but the bus did not move. Children who played in the street came to a stop. A ball bounced unmolested to the curb and came to rest against the back tire of a dark-blue Chrysler. Ears pricked at the music from the ragtag band as the parade marched toward them from farther north on the Embarcadero.

The Socialist Workers of the World, in their militaristic red and brown attire, were striking in their demeanor. Red flags on parade. They marched through the streets of San Francisco and passed out fliers extolling the merits of socialism, the Working People's Party. The fliers provided the date, time, and location of the next Socialist Party meeting. Most people did not pay the communists and unions any more attention than any of the others who had paraded their ideologies up and down the hills of San Francisco since before the gold rush.

As the parade came to an end, ice cream was passed out to the children as payment for swelling the ranks of the anemic line of spectators along the streets. The children sped away on bicycles, or ran a few more blocks to catch the communists' parade and more ice cream.

Few noticed that the marchers in the various factions' parades were the same volksmarchers in various other parades and strikes on other days.

As the parade passed and the congested traffic began to move again the bus driver honked and jockeyed for position among the other drivers. Throughout San Francisco vehicles honked. The noise lapped up against the tall concrete-and-brick buildings and flowed down the wet, city streets. The bus driver attempted to pull the bus around a truck parked in the middle of the street. George looked down, to his left.

There, a beautiful lady was talking to a man in a truck whom George could not see. On the side of the truck, the farm's signage: *McCracken Farms, Madera, Calif., Joseph McCracken, owner.* George lighted on the name of the farmer.

"McCracken Farms! Hey! I know that guy!"

"Lucky you," said the bored bus driver pulling on the unfiltered, Pall Mall cigarette dangling from his lips then spitting a fleck of tobacco from his tongue as he exhaled.

"Jesus Christ!" the driver complained. "Parades, Okies, whores! Can ya'll get the hell out of the damned street?"

"Pull over! Pull over! Let me out!" George yelled at the bus driver.

"'Pull over', he says. Jesus! Hang on, mister. Keep your shirt on. Unlike you and your friend there, I have a schedule to keep. There's laws you know, least in the bigger cities, 'bout parkin' in the middle of the damned street! You might tell him that, 'cause he obviously doesn't know shit from Shinola!"

George jumped from his seat and ran the length of the bus. He was bent over, watching through the split rear windows to see which way the truck might go. He ran back to the front of the bus.

"Did you hear me? You may want to share that with your buddy down there makin' time with the hooker."

Back and forth he ran, agitated, like a watchdog on a lunge line, George paid the driver no attention. He tapped his fingers impatiently on the handhold that extended to the two doors.

"Open the doors!" he demanded, again.

The driver said sarcastically, "You're gonna have to step back, away from the doors, honey. They open inward."

George jumped back to the top of the steps, turned and looked sternly at the bus driver. The doors pulled open and George shot out of the bus and into the street.

Alas, the truck had turned and was long gone. The bus doors closed. George was left standing in the intersection in a cloud of diesel exhaust, like the fellow standing in the middle of the road, who doesn't know if he has found a rope or lost a mule.

Hey! Outta the damn way, huh?" a driver yelled at George. "Go back to your Hooverville, dumbass!" another yelled. "Hey, Okie . . . !"

George stood in the street and looked in the direction of the truck that had disappeared around the corner. Horns continued to honk and echo throughout the streets of San Francisco.

A traffic cop approached the clogged intersection. "Hey, you! What are you doing there? Get out of the street! Get over here, you!" he commanded George who quickly ducked into the crowd of city people and was gone.

23

Since before midnight farmers had been coming from as far away as Tulare and Visalia. Tired men napped in the cabs of idling trucks while others sat at the counter in the diner drinking hot coffee. Still others made small talk with the local prostitutes who had wandered in from all corners of San Francisco and other parts of the peninsula to greet the newly paid farmers.

The prostitutes shoved and pushed each other, like gulls squabbling and pecking one another over anything they could put in their mouths. Farmers waited for the wholesalers to descend from higher up the hill, to open their produce houses.

Joseph arrived at about 4:30 a.m. and slept in the cab of his truck with the driver's window cracked open.

The sun quickly rose from behind the hills of the East Bay. Gulls screeched. San Francisco's Market District consisted of one- and two-story warehouses and encompassed the few blocks surrounding Washington and Davis Streets.

In the span of twenty minutes Washington Street erupted with the sounds of trucks coming and going and horns honking to clear the street ahead. Farmers yelled from one truck to another inquiring how families were doing. A trolley edged its way through the nexus of farm trucks, handcarts, and automobiles clogging up the street.

Wholesalers haggled with the tired farmers over the price of their produce. Prostitutes quietly plied their trade and haggled over their own prices. Wallet snatchers combed the streets in search of a quick pick.

Farmers sitting at the counter of the roach-infested diner waited for their turn to move their truck into position so it could be unloaded. Men mingled between trucks and spoke their minds on the pending war in Europe, Hitler, and the new, sticky, chemical called Dichlorodiphenyltrichloroethane, or DDT. They continued to sip strong, black coffee and smoke cigarettes.

Wholesalers yelled at dock apes to pull twenty, thirty, forty, or even one hundred boxes of produce from a single truck. Untended trucks blocked the street and impeded other farmers from moving their trucks. Wholesalers yelled in Italian, from one end of the street to the other, in a code the farmers could not understand. Farmers yelled salutations to one another and spoke quietly amongst themselves to relay prices they had received and from whom they had received the better price.

Farmers honked and yelled to other farmers to get out of the way so they could get their trucks through the clogged street. The market was a riot of noises that woke the bottom of sleepy, foggy San Francisco.

"Yeah? Well, Hitler is the craziest bastard in the world, I tell ya!" said a farmer while sitting at the counter in the diner.

"Mark my words, we're gonna get dragged into another war by that limp-dick Roosevelt," said another farmer.

Out on Washington Street, "How much ya want for the corn?" the wholesaler barked around the spit-soaked cigar clamped between his teeth.

"You heard me. How 'bout five dollars a box?" replied the farmer.

"How's about you kiss my big, fat, Italian ass and move your fuckin' corn outta the way? I got good people here wanna sell me corn at a real-is-tic price. I don't even wanna look at chew, Mr. five bucks a box."

"Everyone wants to sell corn today. Jesus Christ! Don't you guys ever grow nothin' besides corn?"

"Well, what are ya offerin' then, Mr. Smartass?"

"How's about I make us both happy?" Fangio removed the cigar from his mouth and examined it.

"I was gonna offer ya two-fifty a box, but since you scared me," the wholesaler grabbed both his fat cheeks in the palms of his hands, clipboard tucked under his left arm, "how 'bout I make it three dollars a box and we can both sleep tonight, 'kay?"

The wholesaler grabbed his clipboard and chomped down on his cigar. He looked at the clipboard held against his stomach and ignored the farmer.

"How 'bout four a box and four cents a box cause that's what they cost me?" The tired farmer was worn down from the harvest, the long drive to San Francisco, to speak nothing of the assault from his wife who scolded that he had better make damned sure he did not get taken advantage of by the Arabs in the city.

"How 'bout . . . get the fuck off my street! Four cents a box! What's the matter witch you? Four cents a box. Get the fuck outta here, I told ya! You need help in a big way my friend. I don't need your boxes! Take your boxes! Take your corn!"

"Seriously, does anyone want to sell me their precious produce today?" the wholesaler yelled to the street.

"Get the fuck outta here! I ain't talkin' to you no more. Disappear there sheep shit."

The wholesaler intentionally held his breath to appear red in the face with exasperation. Sweat poured down the sides of his fat head.

The farmer took a moment to think it over, rubbed his chin whiskers and looked up and down the street to see if he could see anyone else selling corn. There were just too many corn growers at the market today, he decided.

"Excuse me, sir! You're keeping me from making a living here!" the wholesaler shouted above the honking horns and arguments between other farmers and wholesalers.

"Look! Pal! There just ain't nothin' special 'bout your corn! It's like them stupid bimbos over there, givin' their coochy away since they was in high school. Now they got kids from half a dozen derelicts and they want us to think there's somethin' special 'bout 'em, ya know, worth the money. Kind o' like you and your corn here, blue jeans."

The buyer grabbed an ear of corn and tore the husk halfway down the cob and stuck his dirty fingernail into the kernels. "It's kind of dry as a matter of fact. Maybe three bucks is too high."

Of course the top ears of corn were drier than the bottom ears after a long drive from the hot valley. "I'm doin' ya a favor here and you need time to think. Com' on blue jeans what's it gonna be?"

The bone-weary farmer was afraid his whole season's efforts would go to waste if he could not sell his corn today. The wholesaler knew that.

After considering the long night on the road and a longer drive back to the farm with a full load of corn, and having to tell his wife the bad news, the farmer caved to the wholesaler's offer.

"Okay, okay, don't have a coronary. I'll take three dollars a box, but you have to take the full load. Deal?"

"Deal!" The produce man said, turning to his apes to get the truck unloaded.

"C'mon get off your butts and get that truck unloaded! That's why you have a fuckin' union, so I can pay you for sittin' on your asses? Ya lazy bastards! Jesus Christ! Doesn't anybody know how to work anymore?"

Wholesalers took the produce for as little as they could, then turned around in a few short minutes and sold it to restaurant owners, chefs, and market owners up and down the peninsula.

Since the time of the Greek agora farmers, having toiled a whole season under the hot summer sun, brought the fruits of their labor to the market with the hope of earning enough money to support what they could not build or trade for themselves. The little money allowed the farmers to continue their labors in the countryside, away from the haughty city and all its problems. The same haggling continued, even today, between farmers and wholesalers to assure the picky, American consumer their fresh fruits and vegetables.

The farmers jockeyed for position and slowly moved their produce down Washington Street, or any of the other streets that made up the market district across the Embarcadero from the wharf.

Gus Fangio was a swarthy, fat man with an unlit cigar mashed in his mouth. He was built like bad Eastern European folk art. His head and stomach seemed to be fashioned from brown clay rolled into balls with the smaller ball planted on top of the larger ball, then a suit and face painted on.

His black, greasy hair was combed straight back and seemed to be torn into jagged edges where it rubbed against the top of his oily collar. The back of his fat head reminded one of an oily pelt that had been rubbed the wrong way.

Fangio stood as if his legs had been shoved under him to prop up his fat body. His clipboard was wedged between the left side of his stomach and his left wrist. The buyers began to meander in behind the farmers, most of whom had already off-loaded their produce.

"Hey! Who parked their truck in the middle of my street?" He yelled. Fangio was only one of the many loud wholesalers yelling and directing traffic along Washington Street.

The street was packed so tightly no vehicle could move without having to wait on three or four other trucks to move first. The sidewalks became mountains of tottering wooden crates and cardboard boxes full of fruits and vegetables hanging out in all directions. It was the same scene for blocks on either side of Washington Street.

On the sidewalk, up close to the wall was a narrow passageway by which the buyers, sellers, and those paid to load and unload the produce could maneuver in and out of the throng of people and vehicles.

"Hey! I said, who parked their . . . oh, shit! Hey, Nicky! That's McCracken's truck, ain't it? Find him, would ya, and see what's on the truck. Shit!"

Fangio waddled to the other end of his self-designated turf, the area just in front of his business, Fangio's Fruits, across the street from Galli Fruit Company. When he turned around to pace to the other end of his turf, Fangio ran into a wall.

"Look McCracken, I don't have time for ya today. You're late! Ya should o' been here a few hours ago. I'm trying to sell some produce here now, excuse me. C'mon. C'mon, let me by here would ya?"

Fangio lowered his head and attempted to go around the immovable object in front of him.

"I don't have a boss, besides Mother Nature, and you look nothing like her. Therefore, I can't be late." Joseph smiled.

"I have Arkansas Blacks. What are you payin' by the box? It was you, wasn't it, who wanted to know what I have on the truck?"

Joseph's voice was deep, calm, and controlled. He continued to block Fangio's way to the corn buyers and slid his hands behind the bib of his overalls, content to wait.

"What? Hell no! Three dollars a box! And that's a final on those apples, by the way. Take it or leave it! Now, excuse me, I have customers who want to buy some corn." Fangio said, wagging his index finger.

"Not anymore. Looks like they're headed down the street," Joseph said. "Everyone wants to sell corn today. Don't you people ever sell anything besides corn?"

"You see anyone selling apples today? It's the end of apple season. You know it and I have the last in the Valley. They were

picked less than twenty-four hours ago and they're sweet, and fresh.
Look how big. I need six dollars a box. And don't point your finger
at me. I'm not one of your dock apes."

"Yeah?" Again he pointed a fat finger at Joseph, "Well, I don't
work for you, neither. In case you haven't noticed McCracken."

Joseph's eyes moved from the fat man's finger to his eyes.
"Do it again and I'll show you the other end of it," he admonished.

His slow and controlled manner infuriated the fat man who
wanted to sell corn before all the buyers were gone. Joseph never
regretted the wicked pleasure he derived from tormenting Fangio, if
for no other reason than to pay him back for the injury he caused
others.

Fangio looked up to McCracken's face, tearing the wet cigar
from his teeth.

"Are you nuts or sump'n? I can't make no money that way,
McCracken! Outta my way, I have work to do here! Can't ya see?"
Fangio tried to look around and over Joseph, to no avail.

"C'mon, McCracken, you're ruining my business here. And
move your truck, will ya! The buyers are trying to get in to load."

The fat man stuck the damp, torn cigar back into the corner of
his mouth and looked up at Joseph who did not move.

Joseph knew Fangio was going to buy the apples at this price.
He just had to wait for Fangio to realize it. Fangio was a loud mouth.
Joseph knew he was prideful and took advantage of that weakness.

Fangio was vain and prided himself for having produce no
other seller on Washington Street had. Joseph knew this and played
to Fangio's ego. Even if Fangio lost money, he at least retained
bragging rights.

"Look, McCracken, I'm not making any money on this stuff if I have to buy at that price. Ya know that. You always know that, and you always don't care. Ya always want too much!"

"I think it's fair, considering what it takes to bring these boxed apples to your front door . . . a year's effort to grow them properly, putting up with the harvest tramps and union agitators, the drive, having to put up with you and those gangsters over there at that roach infested diner."

"Was it you who told them to bust out my truck's taillight last time I was up here?"

"No! And I can't make any money on them at that price! Are you deaf or sump'n?"

"You'll turn around and sell them for six dollars and fifty cents a box in less than an hour. Remember, fat man, you haven't done any work for the fifty cents. Besides, you'll just sell these innocent buyers your other produce at a slightly higher rate on delivery and make your dirty profit."

"I have another truckload of apples coming tomorrow. They're being picked as we speak. Keep wasting my time. I'll take them across the street."

"Okay, okay, McCracken! Keep it down, will ya? Five fifty a box."

The crowd in the street was becoming impatient with the abandoned truck. Horns honked. Buildings sucked in their shadows as the sun continued to rise.

A small crowd of men gathered in front of the diner. A businessman, one of many yelling on the street, was poking a finger at a farmer. The farmer pushed back. The smell from the idling trucks burned one's sinuses. Joseph was not distracted by the action on the street.

"It's still six bucks a box."

"Jesus Christ! Can't you hear, McCracken? I can't make any money that way! Why don't ya just shoot me? You're killing me here!" The fat man screamed and his face boiled.

"Don't tempt me."

"Not funny, McCracken!" Fangio frowned at Joseph. "What's wrong witch you?"

Joseph raised his nose to the scent of the street, the sounds of honking, cussing men, trucks idling, and the yammering of the marketplace.

"Oh, for Christ's sake! Here, take six! You're robbing me here, McCracken. How many boxes ya got there?" Fangio snapped his clipboard in half. "Move da truck, McCracken! Right now! That's my load on there and I want it now!" Fangio threw the broken clipboard to the curb and chomped down on his cigar.

"Let's go ya lazy bastards. Get off your fat asses and do something'! Come on! Get McCracken's apples offloaded! Whole thing!"

Fangio wiped his face and neck with his handkerchief.

"For the love of God! Would you guys fuckin' move? Come on, here!"

Joseph moved off the sidewalk towards his truck. The fat man whipped his dock apes into action and began hawking his newly purchased apples.

"How about this corn? Best on the street! Just look at them yellow ears! Look at that silk!" Fangio yelled to the buyers. "Some of the Valley's finest, right here!" Digging down below the wind-dried ears, Fangio grabbed an ear of corn and pulled the husk down for inspection. He inserted a thumbnail into the kernels, "Ah! Just look at that," he exclaimed with the pride of the farmer who grew it. "Just look at that color, the milk! You may not know this, sir, but that's a fine ear of corn right there." Fangio slammed the ear down in the box. "That's some sweet corn, I'm tellin' ya!"

"Hey! I know what you gents want. Apples! Yes, sir! I got 'em too, brother! Last of the season. And you know what they say, end of the season fruit is the sweetest. I have the best! Tell ya what let's do. You buy the corn at six a box and I'll sell ya the apples at a steal for seven-fifty a box."

"What's that? If you say so. I can only guarantee ya one thing, sir. These apples won't be here in another hour."

Fangio's voice was lost in the noise of the street and other hawkers. Next to Galli's Fruit Company was the diner where farmers mingled with pickpockets, pimps, hopheads, and prostitutes. All were looking for an opportunity to relieve the farmer of his year's hard-earned wages. Behind the diner, next to the trash cans, thugs played craps. A woman screamed. City men laughed.

Men in shirtsleeves rolled to their elbows, baggy, wool slacks, and fedoras stood in a tight circle, shoulder to shoulder. Joseph wound his way through the crowd and vehicles in the street to see.

Joseph's ears pricked to the sound of the distressed woman.

In all the commotion Joseph could not hear Fangio screaming for him to maneuver his truck to be unloaded. "I have a buyer! McCracken!" The street was in complete gridlock.

Voices, horns, then one long blast from a ship in the bay heading out to sea, added to the calamity on the street. The air was filled with the smell of greens, carrots, garlic, and now apples. A cornucopia of produce spilled out of trucks on Washington Avenue. The art of Hieronymus Bosch came to Joseph's mind. Underfoot were torn lettuce leaves, broken garlic and pieces of fruit, along with moldy vegetables no longer distinguishable. Gulls filled the empty spaces on the ground and picked at rotting produce while other birds soared overhead in anticipation. Gull shit splattered here and there on man, vehicle, and produce without discrimination.

"Excuse me, can I get in here?" Joseph asked the backs of the heads before him. No one moved and only concentrated on the action in the center of the group. A woman continued to scream as she was tossed from one thug to another. Joseph headed to his truck.

"Finally! Come on McCracken! Let's go, I need those apples."

"No! Wait! McCracken, what are you . . . where the fuck are you goin'? McCracken! Goddamn it!" Fangio slammed his hat on the street.

Joseph returned to his truck for a club of oak he used to check his tires. He returned to the crowd and placed the club between the legs of the man who had shoved him. Joseph turned the piece of oak horizontally and grabbed the back of the man's shirt collar and lifted the man two and a half feet off the ground. The man came away, no longer a nuisance.

Joseph sat the man down on the sidewalk, "I'd leave if I were you."

Joseph tapped another man on the back and asked him to move. The stranger looked at Joseph. "Fuck off plow-handle! She's ours," he said. He turned back to the action in the center of the group.

The insulting stranger immediately grabbed the lump that rose on the top of his head and spun to face the "plow-handle".

"Hey! What's the matter with you, huh? Are you crazy?" The men in the circle looked from the woman to Joseph.

Joseph pointed his tire thumper at the man's nose. "I asked you to move, politely. Don't speak to me like that again."

Joseph looked to the rest of the assembled crowd and spoke in a louder tone. "I'm gonna ask you all to move away from the lady and leave her alone, now!" Joseph slowly moved the end of his stick to just inches from another man's nose.

As with the parting of the Red Sea, the crowd opened to reveal a young woman. Her blond hair, no longer a neatly combed pageboy, hung in her face.

"Get a load of this guy. You the new sheriff?" The men laughed at the man from the country. From the looks of his overalls he seemed not as sophisticated as they.

"Naw, he wants her for hisself," another man said. Guffawing continued at the country bumpkin's expense.

Joseph's eyes shot to the big mouth dressed in a baggy purple zoot suit over a canary yellow shirt and red tie. The colors were topped off with a white Cab Calloway hat encircled with a black sweatband. A watch fob dangled from the pocket of the pimp's vest.

"You leave or I'm gonna hurt you." Joseph pointed the club at the man. "It's your move."

The pimp smiled. His two front teeth were framed in gold.

"I'm not afraid of you, blue jeans. This is my street. This is my diner. Look around. See these bad-looking men? They're mine, vato. Maybe you better take it back to the farm where you belong. You know, with the other farm animals."

"Move, corn cob!" one of the pimp's bodyguards ordered, stepping in front of the pimp.

The blow hurled the man backwards into his friends and onlookers standing against the plate-glass window of the diner. The pimp's associates came at Joseph and were dropped, like cattle at a Denver slaughter house. One of the pimp's entourage only had time to get his razor open. Joseph's club slammed down upon the man's hand, making those nearby wince at the sound of the small bones breaking.

"I'll put the next man in the graveyard. Believe that if you want to see the end of this day." Joseph stood his ground, looked into the faces of the city men, then finally to the girl.

"Hey, why don't you bite the bullet out of your ass, huh?" Joseph heard the metal spring release the blade behind him. Joseph swung around and smashed the man's nose with his elbow.

Blood squirted from between the pimp's fingers as he grasped his face. Joseph smashed the man's knife arm with the piece of oak. The white hat with black sweatband rolled into the fetid gutter followed by the pimp.

A farmer chuckled atop his flatbed and yelled out, "You city boys may not realize this yet! Y'all are outnumbered!"

"Please, keep coming at him!" another farmer yelled, standing on the running board of his farm truck to gain a better view.

Horns honked and farmers yucked it up as part of the age-old competition between city boys and country boys.

The pretty woman seemed to Joseph to be in her early twenties. He pulled the girl to him and positioned them both, with their backs against the diner window, so no one could get behind them.

The veteran was just getting boiled up.

"Come on now, who want's some of this?" Joseph said.

Some waved their hands in the air as they walked away. Others slid their hands into their pockets and attempted to blend into the larger circle of people who had stopped their transactions on Washington Street to see what had developed in front of the diner.

Washington Street was a riot. Men looked on from their running boards, truck windows, and the flatbeds of their trucks. The farmers thrust their own clubs in the air, pounded on the roofs and doors of their trucks. Horns honked. Catcalls and applause exploded from the farmers.

Business slowly commenced and voices began the banter of buying and selling again. The pimp and shooters were helped up by their associates and hauled away to be mended.

A beat cop, two blocks away, slowly made his way down Davis Street through the crowd.

"I'm sorry for this, ma'am. I can't tell you how much. Name's Joseph. I hope you're not hurt." Joseph tucked the club under his arm as though a walking stick.

"Thank you very much for coming to my rescue." The woman, jaded by years of filthy men from every walk of life having their way with her, had become used to this type of commotion. She dabbed her eyes with a handkerchief, pretending to pay attention to the farmer while watching the pimp and his gangsters in her compact.

"Can I drop you somewhere? This isn't a good place to be any time of day." Joseph looked up and down Washington Street. "Nothing but trouble here."

"Thanks, but no." The prostitute thought for a moment. "Well, maybe just a block or two if you don't mind. If you're done with your work, that is." She brushed her short, frosted hair back while looking in the compact mirror. She evened her red lipstick around her large mouth with her little finger.

"If it gets me away from here and that creepy, little man."

"Come on. I have a truck over here. I can drop you where you like." Joseph took her elbow and guided her. Catcalls and rude comments shot out from the crowd. Joseph frowned at the men on the street.

"Hey, McCracken! What are ya doin' to me here? Jesus Christ! I'm tryin' to make a livin' here and you're trying to kill me all in one day!"

Joseph pulled the hand brake and waited for Fangio.

"This guy causes me more problems than all these yokels put together."

"Sign here."

"Six a box?"

"Yeah, sure, sure, sure. Just, let's get it unloaded!" Fangio screamed.

"Pay me first."

"For the love of God, McCracken!"

Before Fangio's dock apes had unloaded twenty of the boxes of apples, forty were sold for a nice fifty cents to one dollar profit per box.

The produce was coming off Joseph's truck and going straight to the buyers rather than being stored in the warehouse or on the sidewalk.

"Hey Russ! Ten boxes; four large, five medium, and one small, for this gentleman here, would ya? That's four, five, and one. Come on here! Chop, chop my good man!"

Fangio practically gushed while looking at Joseph. The wholesaler counted out Joseph's money. The prostitute watched closely the transaction.

Joseph folded the bills in half and pushed them deep into the front pocket of his bib overalls, then climbed into the cab of his truck. Joseph eyed the pimp's thugs watching from the other side of the street.

"Always hard men when they're in groups," Joseph thought.

"Names Almeda. Thanks for helping me back there. You big, strong, country types always make a slave of me with your farm charm. Anything I can do for you, big man? How 'bout drinks up at my place, cowboy?" His muscular arms were not lost on her.

Joseph skidded his flatbed through the intersection at Ceylon and Sacramento Streets and headed west. Almeda slid across the bench seat and laid her left hand on Joseph's thigh.

"That's quite a wad," she giggled. "Wanna have some fun?"

"You're kidding."

"I know." Almeda pouted. "Innocent looking, huh? Guys love it. Poor, little, innocent girl shtick."

"That's not what I meant. I thought those men were harassing you, back there."

"Who, Manny; that dumb bastard? He was. But he always does. He's always trying to get me to work for him. I just like having boyfriends. You know? The holidays are coming. I don't want to be alone."

"Turn here would you, lover?"

With his face reddening, Joseph turned to Almeda, "How much farther?"

Smiling up at Joseph, "Far as you wanna go, hon." She giggled.

"Need a girlfriend for Christmas?"

"You are gonna come up, aren't ya, let me repay ya for your chivalry. I do so love you big, strong, violent types."

She stopped, as if startled. "Ya do like your jelly rolled, don't ya, sugar?" Almeda blew into Joseph's ear and ran a red fingernail down his neck.

"I'm married, if that's what you mean."

"I don't care if you don't care, hon'." Almeda pulled the loose, short, hair away from her face and tucked it behind her left ear. Chewing gum snapped between her teeth.

Joseph placed her hand on her own lap. "This is as far as we go." Joseph's truck came to an abrupt stop in the middle of the intersection. A parade had just passed and the intersection was in gridlock.

The bus driver hit his horn and waved his hands in wonderment at how these farmers found their way into San Francisco.

"Ah, Jesus! What the hell have we done here? Huh? Move that piece of shit out of the way, pal!" The bus driver threw his hands up as if to ask, "What the hell's wrong with you?"

The bus driver pointed at his own head in a gesture to let Joseph know he thought Joseph was stupid.

Joseph turned to the bus driver with a dark, expressionless face and saw the bus driver frantically yelling at a passenger running up and down the aisle.

Joseph leaned across Almeda and swung open the truck's passenger side door. Almeda slowly blew in his ear and scratched his back as he leaned across her, with no consideration for the commotion now damming up the intersection. Joseph sat up straight as an arrow and tipped his hat to the prostitute.

Almeda rested her elbows on the truck's open window frame, ignoring the mayhem all around.

Unconcerned for others, a driver ignored the streetlight and made his way through the intersection. This mess was not in the man's schedule and everything on his calendar was going to get jammed up.

A beat cop was still half a block away and in no hurry to get to the intersection.

"Maybe you change your mind, you'll look me up some time?" She smiled. Her gum snapped between her teeth.

"I'm right there, lover, on Hemlock." Her hands were small. She pointed a little, slender finger. "Number 13." She threw back her head and cackled as she slowly sashayed to the curb.

The bus edged around Joseph and stopped traffic in both directions. The bus driver said something to one of his passengers as he pulled the side door of the bus open for the man to exit. The driver then yelled at Joseph from the side window of the bus, "You think this is some country road? Asshole!" Horns honked and drivers shook their fists at the bus driver and the farmer.

Joseph ground the gears of the empty flatbed into place, through the red light. He slammed the long gearshift into second gear.

A small man jumped from the bus into the middle of the chaotic intersection.

The beat cop, having finally arrived, asked, "What's going on here, now? Hey, you! Come here!" he commanded George.

The cop walked into the confusion of the intersection. George exited, wanting to put as many pedestrians between himself and the policeman as possible.

"Hold up there!" the police officer commanded again. The little man had vanished in the crowd.

The beat cop turned. "Hey! I said, hold up!" The officer yelled at the businessman whose day planner was becoming unraveled by the mayhem before him.

"You!" the officer yelled, again. He gave a sharp whistle. "Get that bus out of here! Let's go!" The officer waved his right arm as he held the sedan in check with his left hand. His whistle screamed for more attention.

"You think I planned on sitting in this intersection until you came along to tell me what to do?" the bus driver said aloud. "Dumbass." The bus driver continued on his designated route.

The beat cop turned back to the businessman in the sedan and shook his finger.

On Washington Street another cop arrived at the diner.

"What's all the commotion? What sort of mayhem are you gangsters causing me today?"

"Nothin. A guy tripped, hurt himself. These dumb farmers thought it was funny. No problem, officer," the gangster lied. "Everything here is roses."

Inside the diner, in the farthest booth from the front door, the pimp sat with his head back to keep blood from running out of his broken nose.

He wrapped his arm in a towel full of ice and awaited the doctor. He swallowed his blood and whispered something to one of his men as the waitress arrived at his table with coffee. The waitress poured three tablespoons of sugar on top of a good shot of cream and stirred.

"Do I look like I can drink coffee, now? Huh? Stupid, pendeja. Get outta here." As the waitress walked away, "And bring me some more napkins!" Then under his breath, "Bitch."

"Ah! Look at this!" the pimp whined about his suit. "Ruined!"

One of the pimp's gunmen slid through the diner door and onto Washington Street. He looked left, right, then maneuvered through the remains of the crowd in front of the diner and strolled across the street to have a talk with the produce wholesaler. At first the fat man pulled his arm away from the smaller man in the nice suit and wide-brimmed hat.

The smaller man immediately stepped in close and in front of the fat man. He said a few words. He stepped back and opened his jacket and then buttoned it again.

The fat man took the receipt book from his hip pocket. He flipped through it until he found the information the man requested and wrote something down on a separate piece of paper. The little man, with the thin mustache, tipped his hat and crossed the street, weaving in and out of the produce trucks on his way back to the diner.

The fat man wiped the sweat from his brow and neck. He tilted his head skyward and wiped the sweat from the front of his neck. He clasped his handkerchief in his right hand as he braced himself against the building.

"Hey! Come on there! Get those damned boxes in here."

"Jeez! It's hot! Who turned up the furnace? Come on with those boxes, will ya? What the hell am I payin' ya for?"

24

While Joseph haggled with Fangio over the price of apples in San Francisco, the migrants arrived at his farm in Madera for the second day of picking. They drove their cars to the side of the road and parked behind the organizer who waited with his men.

The pickers left their vehicles and congregated around the head of the column waiting for the McCracken's to arrive. Deep down the shaded driveway four flatbeds started up their engines and pulled on their headlights. The flatbed trucks were loaded with newly deputized farmers and ranchers. The small convoy pulled out of the driveway and turned toward the migrants.

The first truck pulled behind the last vehicle parked alongside the road. The second and third trucks stopped equal to the middle of the migrant's column of vehicles. The last truck pulled in front of the lead union vehicle and stopped. The workers were pinned in by the angry farmers.

"Get everyone bunched up here together, nice and tight, see? They won't dare shoot with women mixed in with us," the agitator told his men.

The deputized ranchers and farmers offloaded from their trucks and formed a perimeter around the workers who now stood in a tight group, awaiting the next move.

Angry farmers tapped ax handles in their palms and did not smile.

"This is gonna be like one of our rabbit roundups," a farmer said.

The migrants that heard backed away and hid towards the rear of the group of pickers.

The sheriff stopped his vehicle behind the two flatbed trucks in the middle of the column. He was accompanied by Jack and Bert. The three men walked between the vehicles to address the group of migrants. The union man spoke first.

"We didn't come here to fight y'all, sheriff. As anyone can see we're defenseless and outnumbered. We have women with us too, just so you know."

Then to Bert, "You need to pay a wage that will allow these good folks the opportunity to at least eat! You won't cheat us today, either! Your apples can rot for all we care."

"That one there, Sam. He's not coming aboard. Neither are his cronies. Those four and that big one there," Bert said.

Jack instructed the pickers to file past him and Bert and they would decide if the migrant would be allowed to work in their orchard.

"What's the pay?" the union man demanded.

"Folks, pay's the same as it was yesterday. We're not here to cheat anyone."

"You're not working here," Jack said to the union man.

"You can move on down the road. It doesn't have to get ugly," Bert said.

"Let's go! Times wastin'!" Jack ordered.

"You folks can't work for these cheats. Don't you have any pride?" the union man asked the crowd. "These cheats . . . !"

"That's it!" the sheriff said. "You and your boys can move out on your own or laying in the back of that flatbed. It's that simple."

"Let's go, folks. Time's wasting. Either leave, or let's get to work!"

"We wanna work," the little man with a bushy mustache said.

"Good! Next? There ya go. Stand over there and we'll get you set up with gear in just a few minutes," Bert said.

Hungry migrants made a line toward the front of the column of parked cars.

"Let's go!" the sheriff said to the man with the worm on his head and his agitators. "There ya go. Climb in your vehicles and turn around nice and peacefully."

"Loitering is an offense I would dearly like to cite you with."

Having identified the agitators from yesterday, the selection process went quickly. Within minutes the huddled mass began to move down the gravel drive toward the packing shed, led by Jack.

Bert stood by with the sheriff and his deputies while the agitator and his men turned their vehicles around.

The agitator yelled to the workers, "You poor monkeys! You'll never learn! Starve for all I care!"

The agitator tipped his hat to Bert and the sheriff.

"Move your ass. You're blocking a public thoroughfare, causing a public nuisance . . . and you're ugly. We can add that to the ticket at no extra charge," the sheriff quipped.

Bert smiled and caught the eye of the union man who locked eyes with him as the sedan drove away.

"Shut up and let me think," the union agitator said to the men riding in his vehicle.

"Christ all mighty. McCracken thinks he's gonna give us a rough time," he said.

"I'll bust that big, dumb farmer, right in the chops." Roy said.

"Pipe down! Pipe down, you moron. Where were you when he was throwing me around the road? That's right, stuffing your face. And no, you aren't goin' to bust nobody. We don't need a confrontation. They know what we look like," said the agitator. "I may need more muscle on the wing, you can't do any better than what I saw out there yesterday."

"Ah. I can do better. I was just hungry. You aren't mad at me are you? I promise. I'll do better. You can hit me, if it makes you feel better. Just don't be mad at me," Roy said.

"Shut up and let me think."

The three vehicles loaded with union men arrived at the river and came to a stop above their campsite.

"No. I'm going to get their attention and I'm going to teach these dumb farmers a thing or two about how to treat workers."

"There is a higher law than just that of man they must answer to. Where is their sacrifice and their commitment to their fellow man?"

"Want me to take care of his truck? "Roy asked. "Maybe tidy up his packing shed. I'd like that, boss. I would, if that's what you want."

"Hey!" said the agitator.

"Keep it down, will ya? Get over here before all the pickers get back. Here's what we're gonna do, see?"

Roy moved in closer, anxious to please the agitator.

As dusk turned to night the migrants filed slowly and sweat-dried into camp. Dashiell turned his truck around after the pickers jumped off. Exhausted, he headed home to help prepare the next load of apples for Joseph to take to San Francisco.

After cleaning up from the day's work, men gathered around the largest campfire in the bachelor's camp.

"That's right. It's like I was telling my boys this morning, 'We can't fight them all. We were out-drawn today. They had the sheriff and his vigilantes with them. You saw all those clubs, pitchforks, rifles. It was no good for sure. They needed all that to keep us from winning the day."

"Admit it," a skinny man in overalls said. "Them folks ain't so bad and none of that, what happened today, had to happen that-a-way. They paid us for our work and they even fed us. How many you folks hungry? Uh huh."

The Basque said, "Pay was the same. Food was the same and I don't have to sleep with knots on my head. It was a good day."

"That young feller even gave us a ride back to camp. How about that?" another man said.

The group discussion continued ad nauseam late into the night. Roy and one other of the agitator's cronies separated themselves from the crowd. They moved behind the union men's tents, where they were lost in the dark, then headed to the top of the riverbank. They climbed into one of the union sedans and headed east.

25

Bert grew his rabbitrie slowly. He studied the amount of food, water, labor, and various other "one percenters" as he and Joseph called them. Any small tweaking in the production of animals or produce that might save a farmer's muscle or hours was a "one percenter".

If a farmer could string together enough "one percenters", it made his difficult work a little more bearable.

Bert was rapidly coming to the conclusion rabbits were a damned pain in the ass. Whether raising bees, cattle, goats, or rabbits, it was never a matter of *if* you would be attacked or otherwise hurt, but of when and how many times you would be attacked and injured.

Bert and Ethel dressed dozens of rabbits for delivery to the local meat markets, grocery stores, and restaurants throughout Fresno and Madera counties. Bert beheaded and skinned the rabbits. Ethel dressed the rabbits, then rinsed them and packed them in ice Bert had brought on his return route from Fresno.

While Bert delivered rabbit meat to market and butcher, Ethel dumped bucket after bucket of rabbit entrails and the half-cannibalized baby rabbits into a pit. She sprinkled quicklime over the muck and then a few inches of soil was shoveled on top of the mess. She detested the flies and the smell. When the wind changed direction, the smell was so godawful she could not control her gag reflex. Ethel performed a rough, cursory cleaning of the rabbit pelts which were then sold to make ear muffs, shawls, and glove inserts.

Towards the end of the summer and approaching autumn, the temperature was perfect for an explosion of the fly population. It seemed flies or fly spots covered everything. It was all Ethel could do to keep them out of the house.

Does protected their young and their territory with ferocity and always attacked as Bert removed the mothers so they would not cannibalize their young. Yet, these same does cared not that their young might wander off to be eaten. He never understood that.

Bert and Ethel talked of transitioning to broiler chickens and layers.

"Just a few dozen or so to begin," Bert suggested. "You know, get a few eggs, and sell a few birds. Besides everyone's raising rabbits in their backyards now," he said.

"I'm damned tired of getting bitten and having to haul out all those half-eaten baby rabbits. The reproducing process and dealing with the does is just a lot of work."

The veteran did not share with his wife the dark memories the half-cannibalized baby rabbits conjured in his mind while he cleaned cages.

Ethel held out her hand to receive a half-eaten baby rabbit from Bert. His mind snapped to a reconnaissance with Joseph, George, three indigenous tribesmen, and their interpreter, scouting in front of the main element.

Recent warm fires and fresh scraps of food suggested they were close to Aguinaldo and his band. Broken leaves and branches, not yet withered, spoke to the proximity of the enemy.

An explosion not more than ten feet behind Bert killed one of the tribesmen. Bert, regaining his feet, turned around to see what had hit him in the back. The hand of the tribesman was palm up and looked, to Bert, as if it was begging for help. Upturned palms would haunt Bert for the rest of his life—every upturned palm. For the rest of his life, cannibalized baby rabbits would remind Bert of the tribesman's upper body which had been stripped of clothing and flesh.

After supper, Ethel worked in her kitchen. Bert checked his meat rabbits by lantern light. He checked the water system and spread more kitchen scraps and garden refuse for the rabbits to eat. He separated the rabbits that would be butchered in the morning. No need to feed them. He put on a heavy leather glove to fend off an aggressive doe while removing her dead, half cannibalized baby.

"Jesus Christ!"

Bert tried to sing songs, whistle, anything that might distract him from his chores. But that incident in the jungle, years earlier, always awaited him.

Bert was singing, *Don't Fence Me In* when a lone vehicle turned left, away from the San Joaquin River. A mile or so north the driver pulled to the side of the gravel road then pushed in the knob that killed the headlights. At a low spot within the rolling foothills below the Sierra Nevada Mountains, invisible in the low-lying fog covering the Valley, the big man quietly exited the vehicle.

Ethel climbed the stairs to their bedroom to light the kerosene lantern.

The big man, concealed by the darkness, climbed through the barbed wire fencing. He worked himself into and through a stand of live oak trees and granite boulders.

Coming out the other side of the trees Roy walked quickly to the back of the barn, all the while peering around lest anyone should find him out. He peeked through knotholes in the barn's wooden, board-and-batten sides. Roy could see one of the farmers they had confronted earlier at the McCracken farm. He ran back to the road and the man waiting in the sedan.

"This is better," whispered the fighter.

"Gimme that can. I'll get her goin' in no time. Turn the car around. This is gonna be easy," he whispered.

Roy prowled silently around the barn. Sacks of quicklime were quietly stacked in front of the large double doors of the barn as Bert whistled his tune of distraction. Roy slipped the padlock into the hasp of the door latch on the main door to the barn.

Roy then unscrewed the lid on the can of kerosene and pried out the seal with his penknife. He splashed kerosene around the northwest corner of the barn. The liquid trail lit, the corner of the barn exploded in a flash of yellow and blue flame. The kerosene caught then ran around the perimeter of the barn.

Rabbits screamed. Bert ran into the door that had been secured by Roy returning the lock to the hasp. He tried again. He ran to the double doors and removed the wooden one-by-one that served to secure the big doors. He could not push them open. The barn quickly filled with flame and smoke.

The fighter threw the kerosene can to the side and trotted into the folds of heavy yellow and grey smoke.

26

The sun still sat behind the Sierra Nevada Mountains on the eastern side of the San Joaquin Valley when three flatbed trucks, like menacing ships of war full of angry Greek warriors, pulled to a stop at the ledge above the hobo jungle where the trestle bridge intersected the San Joaquin River.

The trucks were filled with farmers and ranchers laden with ax handles, pitchforks, rifles, and machetes. The farmers stood in the backs of trucks aching for a fight. Their skin was tanned and work hardened. No-nonsense faces creased by their labors under an austere sun only awaited the order.

Dust danced in front of the headlights. Horns honked. The men unloaded from the trucks and lined the top of the riverbank. Still others followed the sheriff down the animal trail in a cloud of dust.

"I'm gettin' too old for this shit," the sheriff said to no one in particular, as he bounced down the switchback. The farmers and ranchers reached the bottom, spread out, and encircled the bachelor's camp, leaving only the swift San Joaquin River as the trespassers' only escape.

"Awe heck, sheriff, we been here all night. You can ask any man, woman, or child here." A union man stretched and farted. Tin cans and fryware sat on smoky fires along the river's edge.

"What are you lookin' for sheriff?"

"A man was murdered in his barn last night." The sheriff spoke loudly. "Got caught inside while his barn was set on fire!"

The sheriff's deputies rousted the remaining single men from their sleep rolls and tents. "Get 'em over here. Every one of 'em." The men were told to dress and gather together as the deputies searched their belongings.

"Spread out a little! Come on! Spread out, I said!" a deputy commanded the slow-moving, lethargic men of the camp.

The sheriff instructed a deputy to hand his revolver to another then go in amongst the transients and search pockets, waistbands, and boots. Sleep hung on the transients' faces, hair like tossed leaves. Yawning and crotch scratching continued as the last of the single men gathered together from the farthest reaches of the hobo jungle.

Fog and wood smoke filled the encampment.

"I say, what are ya lookin' for sheriff? Maybe we can help."

"Any man here that smells of kerosene might just be beginning a bad day," the sheriff replied.

"Sure there was a little altercation at the McCracken farm, but we all been down that road before, right? You told us to leave yesterday. We left, just like you ordered. We've been here all night. Ask anyone. Not a car has moved from here. Everyone in camp would of heard it. Go feel the hoods on the cars," the agitator said with confidence.

"Who said anything about the McCracken's farm?"

"Well, that's 'bout the only place any of us worked yesterday. Now, it sounds like we're out of work again. There just seems no end to it all, sheriff."

He looked at the agitator with disdain. The sheriff had already come to the conclusion none of these jalopies could have been used by the culprits of Bert's murder. All the vehicles had heavy dew running down their hoods and windshields. The ground around the cars showed no recent activity. None of the men smelled of kerosene.

"Where's the big ugly man that was with you yesterday?"

"I'm not sure who you refer to, sheriff. I do remember a big man that was attacked by one of those rough farmers. I assure you all my associates are here and accounted for."

The agitator addressed his cronies. "Do any of you gentlemen know who the sheriff is talking about? There, you see, sheriff?"

To the other single men in camp, the sheriff said, "By the time the sun reaches this "X" here." The sheriff gouged an "X" in the shady sand with his boot. "I want you gone from this county or there will be hell to pay." The sheriff looked at the union man with the worm on his face.

"You and your assistants need to come with me."

A general grumbling came from the union men. The agitator raised his hands.

"We'll go. We haven't done anything wrong. We have nothing to fear. Right, sheriff?"

"Let's go."

The sheriff explained to the families camped on the other side of the hobo jungle they could stay, but just for a while.

"Seeing as you have families and all. You folks might be okay, but I can't guarantee your safety down here, so ya gotta go too. The folks here about are mighty angry right now. I'd be leaving as soon as possible."

Sam Westfall had many regrets as the sheriff of Madera County. Rousting families from the only home they had with winter coming on was one of his biggest regrets. He offered the small group addresses in Fresno where food and shelter might be sought.

"But, folks, you gotta go. There's just too much bad blood for transients here now."

"You know? People getting' killed, barns burned, crops ruined. Folks are about at the end of being neighborly. Visitors don't treat their hosts this way."

Then, turning to three deputized farmers, the sheriff said, "You boys follow the trucks back to town with their vehicles, where we can give them a good goin' over."

"Hank, get them signed in for me."

"I'll be at Bert's place."

The accused were told to tear down and pack their belongings in their vehicles that they would not be coming back to the jungle. The union boss and his remaining five assistants loaded onto Cyril's flatbed truck. Smoldering farmers filled the lead and trail vehicles.

27

George was at the corner of Washington and Davis Streets just before sunrise. Looking for a ride to the Valley, he engaged a farmer who was headed south of Fresno and knew where Madera was, though he did not know Joseph McCracken or the location of his farm.

George paid the man a dime for gas then climbed atop the flatbed and sat on his bindle, his back to the driver. George enjoyed the beautiful San Francisco bay. Across the Oakland Bay Bridge, the farmer drove with George in tow. They crested the last hill on the east side of the Pacific Coastal Range. The sun had risen and was now headed west.

The farmer banged on the back window of his truck and yelled to George. "That's the San Joaquin Valley!"

George turned and stood in the back of the truck holding his hat in the breeze and looked across the Valley. He had worked the San Joaquin Valley over the years he had spent on the road, but he had never seen the magnificent San Joaquin Valley from this vantage point.

As far as he could see the land was as flat as the ocean on a calm day. Irrigated land, parceled and divided into nice, neat sections; some to row crops, some to tree fruits and nuts, still other sections to vines, grasses, and grains. George could not tell all the different varieties he saw along the road. The orchards were as neat and orderly as a military formation standing at attention, awaiting the veteran's review.

At sixty-miles wide and five-hundred-miles long, the San Joaquin Valley was left unexplored and relegated to "future exploration" until the likes of men such as Savage, Bunnell, Walker, Carson, Fremont, and Smith . . . until gold was found north and east, around Sutter's Fort.

The Pony Express did not consider California important enough for a mail route until the 1860's. Indeed, Father Serra, mission-building his way north, evidently did not find it prudent to venture too far down the eastern side of the Pacific Coastal Range into that burning, brown desert. But that is not how the agrarians and ranchers, like Miller and Lux, understood the potential of the San Joaquin Valley; the vast unirrigated desert of central California. Some dreamed of what could be done with a few good men and water, but that was also all hell needed.

The great, agriculturally rich San Joaquin Valley had been a virtual backwater to the tide of civilization that flooded in from the East Coast and the rest of the world. The blistering summers of the San Joaquin Valley could strip the hide off a man's back and boil his brain. In the hot Valley the landscape changed men as much as the men changed the landscape. Temperatures reached well over a hundred degrees for days on end.

Averaging only ten to twelve inches of rainfall a year, one fourth of that annual amount could come in a single day. The lack of rain was compensated for by the magnificent snowpack held by the

Sierra Nevada Mountains that rose directly to the east. Eventually, dams were built to hold the snow melt until the farmers had need for it. The infrastructure of California would need to be continually tweaked to allow for the growth of more agriculture and the burgeoning numbers descending on the state and her resources, but that task would be left to successive generations.

Early agrarians and ranchers harnessed the waters of the Sierra Nevada to grow their crops and raise cattle for the exploding populations of and around San Francisco and Sacramento during the gold rush of 1849. Later, water would be sent farther south to barren Los Angeles, San Diego, and beyond. The railroad and refrigerated boxcars opened the doors of the San Joaquin Valley to markets back east. International markets were accessible through Stockton, Los Angeles, San Diego, and San Francisco Bay.

If one took a giant knife and stabbed California in its geographical heart, one would slice through the northwest section of the McCracken farm.

The farm was situated north of the San Joaquin River and continued north beyond Cottonwood Creek on the eastern side of the Valley, or approximately halfway between Fresno and the old coach road that led Teddy Roosevelt and company to the recently discovered Yosemite Valley.

"My God," George said to himself. "It's like a modern-day Mesopotamia."

Still holding on with one hand, he stood in the back of the truck with the brim of his fedora held in the other. The truck descended into the San Joaquin Valley. George could feel the temperature rise.

The orchards stood at attention, ready for inspection.

28

Joseph made the final turn, north, toward home. His eyes burned and were red from lack of sleep. Instead of the lonely, empty road to which he had become accustomed his whole life, he spied vehicles all along the sides of the road up ahead. It looked to be a country fair of some sort, or an auction, though Joseph knew it had to do more with the union men coming back to make trouble for his family and the families of those who had come to earn a little money.

Joseph pulled his truck onto the shoulder of the road in front of Bert's farm. He rolled down the window of his truck and tried to see through the fog and smoke.

"Oh, my God!" Joseph exclaimed.

He jumped from his truck and heading towards the farmhouse saw Floe's car in the driveway with the sheriff's car pulled in behind hers. Joseph saw the burned remains of Bert's barn, embers still smoking. Joseph looked north to his farm as he proceeded to Bert's front porch.

"Joseph! Thank God you're back! Where've you been? Bert's dead! In the barn fire."

"What happened? Where's Dashiell and Pa?"

"Why didn't you come home last night?"

"I had trouble with the truck and slept on the side of the road. How's pa, Dashiell?"

"Ethel, what's happened here?" Joseph's eyes darted between Florence and Ethel. "Floe?"

"They're fine, Joseph," Florence said.

Ethel began to speak. "I ran to Floe . . . ," but she could not finish her sentence and started crying again.

The tired, jaded sheriff entered from the back porch. It appeared to Joseph as though Sam had been rolling around in the dirt and ashes outside.

Joseph looked to the sheriff. "Sam . . . Bert was inside? What happened?"

"Joe . . . ," Sam nodded towards the ladies. "Excuse us ladies. Let's talk outside, Joe, give these ladies a moment."

Once outside, Joseph stared into the ashes from within which he hoped his friend, Bert, would somehow rise. The sheriff noticed Joseph's stare and gave him some time.

After a moment he spoke. "Uh, Joe? I just wanted to let you know, the barn doors were secured from the outside before the fire was set."

A darkness fell across Joseph's reddening face.

The two men walked around the barn's ashes. "See here?"

The sheriff explained that sacks of quicklime blocked one door. He stirred the ashes with a stick so Joseph could better identify the lock that still remained open, just simply returned to the hasp baring anyone's exit from inside.

"See?" Sam said. "One man came in from that direction. One man carried the lime sacks and stacked them in front of the door here. Over here," the sheriff walked Joseph through the sequence of events, "is where he threw the kerosene can on his way out."

"One man."

"Here's a boot print. Should be easy to find."

"How's that," Joseph asked.

"The soles of the boots don't match. See here? Big man, too. Seems to me there was one of them union types, a big, ugly fella, was with them."

"Should be easy to ID him, ugly as he is, from what Jack and Dashiell said."

"Where is he, Sam? Did you go to the camp down by the river?"

"We went to the migrant camp down at the river," Sam said. "Hauled the agitator and his crew in. The big, ugly sonofabitch wasn't with them. I suspect it was him, maybe one or two others with him. If it was him, he's long gone and has been since last night."

"Only families there now. And they were supposed to be out about noon today."

"Where did they go?"

"No one's talkin' to us. What I need to know is what do you know?"

Joseph told the sheriff of the argument at the orchard after the first day of picking. Joseph confirmed he had been in San Francisco.

"Sam, you know as well as I . . . ."

"Now, wait a minute, Joe. We don't *know* anything."

"So, no one could fill that boot except the big, dumb guy with them?"

"I don't think so. There wasn't a one of them taller than about five, nine. Do you remember any other big dude that could wear a size twelve boot that looked like the agitator's muscle?"

"No, I don't," Joseph lied. "I was busy in the shed . . . with the women and old folks mostly." Joseph averted Sam's eyes and stared into the ashes.

Sam and Joseph had known each other all their lives; played football together. Sam sensed Joseph's uneasiness. "I'll let you know what we turn up. I got a good description of the guy we suspect. Put it out on the radio this morning, notified all the offices between Sacramento and Bakersfield."

The sheriff patted Joseph on the back as they walked to the squad car.

"I know this is hard for you. Let me know if there is anything I can do. I imagine Bert would want a veteran's funeral. I'll talk to Ethel. We got Bert, what's left of him, over at the funeral home. You don't want to see him. I'll make a call on the veteran's group."

"Thanks, Sam. I got another load of apples headed for San Francisco. I'll get back as fast as I can. I have to talk with Floe, Pa, ya know?"

Joseph, ever so gently, closed the door to his flatbed truck. He sat thinking of the fighting man he had encountered previously in the ranks of the agitator and his crew. Joseph slowly pulled away. The truck whined as Joseph kept the truck in low gear, staring straight ahead, on the short drive north, toward his farm.

29

After jumping off the flatbed truck at the hobo jungle in Madera, George gave thanks and waved to the Swede who waved back and created a cloud of dust as he continued south of Fresno to his tree farm in Selma.

It was late afternoon and fast heading into evening when George descended the switchback that took him to the bottom of the river, sliding most of the way on his feet. He seemed to enjoy it as a young boy might.

A woman watched the stranger from a distance. Only a few, those too young, tired, or broken, remained in the hobo jungle.

George pulled his coffee pot from his bindle and set it, full of water, on the abandoned, smoldering fire. He then stood washing at the river. The soap did little good as the road grime had worked its way into the pores and scars of George's face, yet he scrubbed on, diligently.

George pulled a clean, but highly wrinkled, shirt from his bindle. He turned to face the river. He unbuttoned his trousers, tucked his clean shirt in, and turned back towards the camp. He buttoned his shirt as he approached the large-breasted woman bent over tending a pot of opossum meat and beans.

"Someone's eating high times tonight. That smells delicious, dear woman. My name is George."

The woman looked up from the steaming pot. She viewed the single man with a tired indifference.

"The others have either gone off pickin' or headed out for greener pastures," the old woman told George. She wiped her hands on her apron. "You by yourself?"

"Yes ma'am, I am. But I won't be staying. I'm looking for a friend."

"Just the same." She straightened up and arched her back and wiped her face with a handful of apron. "You single men stay over there." She pointed with her head toward the bachelor camp. "You men been causin' nothin' but trouble around here lately. Watch yourself."

"A bunch of fellers was up top earlier throwing river rocks down on us. I yelled at them we couldn't go nowhere till we get this old bucket of bolts fixed. That seemed to do them for a while. But they mean business, mister. They quit and said they'd be back tomorrow for some more."

The grey water was just coming to a boil. Bone-colored bubbles and foam collected on the inside of the pot. The overworked woman stirred her pot of stewed opossum meat.

"Said they would wait till we was sleepin' then sneak back and smash our heads in like pumpkins with them big round rocks." Her hands were in front of her, as if she was about to choke someone. "I mean them big ones too!"

George doffed his hat. "Now, what's goin' on here?"

"Ah!" She threw her hands in the air. "Them union men came in here a week or so ago. Man says to everybody, he says, 'We'll stand by you! Higher wages for all! We're here to he'p ya!'" She shook her head and bent over her fire. "Ya ever notice, someone says they're here to he'p ya, it ends up costin' ya more than if they didn't he'p ya 't all."

"Ma'am? I'm not trackin' with you. What do you mean?"

"Well, I mean to tell ya. It was godawful!" She shook her head.

"One of them farmers, where everyone that wanted to work was? Farmer gets hisself killed in a barn fire. Course, union men are to blame. Everyone knows it. No one's talkin'. Sheriff and a bunch of angry farmers, vigilantes you know, hauled them all to the calaboose about dawn this mornin'."

"Then them knuckleheads showed up and started throwing rocks down on us!"

"Now any man wants to work can over at the farmer's cause the union men got hauled away and the other men took off."

The old woman raised the dirty, grey apron and wiped the sweat from her face and neck. She brushed the loose strands of hair back into place and repositioned a pin in the bun behind her head.

"Who was killed? I'm looking for the McCracken farm . . . Joseph McCracken. Was it that farm?" George asked, becoming agitated.

"Don't know his name, Scotch, I think."

George stiffened. "Where is this farm?"

Her features were as brown and grey as the clothes she wore. The old woman pointed to the northeast with her wooden spoon.

"'bout eight or seven mile or so, I reckon. As the crows fly. Take the road up top that-a-way. Keep the river on your right, then north when the road dies. Least that's what the men were sayin' ta other day."

"You a union man?" the lady asked. She unfolded the paper she pulled from her apron and handed George a copy of the union flyer announcing the meeting in Stockton. George took the flyer thinking he might stuff it in his shoe later.

"Them boys was passin' these out the other night when they were here. Says there's gonna be food after." She looked beneath her brow at George's thin physic.

"Just sayin'," she said.

George, scrambled to the top of the switchback. After walking for an hour he noticed the dirt road died at a T intersection up ahead. He instinctively surveyed the landscape north and estimated the trek farther down the road and bisected the distance with a forty-five degree alteration of his advance.

Another hour went by and George found the road north. He moved off the road as a train of four vehicles loaded with pickers passed, headed south. A picker yelled out the window of his vehicle that the work, down that road was all gone, now. The walking man waved and continued on for a while longer.

George squatted on his haunches and watched the activity at Bert's farm. He saw a young migrant couple walking toward him and stopped their retreat.

"Is this the McCracken Farm? What happened here?"

"No, no. That's not McCracken's farm. That's up the road. This here farm is the other guy. One of the farmers who was helpin' pick the other day when the fight broke out between the farmers and the union men. Don't know his name."

George thanked the young people and continued on.

30

While city folks were warm and settled in after their comfortable dinner, radios were turned on for the evening's entertainment and Roosevelt's fireside chat. Tule fog blanketed the Valley floor. Dashiell readied another load of apples for transport to San Francisco.

Most of the picking crew brought in from town to help with the last of the apple harvest was gone. While the truck was loaded with the last of the apples and secured with ropes, a few friends and neighbors stayed to pay their respects to Ethel and help clean up. Now and again a pickup truck or sedan arrived at the McCracken farm to retrieve a family member.

Florence busied herself gathering dishes and napkins. Her hair had fallen with her countenance. She looked little different than the migrants. Her feet were swollen within her granny shoes. She ached to take them off.

Jack looked at his son then kicked the ground beneath his boot. "Been a long day, son."

"Cy and his boy went to the park and brought in fellers who wanted to work. He guaranteed a ride back into town when the work was done and an ass whoppin' if they caused us any trouble. Word spread at Gigio's diner too. So, hell, must have been forty, fifty people showed up to give us a hand today."

"Pa, talk to me. What happened after the fire?"

"Yeah, well, Ethel showed up screaming and crying. Said Bert was in the barn when it caught fire. We saw the smoke, but there just wasn't anything we could do. When the sheriff showed up at that camp down by the river, hell, they were all sound asleep. Cars were cool. There wasn't anyone there *to* arrest. Big sonofabitch took off already."

"The one who burned Bert's barn, he must have just kept goin', huh?"

"That's right, but who knows where? Sam said the man who started the fire had two different boots on. None of the men he took in were wearing anything like those boots, nor that big."

"That barn-fighter, Roy, was the biggest man I saw with 'em."

"That big brawler was long gone. I suspect it was him. And they didn't find any boots, like what they were lookin' for, in any of the gear." Dashiell added.

Joseph took a minute to absorb this information. He noticed Jack and Dashiell were both strapped with Colt revolvers.

Farmers waved or saluted and were gone, headed home to their own chores.

"Thanks, folks. I won't forget ya," Jack said as a car passed slowly by.

The burnt orange sun sank into a grey haze where the earth and sky met.

"It was perfect. Make sure the sheriff couldn't find the person wearing the boots by having them hightail it out of the county directly. Don't even come back to camp. Search all you want, the evidence, the boots tying them to Bert's murder, can't be done."

"That's about the size of it. Sneaky little bastards; could be in Kansas by now." Jack sighed.

Florence came to the back door and called for the men to come have a cup of coffee. She had made a cinnamon Bundt cake. Slowly the remaining crowd behind the McCracken home dispersed and the last of the day's help headed down the gravel drive. Coffee, bread, honey, and a venison stew brought over by Gigio and his wife, Maggie, remained on the kitchen table. Joseph replaced the lid on the stew.

"Joseph, I've packed a basket for you to take with you." Florence said quietly. "You're going to need some sleep too."

Joseph half smiled at Florence's continual concern for her family's wellbeing.

Ethel stared out the blackened kitchen window. Florence and Joseph looked on.

"We'll be okay," Florence said as she approached and wrapped one arm around Ethel's waist.

"Well, thanks . . . I guess I'll be headed out then. I need to check my load and the truck." Joseph said. He reached for the lantern by the back door.

"Joseph! You need sleep first!"

"I know, dear, but I gotta get going. If I get tired, I'll nap along the road, or at the market."

"Dashiell and I just checked it. Good to go," Jack said.

"A little nap, then get that last load off the truck and get back here."

Turning to Ethel, "I truly am sorry about all this," Joseph said.

Ethel was lost in her nightmare, "Oh, Joseph! I don't know what to think." Ethel's eyes were red and it hurt Joseph to look at her.

"It's just been a long day, dear. Let's get you a nice hot bath and then to bed."

"Dash, would you be a dear and get the hot water when you're done there?"

Dashiell was dunking chunks of torn bread into his stew and taking big gobs into his mouth.

"Of course."

"Maybe you two ought to take shifts. Leave the dogs out." Joseph said. "Dash, hang some lanterns out in the trees. Watch for movement."

"Keep an eye out, yourself. Those bastards'll steal half that load off your truck before you can whistle Dixie," Jack Said.

Joseph raised his hands in consternation. "Remind me to tell you about the pimp and the prostitute I ran in to in San Francisco yesterday. Tomorrow ought to be great."

"Prostitute?" Dashiell straightened up and gave his full attention to what Joseph was saying.

"Easy, cowboy," Jack said.

A knock at the back door sent Joseph to the living room where he grabbed the shotgun from over the mantle and chambered two rounds. He returned to the kitchen porch. The dogs, normally attuned to strangers, were not concerned by this stranger's appearance on their property. A result, no doubt, of the coming and going of visitors all day and night the last couple of days. Jack and Dashiell palmed their revolvers.

"Floe, can you take Ethel and step into the living room while we see what's going on here?"

Joseph nodded his head to Dashiell, who opened the door with a jerk, as Joseph leveled the shotgun.

It seemed to the men the grimy fellow at the door was just another migrant looking for a handout and a place to stay the night. He had nothing in his hands that looked like it could be used as a weapon.

Dashiell and Jack relaxed a bit, but remained vigilant. Joseph brought the barrel of the shotgun up and rested it against his right shoulder.

The small, dirty man stood at the bottom of the steps leading to the back door of the McCracken home. He took the round glasses from his face and cleaned them, as best he could, in his soiled handkerchief. Once his glasses had been replaced the man removed his hat and straightened his shoulders.

Joseph noticed the man needed a shave and could not understand how the man could see through his filthy glasses.

George brought himself to the position of attention. "If this is the McCracken farm, then I am Corporal George Root, United States Army, tried and trusted friend of Sergeant, Joseph McCracken!"

Astonished, Joseph pushed from around his father and son.

"Sergeant McCracken! Is that you, Joseph?"

The little man moved closer to the bottom step that led to the back porch. "Well, sure it is! Sergeant Mac!"

"Root?"

The little man squeezed his filthy, dove-gray fedora between his hands, in front of his heart. Jack, Dashiell, and the women, back now, looked on, curiously.

The small man offered his best grimy and thoroughly exhausted smile.

"It is I, Sergeant Mac. At your service," Corporal Root said.

31

The men hugged one another as veterans do when reunited after many miles and battles, only then realizing the other still alive. Introductions followed with a brief synopsis of what brought George to the McCracken farm that night.

Joseph explained to George what had most recently taken place concerning the death of their friend, Bert.

"I understand, Joseph. I passed by Bert's place earlier without knowing that was his home," George said.

Then directly to Ethel, "A shame, what happened to ol' Bert. He was a fine man. Damned few like him, ma'am."

"None better," Jack said.

George bowed to Ethel and Florence and excused himself for using such rough language in front of them.

"I have enjoyed a thoroughly difficult and miserable existence in the wild and spent too much time on the road and in the company of rough and wretched men. I have been informed, I may no longer be civilized, ma'am." Turning toward Florence, "Please forgive me ma'am."

Florence thanked him.

"Sergeant Mac, what is being done to catch the scoundrels who murdered our dear friend, Bert?"

Joseph, along with Jack, brought George up to date on the sheriff's investigation. George ate venison stew and drank hot coffee. Jack told George that while Joseph was in San Francisco with the first load of apples, the sheriff and his deputies had gone to the river, suspecting the union agitator and his men were responsible for the barn burning and Bert's murder.

"Of course, when they arrived, the sons o' bitches who did it were long gone. They caught ol' Bert's barn afire and took off as fast as they could. They never went back to that camp below the train trestle, by the highway," Jack said. "Sorry, Floe, Ethel."

"You men! Just go on, I've heard it all before," Florence said. Ethel hardly paid attention to the conversation.

"An old woman at the migrant camp, down by the river, gave me this flier earlier today," George said. He handed the flier to Joseph.

"What you got there, son," Jack asked, after a moment. Joseph handed the flier to his father. Dashiell read the flier over his grandfather's shoulder.

"There's a chance they could rendezvous."

"George, I know you've been on the road and are dog tired, no doubt, but I'd sure like your company on this next haul to San Francisco, if you wouldn't mind." Then for the sake of Dashiell and the women, "I haven't slept in two days. Maybe you could help drive a bit."

"I would be honored, Joseph. It will give us a chance to catch up, old friend."

Florence busied herself preparing a meal for George to take with him on his travel back to San Francisco with Joseph. Ethel sat at the kitchen table and was lost in all the commotion.

"I'd like to go," Dashiell said.

"Not this trip, son. I need you and grandfather to keep an eye on things here."

"Son? The hot water, for Ethel?"

"Oh, right! On my way."

Once on the Golden State Highway, Joseph told George to continue north.

At all hours, seven days a week, the small two-lane Golden State Highway was choked with trucks moving produce to places as far away as Los Angeles, San Francisco, Stockton, and Sacramento. The drive one way from Madera to San Francisco was equivalent to driving from Staten Island to Baltimore and back, twenty to thirty times a year. Thousands of tons of perishable produce traversed the state and was bickered over daily. Joseph napped as George drove north.

The Golden State Highway was known as one of the most dangerous roads in America and would have that distinction for the next one hundred years due to an ever distracted governance.

A driver fell asleep while hauling a truck and trailer of turkeys that wiped out a family of four headed to Los Angeles.

Brakes failed and twenty tons of produce, metal and fuel slammed into a cattle trailer killing the drivers and twenty-four head of cattle.

There was never a guarantee the farmer's produce would sell at the San Francisco produce market once it arrived. From various California ports, San Joaquin produce, grains, nuts, fowl, and beef found their way to the four corners of the world. One agrarian, in the backwaters of the San Joaquin Valley, fed a hundred people in the cities.

Tired, tanned, and dirty farmers with trucks loaded with produce drew not the slightest attention as they pulled off the road. Here a driver checked ropes, knots, or chains. There a farmer checked his brakes, oil, and the water in the truck's radiator before continuing on to Sacramento with his load of eggs. Over there a farmer checked a map for directions on where to deliver a ten ton load of garlic. Another farmer napped before continuing home.

The night was pitch-black, the side of the road littered with trucks, both loaded and unloaded. Headlights, blinkers, brake lights, all were a blur as men's eyes constantly adjusted between the pitch of night and the high beams of an oncoming truck.

Another farmer pulled his truck onto the shoulder of the Golden State Highway and stopped. The harvest tramp jumped out of the cab and waved to Joseph who scooted over to the driver's seat. He headed back on to the Golden State Highway and continued his journey to the San Francisco market and the promise of a quick sale.

George read a sign in the window of a Stockton diner. "No Dogs or Filipinos Allowed."

George walked Stockton as might a tourist.

"Where is it, now?" He checked his map.

"There it is. East Main Street to South Sullivan."

"Your day of eternal darkness has arrived, cousin."

George's psyche darkened, eyes dead. His skin tingled as adrenaline pumped into the veteran's system. His heart pumped faster, like an athlete in anticipation of the competition.

His reflexes sharpened. His sight caught all movement. He smelled the night air and paid attention to its flow. God, he loved it and never felt more alive than when on the hunt. He became more conscious of his steps and breathing. He felt for the knife in his pocket and the razor in his boot.

"My sweet Lord, steel my heart so that I may lay low those that rise against me on the field of battle. Give me Your lightning, Your thunder to combat this evil. In Your name."

"Welcome, brother! Come on in! It's about to get hot!" a union man greeted George.

"Amen to that, brother! You have no idea."

George walked through the crowd, hat pulled low across his brow, indistinguishable from the other fruit tramps or walking men gathered for the evening's sermon and meal. George knew the routine: opening prayer, speeches, more prayer, more lectures, then food, songs, and cleaning afterwards.

The small church was filled with the hoboes, migrants, fruit tramps, and young families seeking what one might expect where free food and shelter were being offered. A young family with three small, dirty, children sat huddled together at a picnic table, eating their first hot meal in two days. Small fires dotted the front of the churchyard.

It was a little past nine o'clock when George arrived. The lectures had already begun. George listened to the agitator work the crowd for membership.

"With your membership we'll issue you a union card that will speak for you when applying for work. It's a brotherhood of workers who believe in fairness for all workers," the agitator said. "We must stand together! This card is your membership that says we're here for you and will protect you from the greedy businessmen and farmers. We'll demand a sustainable wage for all workers."

"They've made too much money. It's time they shared their filthy, ill-gotten money with the workingman. The result will be equality of all workers and owners! A coming together for the betterment of mankind. Our vision is clear as we move forward."

"At some point they have to realize they've made enough money and sharing will raise the standard of living for all people."

George looked for the free food before it was removed. Another union man got up and spoke of the strife between various factions of the Communist Party, Socialist Democratic Party, CIO, and of Roosevelt's New Dealers. He apologized for the mistake by the Communist Party that backed the Hitler-Stalin pact.

"Why would he apologize for the communists?" George wondered sarcastically and lowered his head, shielding his eyes from others' view and scanned the feet of the men assembled around the agitator and other so-called dignitaries there to speak against the state of America and her failed dreams.

The dilapidated Little Church of Hope was made of adobe bricks painted white. The flock was managed by Pastor Alexander who had been exiled from his church due to his less than popular views on politics, the economy, and of course, the mishandling of events unfolding in Europe.

Like his friend, Tom Collins, Pastor Alexander held a romantic notion of the way the world should be and did what little he could to assist in that cause, where and when he was able.

When it was Pastor Alexander's turn to speak, he asked the downtrodden men to look to Russia as their example. He droned on about Stalin's Communist Party, the robust Russian industry juxtaposed with the many cold and silent American factories. He railed against Hitler's fascistic, Nazi Party.

There was no mention of the genocide being carried out against the Russian kulaks, or the famine, and of course, order number 00447 entitling Stalin's Russian government to murder "enemies of the people" and "anyone deemed a harmful element." Of the murder that would eventually be found to rival the genocide undertaken by Hitler's Nazis, Pastor Alexander spoke not at all.

As he got in line to receive the last of the food being offered for the night, George thought it odd a pastor would promote the atheist nation as an example for the children of God. The pastor and four of the union's men helped serve the evening's meal. Once the last of the food had been scraped together and spooned onto George's plate, he moved to a chair on the edge of the gathering to better see the men's shoes. The pastor, again, approached the pulpit and thanked the union for providing the evening's meal.

"Truly the union is here for us all, as is the church. If only society could come together as we've come together tonight. Those who have, sharing with us, who have not."

It was nearly 9:45 p.m., when Tom Collins, spoke to the bored occupants in the church's pews. There was scant applause from men more interested in the warmth of the church and the hot meal. Collins proceeded with his lecture promoting migratory camps. He explained the idea behind the camp in Arvin and advocated for more camps.

Pastor Alexander allowed traveling men to sleep in his little church. He only required they do all the menial tasks that would fall to him if not for those working off penance or earning a day's respite. He was comforted when surrounded with like-minded souls.

The pastor used the church's donations to support his political causes.

George watched the interaction between the pastor of the church, the union boss, and Tom Collins. The unassuming veteran spooned up a large piece of fatty meat from his plate. He saw the big man as he came out of the kitchen with a sandwich not offered to the migrants and road tramps.

"Yakima! We meet again," He said to himself. A slight grin developed in the corner of George's mouth.

He winked at Roy, the big man, whose shoes did not match. George nodded to the barn-fighter and raised his cup of coffee to him. Roy looked away uninterested. George took the big man's measure as he sipped from his coffee.

George finished his free meal and deposited his plate and utensils in a tub to be washed. He wandered around the church, sipping from his cup of coffee, keeping an eye on his prey.

The union boss gave Roy a fistful of fliers to pass around while he explained the details of the upcoming Agricultural Workers Union strike on Waterloo Road.

The hungry, dirty, and tired transients sat through another lecture from one of the teachers from the high school as he explained how they, on the backs of the already destitute, would right society's ills.

All the requisite emotions were appealed to during the speeches from the lecturers. The fairness of factory owners and farmers keeping the lion's share of profits was questioned from the perspective of those who wanted more of what others had without having to do the work or take on the risks to earn it themselves.

"In a better world our ideas will prevail, I promise you, by any means necessary," the teacher argued. "We will not yield to the demands of the greedy corporations and factory farms."

No mention was made of the money Steinbeck would not be sharing as a result of his report on, and exaggeration of, the treatment of the migrants at the hands of the evil farmers. Three applications for union membership were taken.

Here and there, the filthy littered the front and side yard of Pastor Alexander's small church. Some staked out lean-tos in the front churchyard, away from the stink at the back of the church.

"Finally," George thought, "Your moment has arrived."

He watched the big man head to the back of the church's grounds to a line of men snaking out from a single outhouse. Roy pushed into the surrounding bushes upwind from the line of stinking men. Outside the periphery of the church's backlights George was hardly noticeable in the evening's dark.

"Oh, excuse me. It's kind of dark back here ain't it? I didn' see you there big man," George said. "Almost peed on your leg."

Roy looked over his shoulder and peered down on top of a hat and, like most, paid the smaller man no attention.

"I'll be done here in a minute. Tie a knot in it," Roy commanded.

"It surely is dark. No moon shining down on us tonight, is there?" George asked. "Scary, huh?"

"Seems strange, a man can wake up one day never realizing that the sun which would soon set would be his last."

Roy paid the derelict no attention. His lower lip hung lower than usual as he concentrated on peeing.

"Like you, for example. I bet when you woke up today you never once gave the warmth of your last sun a second thought. Now your last day is done and that opportunity is lost to you, for eternity. Isn't it?" George asked.

"Go away." Roy frowned.

"Say," said George, "Don't I know you?"

"I don't think so."

"Why, sure I do. I saw you up in Washington a couple of years back? You're a fighter aren't you? That was some fight. You survived."

"Yeah, well I'm retired now, workin' for the union."

"Yes. That's a good thing." George paused. "I mean you retiring and all. Then I saw you and that union man talking over in a Hooverville, outside Sacramento, just a few weeks ago, too, right?"

"Might o' been," Roy said.

"We move around a bit. We do a lot of talkin' around the state; mostly the Valley, now. You seen me fight, huh?" Roy enjoyed the notoriety. "We're with the AWU. You got your red card?" Roy asked.

"Are you crazy! Always have my red card," George lied.

"That man cut you to pieces up in Washington. I didn't think you would survive the punishment that man dealt you."

"That was nothin'."

"Scary, is what you are, sir. My goodness!"

In the darkness George relieved himself next to Roy. "Now, weren't you and those other union boys, back in the church there, down in Madera just a few days ago?" George asked.

"I did see you folks! Down in Madera the other day, pickin' apples, wasn't it? Boy what a mess. You know, someone killed a man, down there? Kind of like the mess you boys are about to start up here with the canneries and farmers . . . Waterloo's gonna be the next drawer you all shit in, isn't it?"

Roy finished and turned towards George in the darkness. The tone of his voice changed to a guttural monotone, more like a growl.

"You got the wrong Joe, brother. You ought to go back to the church, where it's light and a lot safer." Roy came to an abrupt stop by George's next words.

"Indeed. It is dark tonight. I'm sure you know the saying about the dark before the light."

George finished. He shook himself and buttoned his fly. "My, that is better," he said and turned to face the barn-fighter. George took a deep breath, as a man about to start an arduous task.

"It's about to get even darker for you, cousin," George said.

"What?"

"No, no. I have to tell you, now, I feel I have the right fellow." George pushed his hand into his pocket.

"You're the sonofabitch who threw the empty kerosene can the other night at my friend's farm, aren't you? Then you headed back to the road where your partner was waiting for you. What's his name? Where is he? I would dearly enjoy talking with him."

"You don't know nothin', little man. You don't know what you're talkin' about."

"I found you by those fliers you passed out at the migrant camp where the railroad and the river meet, you know, down in Madera. They're blowing all over Madera County. Surprised the sheriff didn't pick up on that. Well, that, and of course, your boot prints, if I'm to be totally honest."

"Watch your mouth little man. You don't know nothin'."

"That may be," George said, "but I do know from watching you walk around tonight, the soles of your two boots don't match, just like the boot prints at my friend's burned-out barn. Same size too. Curious isn't it? Is that curious to you? Because that seems curious to me."

Roy's musky smell hung in the cool autumnal air. His breath was sour and smelled of alcohol and stale cigarette smoke.

"Your breath is kind o' smelly, if you don't mind me saying."

George achieved what he had sought. Roy lashed out with his big right hand. George ducked as the greater part of the big man's blow grazed the crown of George's head and knocked his hat off.

"You little bastard!" Roy growled, "I'm gonna fuck you up!" The big man leapt at George with his fist held high.

George saw the big fist balled before him. As the bigger man's arm came down in a pounding motion, George moved to block Roy's right forearm.

A blur of lightning-quick motion. George's knife glinted off the lights of the church. The little man made a swift wave with his hand. The butterfly knife cut deep under the arm of the bigger man, severing the large artery and tendons.

His right side started pumping blood before the big man realized the fast, little man had just killed him. Roy's arm curled in his darkening shirt. He looked at George oddly and lunged. George took a step to the side of the bigger man. With a backhanded motion the knife blade sliced through the larger man's trousers and severed the tendons behind Roy's right knee. Roy grabbed at the nearby shrubs for balance then fell forward with the thud of a bull beaten in the ring.

The veteran quickly moved behind the bigger man and poked the fingers of his left hand into Roy's eye sockets and pulled the man's head up. The wounded animal groaned. With one quick pull of the knife the veteran relieved the larger man from his mortal obligations and his servitude to his union handler.

George whispered in Roy's ear. "Bert was a good, brave man. I sense your life has been quite difficult and your future prospects don't look good either. I'm releasing you from this bitter labor." George wiped the knife clean on Roy's shirt and tucked the big man into the shrubs.

The history teacher's lecture was finishing up. The crowd slowly faded into the side yard and front of the little church.

The veteran ducked into the bushes and was lost in the night beneath the overpasses and through the alleys of Stockton; just one of the one million migrants blowing up and down the San Joaquin Valley.

He slept, covered in newspapers, in the park, among the army of migrants and fruit tramps who had come to California in search of treasure and who had found only fool's gold.

Shortly after noon the next day, a truck pulled off the Golden State Highway and came to a stop at the entrance to Sequoia Park.

A small man with small round glasses asked the driver, "Headed to Madera?"

"Exactly where I'm headed. You got family there?" Joseph asked.

"Yep! The best kind. An old Army buddy lives down there. Has a farm."

"Says he might have some work for me since all my work here is done."

George folded, then laid, the newspaper so the article of the previous night's murder at the church showed.

Joseph nodded his understanding that George had taken care of the business they had discussed.

"You know, you watch a man fight, sometimes he lets you know what his predilections are, Joseph. It wasn't hard work, but it was honest, the good Lord knows. God gave some of his angels weapons for a reason."

George leaned back his head, which within moments rested, cradled between the back of the truck's seat and the passenger door that felt like a large cotton boll.

Joseph looked to his long-lost friend and wondered at the events that had taken place in his life since they had last seen each other. Joseph thought of the German photographer who had taken their photograph standing onboard ship after a nasty three-month fight in the jungle.

Joseph looked at the bloodstain on George's right hand and coat sleeve as he rested peacefully, a thoroughly worn soldier.

32

The sheriff's car came to rest at no particular angle in the gravel drive. Florence wiped her hands on her apron, after putting her dusting rag in her apron pocket. She pushed her hair into place with the back of her hand and repositioned a bobby pin while she checked her look in the mirror by the front door.

"Well, hello, Sam. What in the world brings you way out here?" Florence smiled and waved her right hand above her head.

"Hi ya, there, Floe!" Sam looked around Florence for Joseph, "What are the boys doing today? Up to no good, I reckon." He smiled.

"Joseph and the boys are out cleaning the gardener's cottage, by the pond," Florence said. She herded the sheriff into the kitchen.

She loved company and catching up with what was going on in the world, or at least the county. They spoke of Ethel and discussed her options now that she was alone. Floe told the sheriff of Joseph's old friend and army buddy, George, who had arrived out of thin air only a week or so earlier, *deus ex machina*.

"Name's George. Looks like he may be staying a bit. A little down on his luck, you know? Joseph says he works harder than two men and would trust him with his life."

"That's a pretty good reference."

"Boys should be back any time. I'm fixing food now. Do you have time to share a meal with us? Have a cup of coffee while you wait?"

The sheriff took off his visored patrol hat and took a seat at the kitchen table. He stretched his neck from side to side. "I always have time for your cooking, Floe."

"The times have changed. How people can come in here from all around and raise so much trouble is beyond me. The last few years have been a lot of work."

"I've seen them blow up and down the valley. Some of them get quite angry when you can't help them out." Florencee thought better of herself. "I mean, not all of them, but doggone it, anyway."

"Here." Florence poured coffee for the sheriff. "We'll fix all the world's problems right here and now, by golly."

"Tell me, how's Ethel getting along?"

"She's doing about as well as anyone could expect. Plans on heading up north, Grass Valley. Has family there. She's gonna stay for a while, figure things out. We'll look after her place while she's gone. The boys are going to clean up the mess from the barn fire."

The men came from around the barn. Dashiell stopped to gather eggs from the chicken coop as they passed. The men took turns pumping water, one for the other, while each washed away the sweat and dirt from himself. Floe had left towels on the table that also held soap and brushes. Dashiell gathered up the collected eggs in his fedora and, along with his grandfather, headed to the back door.

"Wonder what the sheriff's doing here," Jack said.

The pump handle George was working stopped pumping water. He swallowed, and looked over his shoulder and down the gravel driveway.

Joseph stopped. He slowly rose from his washing as fresh-pumped water ran off his head and face to his shoulders and back. George and Joseph looked to one another.

"Morning, Joe Mac, Dash, Mr. McCracken," The sheriff said as the men hung their hats on the peg at the back door. The sheriff eyed George.

George only glanced at the sheriff as he passed and tipped his hat.

Feet shuffled on the wooden floor as the men jockeyed for position around the small kitchen table.

"Sheriff, this is Mr. Root, uh, George, George Root. He and Pa were in the army together," Dashiell offered.

The sheriff and George exchanged handshakes and glances before George took the seat closest to the door that led to the back porch and freedom. The sheriff enquired as to George's particulars with a few preliminary questions regarding his origin, where he'd been, and his plans.

"George is a friend, Sam," Joseph said, defending George.

George felt the heat rise within his clothes and hoped his sweat would not be noticed. He answered the sheriff's questions in a stoic tone.

"I'm more than happy to answer the sheriff's questions, Joseph." George smiled his trademark, toothy smile. Joseph had given him a chance to prepare himself.

"Well, I lost my farm a few years ago; went back to the bank. Banker said I had to keep growing. He says to me, 'Just add those implements onto the mortgage.' Problem was, when I couldn't make the payment on the mortgage, they came after my farm, not the implements I couldn't pay for." George shook his head at his bad luck.

"Both parents are dead. That's why I joined the army and where I met my friends, Joseph and Bert."

Turning to Joseph, "We were really something back then, weren't we Joseph?"

Joseph nodded and sipped at the coffee Florence had brought to the table.

"You see any action?" Sam asked.

Joseph intervened and looked to Dashiell, "Well, all the stories we talk about while we're out hunting by the river and whatnot," Joseph said. "Ol' George here was with Bert and me all the way."

"Joseph and I spent a few years traveling around together while in the army. Bert was with us," George said. He sipped his coffee. "Damned shame what happened to ol' Bert. I wish I could have seen him one last time."

"Please excuse my rough language, Mrs. McCracken. I confess, I must not know what it means to be civilized."

Joseph and George shared a few stories of being in the Army with Bert. They spoke of Bert's courage and the work he was doing at his place and his plans for raising chickens. The veterans shared the obligatory stories of being drunk and of doing stupid things.

Dashiell listened intently to George's stories, some of which he had never been allowed to hear before.

Florence set out bread, butter, and a small jar of Dashiell's honey. Joseph spoke of their plans for working together and the future. They talked of what Ethel planned to do with the place, now that Bert was gone.

The men dug into the coffee and bread. "What brings you out here Sam? Have you heard anything on Bert's murder? Did they find the men who did that?" Florence asked. She placed a serving bowl of chicken and dumplings on the table.

George looked to Joseph while buttering his bread.

"Yes. As a matter of fact, I just read the police bulletin from Stockton this morning about a fella who fits the description." Then, looking to the men, "Remember? I told you we went down to the river where all those undesirables and drifters camp out and ran the lot of them out of there. But, as I said, the fellas I was telling Joseph about, those fellas who we suspected did this, were long gone." George pulled his butter knife across his bread.

"No one was talkin' to us about where those union men were off to. So, I put the word out. I wasn't hopeful."

"I thought, well, maybe they headed to San Francisco, you know. So I call a friend, works for the SFPD, and tell them what I'm looking for. Man says they haven't seen anyone fits the description of the man with two mismatched shoes." The sheriff took a sip of coffee.

"Then he tells me what it is he's lookin' for. Asks, have I seen him." The sheriff looked at George. He tells me, says they're looking for a man. He gave me a good description too, who cut the ear off the police chief's cousin in broad daylight with about fifty witnesses watching. Man works for *American Concrete and Pipe Company* or something like that, up there."

George felt his heart stop. Joseph stopped breathing and looked at George.

"In broad daylight, really?" Joseph asked the sheriff while looking at George.

"Yeah, Imagine that. Broad daylight," Sam said, looking at George.

"Well, anyway, little bit ago I get a call from the police up in Stockton. Said they found a man yesterday, a big man, wore size 12 shoes. The soles of his shoes didn't match. Sheriff said he looked like a professional fighter from his scars, cauliflower ears."

"Did they arrest him?" Florence asked.

The men stopped their eating and drinking. Sam looked at Florence.

"Uh, no." The sheriff took a minute to finish chewing.

"Anyway, someone cuts the man three ways from Sunday. Police said it looked like a pro. Just made a mess of him. Killed him behind a church, of all places, where the union men had gathered to lecture and feed the hungry families."

"Imagine that. A church!" George said.

"At a church? Really?" Jack asked.

Florence pressed the back of her right hand against her mouth and busied herself around the kitchen.

"Imagine someone going up against a big man like that?" The sheriff shook his head in contemplation. "Must have been a scraper himself, you know?"

"Got something on your sleeve there, Mr. Root."

George slowly moved his right hand under the table. "Hard telling what that is. There's always some kind o' killing needs to be done on a farm."

The sheriff looked from one veteran to the other. He shrugged. "Somebody cut that man like a watermelon. Seems the fella with the knife did us all a favor."

Joseph nodded. George sipped his coffee.

"You reckon that was the guy that killed Bert?"

"I think so, Joe Mac. Funny, two knifings close together like that. Strange, huh?"

"Any idea who took out the fighter up in Stockton? Any leads, yet?" Jack asked.

"Maybe he was in one of those fights those fellas get paid for, you know? Did you say he looked like one of those barn-fighters?" Joseph asked.

The sheriff took a sip of coffee while eyeing George.

"No idea who it was. Not a clue," Sam said. "My guess is they'll never catch that fella. There's just too many people running up and down the Valley. It's easy for some of them to just blend in, get lost in the crowd."

"Justice will be done," Jack said.

"Why, I wouldn't even know where to begin looking. Doesn't fit any of the folks around here. Been doing this for almost thirty years. Never knew of a knife man around here before now," the sheriff said.

"Looks like you probably could use a new pair of glasses. Those round frames are nice. You sure stand out in the crowd. Pretty scratched up I'd guess, from all your traveling around." Sam said.

George removed his glasses to inspect their condition.

"You folks know anyone like that?" Sam looked to George. "How 'bout you, Mr. Root? Sound like anyone you could identify?"

"Not a soul, sheriff. Sounds thoroughly dangerous to me. The likes of which I would shun, sir. I'll probably have nightmares just thinking about him."

Joseph slowly shook his head. "Not me. Not that I recollect, anyway, Sam."

Changing the subject the sheriff continued. "You boys get all those apples to Frisco, did ya?"

"We did," Joseph said.

"Heck, you boys might have run across that man's killer, yourselves. Didn't you go that way, up through Stockton? How do you like that new bridge that takes you into San Francisco? It's a dandy, I bet."

Florence stood at the kitchen sink and listened to the men over her shoulder.

"Best dumplings ever!" Sam declared.

"Well, Floe, Joseph, the reason I came out to see y'all today was not only to tell you of the body up in Stockton. I got another little problem," the sheriff said.

George, still in survival mode, slowly moved his hand resting on his leg to just below his knee and inches from the boot that held his razor. Joseph noticed the slow conscious movement of George's right hand.

"George, could you pour some more coffee there?" Joseph asked. "Thanks."

"I know you all have had quite a time here with Bert and all that's been going on. I'm truly sorry. A situation has come up I needed to come see you all about."

George's face drained of emotion.

"There's a young lady, name's Martha. She's staying at a boarding house in Fresno. Sheriff down there, name's Ben, says she needs a home. Fresno PD put out the word. Good girl and all. So, Ben was talking to the owner of the Chicken Pie Shop and your name came up. He called me, gave me the particulars, and was asking about you, so I told him."

The sheriff stuffed a lump of dumpling into his mouth.

"I told him you and Joseph been lookin' for a young lady to help ya'll around here and that I would trust you with my own. Said he thinks he might have found just the one you been lookin' for. Hard-luck case, Ben says. We'd hate to see her end up in some orphanage or state home."

"How old is Martha?" Florence asked.

"She's thirteen . . . no." Sam scratched his brow and searched his brain. "Hell, I don't know. Fourteen, I think. I was in Fresno transporting a burglar and petty thief. Stopped by Ruth's boarding house and met her."

The sheriff grinned remembering her. "Cute kid."

"Oh, dear. How long has she been in Fresno?"

The sheriff swallowed a lump of chicken. "Not sure. Few weeks maybe."

"If you want, I'll call Ben as soon as I get back to the office and tell him you'd like to meet her."

"Whatever Floe says."

Florence acknowledged Joseph with a smile.

"What's she like? What happened? Where are her parents?"

"Just another hard-luck case," the sheriff said. "She and her brother took off looking for their pa, I guess."

"There's a brother too? Where's her brother, who should be lookin' out for her?" Jack asked.

"Can she read and write? Any police record?" Joseph asked, rising from his chair.

"Oh, sure!" The sheriff then looked perplexed. "Uh, oh. I guess she can read and write. No, Joe, she doesn't have a record." The sheriff looked to Florence and rose from his chair.

"Brother's dead. Fell off a train. They retrieved his body."

"That's horrible! The poor dear!" Florence exclaimed.

"Whatever Floe decides, we'll go with. We just need a place to put her up." said Joseph.

"George just took over the gardener's cottage. He'll be working with us on Bert and Ethel's place until she decides what to do with it. You know? Cleaning up that mess the fire caused, the rabbit cages, and whatnot."

The sheriff looked to Joseph and the rest of the group with raised eyebrows.

"Good thing Mr. Root showed up when he did, huh? Plenty of work for him."

"You men go on and finish up getting that drafty cottage set up for George. I'll be needing you to help with the porch as soon as you're done. I want it shipshape for that young lady!"

The men milled about giving each other room, grabbing for hats, shaking hands. Florence was reminded of heavy animals stomping around on wooden barn floors, antsy to get outside.

Sam shook hands with George. "Welcome to Madera! Any friend of Joe Mac's is a friend of mine."

George tried to pull his hand away, but Sam squeezed tighter and looked into George's eyes.

"Get yourself some new glasses," the sheriff said. "Those won't serve you very well here." He made a quick glance at Joseph. "They're all scratched up!"

"Yes, sir. A very good idea," George agreed.

"You stay out of trouble, ya hear?" Sam said. "We won't have any problems." Sam nodded toward George.

"Yes, sir. You won't have a problem with me."

George was the first out the door.

"I like to hear that." The sheriff swatted his hat against his thigh.

Joseph and his crew headed out the back door and left the sheriff standing in the kitchen.

The men returned to their various chores and to painting the gardener's cottage for George. The work droned on for over an hour without a word passing between them.

Florence continued to ply the sheriff with questions of the young lady named Martha.

"I've already decided. She'll be staying in the sewing room, right off the kitchen here." Florence looked at the sheriff.

"I want her close in the mornings and evenings. A young girl needs family. She doesn't need to stay out in that drafty old cottage. Fit for a man, but not a young lady. Too far from the house." Florence moved excitedly about the kitchen cleaning.

The sheriff nodded and raised his coffee cup which contained the dregs of his now cooled coffee.

"Thanks! I hope she won't be a problem for you all." He absentmindedly took two steps then turned and gave Florence her coffee cup.

"Times are tough and if anything happened to me I would want someone to look after my family," Florence said, "We're all God's children."

"Well, Amen to that! You may have to put a little meat on her, though."

The discussion continued as the two walked towards the sheriff's car.

"I think we can get Martha out here in the next few weeks or so, for ya. The court you know? Takes time with all that paperwork and whatnot. You all will probably have to go to court too. I'll give Ben a call and set it up. Thanks! Tell Joseph and company thanks, too." The sheriff smiled.

"Whatever we have to do, we'll do."

"Sam, be a dear. Next time you're in the diner tell Millie I'll be in to get her order in a few days. Maybe I'll have a young lady to take to town and show off."

The sheriff raised his left hand, acknowledging her request. "I'll be there in the morning for breakfast. I'll let her know."

Floe remained standing at the bottom of her porch steps with her hands clasped around a bunch of apron as the sheriff turned out of the driveway. A thousand questions jumped around in her head. Florence would finally be getting the girl she had wanted for so long.

33

The foggy, grey mornings of the San Joaquin winters burned off slowly to reveal emerald-green fields, chocolate-brown, freshly turned earth, and a sapphire-blue sky.

Dew dripped from tree limbs and splashed atop the carpet of yellow, red, purple, and brown leaves. The orchard floor appeared as though covered in stained-glass. The harvest completed, the farmer and his orchard would rest a bit before the work of pruning was begun.

With the McCracken's apple harvest and court dates for Martha's guardianship behind them, the men went on a hunting and fishing expedition along the San Joaquin River.

They drank too much alcohol and sat around watching the tips of their fishing poles slowly bob up and down, their lines taut in the current. They hunted and trapped for a few days while they worked their way west along the south side of the river.

"Tell you what, George. You clean my fish and kills and I'll clean yours."

Joseph proceeded to spend his evenings cleaning and dressing George's takes.

"I'm surprised at you, Joseph. In your own backyard."

"May I pour you a little more J. D., Joseph?" George grinned. "I find myself with very little to do this evening."

Gigio prepared a soup of malva and dandelion weeds that grew along the river. He included carrots, onions, celery, and some seasonings from his tote sack. He seared wild boar steaks in a black-iron skillet with butter and mushrooms.

Dashiell collected honey from the beehives. He packed Mason jars with thick, heavy honeycomb. The jars were packed and sealed, then washed off in the river. They were then boxed to sell to the markets in Madera and Fresno.

Jack stayed behind with Florence and busied himself sharpening cutting tools for the upcoming pruning of stone and pome fruits. He fed the animals and enjoyed listening to Florence sing "Somewhere Over the Rainbow" while she was hanging out her laundry to dry.

After dinner they would walk to the end of their long driveway and back. Jack required a cane to steady himself. Florence wrapped her arm in his left. They took their time and when they returned to the porch after their walk Florence brought Jack a shot of bourbon. Jack told Florence what arrangements he wanted for his funeral. Florence helped Jack to his bedroom that had been moved downstairs to make it easier for him.

Florence removed all the belongings from the sewing room in anticipation of the men painting it for Martha's arrival.

Roosters and hens scratched around the freshly turned fields and crowed their approval of the cooler weather. The Creams put on winter fat and began to grow their winter coats.

George walked down to the river where Joseph was working, head down.

He shook his head, slowly. "Joseph, in your own backyard? Well, I suspect I am a bit hungrier than you."

34

Martha's story was not so different from the nearly quarter million children roaming America during the Great Depression. They seemed like rats, having no direction or destination. Those in the east moved west and those in the west headed east.

Martha's father left home, as did so many men, in search of work. Martha's mother, Lillian, was attacked by the drunken super of the tenement in which they lived. Lillian removed herself and her children from the filthy tenement, posthaste. They would settle in with an aunt and uncle of Martha's, her mother's brother, until their father returned from his sojourn.

Martha and Frankie marveled at the living conditions provided by their uncle and aunt and only then did they realize the dire straits of their existence in the humid, inner-city tenement from which their mother had sprung them. They were finally, at least temporarily, happy again. Martha enjoyed listening to her uncle talk about the family's history and his adventures growing up.

Martha felt mature being with the older women, helping her mother and aunt prepare meals, setting the table as if royalty was coming to dinner. When the dishes were cleaned, the family sat together and listened to their favorite radio programs and to Roosevelt's fireside chats. Martha's favorite radio programs were

Abbott and Costello and *Amos and Andy*. She was too young to enjoy *Girl Alone*, but listened anyway, with her mother and aunt. When not listening to radio programs, her uncle listened to music. The radio was always on.

Lillian took sick soon after one of the subsequent and smaller stock market crashes after the big one of 1929. The doctor, a tall, thin man with a handsome, white mustache, made many visits to their home to check on Martha's mother and her deteriorating condition. Martha's aunt and uncle would not talk to the children about their mother's condition and only said things would get better with time. Martha was too young to fully appreciate what that comment meant.

Martha's aunt became unhappy at the financial burden Lillian's illness placed on her. The doctor's visits were expensive, as were the medications Lillian required.

Shortly after Lillian's funeral Martha's aunt became angry at the inconvenience the two children imposed on her and the children's uncle. Martha's aunt, Ida Mae, withheld from the children the little money Lillian had given to her sister-in-law to take care of the children after she died. Ida Mae omitted having received the money and hid the money away, even from her husband.

After Lillian's death Martha and Frankie listened to their aunt and uncle argue through the thin bedroom walls. Ida Mae complained about what needed to be done with the two children that caused her financial burden. Martha's aunt was jealous of the attention their uncle paid the children. Ida Mae did not look at them and withheld all affection. When Martha tried to hug her aunt, searching for some small affection, her aunt pulled Martha's hands away and spoke about being too busy, now, with all the extra work and hungry mouths to feed. No eye contact. "You're too old to kiss."

Bill took Frankie on excursions into the city in search of work for the still young and skinny kid. Bill spoke to Frankie about joining the military and seeing the world, but he was still too young to join.

The children worked for their unhappy aunt and received no compensation for their labor. Their food portions were cut in half. Ida Mae explained there just was not enough to go around, though Lillian's death removed one plate from the dinner table. The doctor's visits and medication were no longer a debt.

Ida Mae instructed Martha to take in all the laundry and sewing for the family and that of the neighbors to whom Ida Mae sold Martha's services. Martha ironed her aunt's house dresses and aprons. Together Frankie and Martha enlarged the garden to grow more food for the family. The crops had just not come in yet.

Frankie brought coal to Ida Mae's neighbors that had fallen out of the gondolas or had been tossed down by the workmen in the railyard. He ran errands for his aunt's neighbors. He raked leaves and shoveled snow from sidewalks. Ida Mae hired Frankie out for any jobs she thought he could do for a few extra cents.

Martha's aunt would not be placated and argued that the Great Depression was created because of greedy people like Frankie and Martha, always wanting more than their fair share.

Ida Mae and Bill argued daily, it seemed. "I can't wait till those little sonsofbitches are the hell out of here!" Martha's aunt was heard to yell. Frank needed to be a man.

One particular night after a hard, and rather difficult, day in which his aunt had become exceedingly brutal towards him, and after everyone had gone to bed, Frankie decided to steal away in the night. He would no longer be a burden and the money saved would go to his sister. Frankie was still young and naive.

Martha, who was headed to the bathroom, heard her brother. He had his boots and jacket on. His bedroll was slung across his back and he was just pulling on his snap-brim hat.

"I'm going with you Franklin! You wait right here!" Running back to her room, to pack her few belongings, Martha ran into her aunt who was all of a sudden happy to help the children on their way. She even gave Frankie and Martha a little of the change Lillian had left for them, to help with expenses.

The road kids worked their way across America, catching trains as their father had. They caught rides in the backs of trucks. Sometimes riding in automobiles, a man would place his hand on Martha's leg as she sat between the nefarious driver and Frankie.

Their father's last postcard was from Fresno, California. The road kids headed west. Sometimes they walked for days and ate little or not at all.

They worked at whatever jobs they could to keep food in their aching stomachs. Once they worked for a farmer who allowed them to sleep in his barn. At the end of the week, the farmer told them to get lost and that he was not paying.

They slept in hobo jungles, in parks, along the highways under billboards, in barns, and train stations until finally, and after many months, they reached California. They had continually dodged predators who wanted to entrap the children as free labor or for sex.

It was in California where the latest tragedy played out for the young lady. The railroad police found Martha in a heap, crying in the crushed rock of the switchyard at the Fresno train depot. She became a ward of the court until it could be determined what to do with her.

"Here. See?" Martha handed the police officer the last post card her father had sent, over a year earlier, and told of him working in Fresno.

"No, sir. I don't have any other family," she lied. "My mother died and I don't know where my brother is."

The thought of returning to her oppressive aunt's home was unthinkable.

Ben Parker, from the Fresno Sheriff's office notified the Madera sheriff that he had a road kid that he thought deserved better than ending up in an orphanage.

"She needs a family, Sam. Fresno P.D. says she liked working on the farms and were just wondering if we knew of anyone that might be willing to take her in."

"Ol' Al, at the Chicken Pie Shop, told me about some folks in your neighborhood."

35

"Martha, Sheriff Parker is here for you, dear. Are you about ready?"

"Yes. Thank you!" Martha yelled down from her room. "I won't be a minute!"

Martha wrapped a box in one of her work shirts then placed the box in the bottom of her flour sack on top of her overalls. Martha looked back at the room that was as much a home as could be during the short time she had helped Ruth with the chores around her boardinghouse.

The early morning air was thick with moisture. Giant sycamore trees dripped dew on the sidewalk in front of the boarding house and sounded, to Martha, like fat raindrops as they splashed atop the squad car. Underneath the big trees pedestrians bounced around dodging the area on the sidewalk directly below the tree's canopy.

"Hello, Martha. How are you?" the sheriff asked.

"I'm fine, thank you." Martha responded.

A young boy walked by with two large bags, one in front and one behind him. The bags were stuffed with as many newspapers as a young boy that size could carry.

"Good morning, ma'am," the young man said to Martha. He handed six copies of the by-weekly *Fresno Shopper's Guide* to her as he passed.

She ran the newspapers up to the porch where Ruth stood.

"No! Don't you dare! I'll put one in their mailboxes. You have bigger things to do today. Thank you anyway, dear!"

Martha ran back to the sheriff's car.

Ruth stood on the wooden porch beneath a sign that read, "NO Musicians". The street lamps were still on. Martha struggled with the sack until Ben grabbed it up with one hand and deposited it in the trunk of the squad car.

"What's in here?"

"Everything I have."

"Oh, dear!" the widow, Ruth, yelled. "Hang on a minute there, Ben," and ran back inside the boarding house, leaving the screen door to slam shut. Within a minute Ruth returned with a sack of treats for Martha to share with the McCracken family.

"What a thoughtful idea!" the sheriff said. "Did ya think to make up a bag for me?" he asked cheerfully. He watched the women before him. "Course not. Why would a single guy want homemade cookies?"

Martha and Ruth hugged again. From Ruth, Martha seemed to derive strength.

"Good luck to you, baby! You be sure to stay in contact with me, 'kay? Of course you will." Ruth pulled Martha's sweater closed and buttoned the top two buttons.

"Don't give her room away yet." Ben said. He immediately regretted his comment. "I mean, Martha may decide this is not the family for her, is all I'm trying to say."

The widow frowned.

"I think it will be real nice for Martha. Sam had nothing but nice things to say about the whole McCracken family. Said Florence is one of the jewels of the Valley. A real nice lady, Martha."

"She seemed to be very nice." Martha remembered back to her first meeting with the McCrackens at the Fresno courthouse.

The widow gathered her shawl in her hands and protected her head from the falling dew. She gave Martha a thumbs up and smiled.

Martha pressed down her new cotton dress and admired her new patent leather shoes and white socks. Ben and Ruth were pleased with the work they had done cleaning up the road kid. Martha turned out to be much more fragile than the grubby-looking kid hidden beneath the road-worn, work clothes in which she was found in the Fresno railyard.

The collection taken up by Trudy and Al at the Chicken Pie Shop rounded out Martha's new wardrobe. There was even enough money for a new pair of work boots.

"You look fine!" Ben said. "Nervous?"

"I didn't sleep at all last night. And thank you both, again," Martha said. Her palms were damp.

Ruth and Martha waved as Ben hit the throttle and was gone.

"Well, mostly I don't know what to say. What if they don't like me?"

"They'll love you. Mrs. McCracken can't wait to have you stay with them."

"How could they not like you?" he asked rhetorically. "If you don't want to stay, thank them for their time and say you would like to think things over." Being mischievous, he continued, "Then you and I'll get up and back out real slow-like, see?"

Martha grinned.

"Give it some time, at least. They all seem so nice and look forward to you living with them."

"You don't have to take your things out of the trunk unless you decide you want to stay. We'll take a look around when we get there, but from what Sam told me, the place is beautiful. And hey, remember the Madera sheriff and I are going to be out to see you. It's part of the court order, if things work out, and you want to stay, that is."

Martha splayed her hands out in front of her then rested them on her lap, palms sweaty with anxiety. The middle finger of her right hand worked at the torn cuticle of her right thumb. She thought she might be sick. Ben turned onto Olive Avenue.

The two stopped in for breakfast at the Chicken Pie Shop and to thank Trudy and Al, the owner, for all they had done for Martha.

Martha disappeared in Trudy's bosom. "You better come back and see me, or I'm liable to come up there and paddle you!" Again, Martha was pressed into the folds of the big waitress's uniform. Trudy planted a big, red kiss on Martha's forehead.

After breakfast, coupled with promises to return and being squeezed by big Trudy, Ben and Martha stopped by the cemetery on Belmont Avenue, southwest of Roeding Park, to visit Frankie's grave.

Afterwards, the two headed into the country north of Fresno. On either side of the gravel road, as far as the eye could see, there was rocky, green land, suitable only for grazing.

The fenced land was littered with McCracken bald-faced Hereford cattle. Steers were scattered, like rough chips of cinnamon, in the pasture. In the distance, cattle dotted the rolling foothills beneath the snowcapped Sierra Nevada Mountains.

Shattered stained-glass littered the post-harvest, orchard floors. The trees, having carried their fruit the entire season, rested.

Groves of citrus, ready for picking in a few weeks, reminded Martha of ornaments. Yellow and orange citrus gave way to giant, naked walnut trees planted up close to the McCracken farm house, harvest completed.

Large-leaved malva weeds, used to store moisture in the ground for summer use by the walnut trees, were nearly two feet tall.

Flood irrigation and the large canopies of the walnut trees reduced the ambient temperature around the perimeter of the home and barn during the sweltering, hot Valley summers. On the north side of the McCracken home, row crops of every variety had been planted and alternated according to a four-year crop rotation. Freshly turned Hanford loam, in tight rows, rested. Joseph and his father watched the temperature, the seasons. The weather was the orchestra, the McCracken's were the conductors, coaxing a little here and a pinch there.

At the far eastern end of a long field, Ben saw men wearing light-colored, broad-brimmed hats above lightly colored shirts rolled to the elbows. The farmers worked teams of large, white horses, the likes of which Ben had never before seen. George worked the horses and used large chains to rip tree stumps from the ground. George and Dashiell then cut fruitwood for warming fires and stacked it on their wagon. The rest would be piled into a large bonfire to be burned later, when it had dried. Granite boulders that posed a threat to and impeded the plow and harrow were blown out of the ground with dynamite.

Ahead on the gravel road, Ben could see the beginning of the rolling hills and granite boulders that began the ascent to Coarsegold, Oakhurst, and finally to Yosemite Valley.

"Now, just as you drive past the oranges and lemons, you'll come to two giant palm trees on either side of a gravel driveway. Drive between them. That's their driveway," Sam Westfall said into the land based radio in his office.

"Roger!" Martha said into the microphone, or lamb chop, as the sheriff called it.

Ben smiled. "Tell the sheriff we can see the palms and can take it from here, deputy."

"We can take it from here. Over." Without releasing the press-to-talk button on the lamb chop, Martha remembered, "We can see the palms. Over."

"Roger," the sheriff replied with a laugh. "You'll be fine, now. Can't miss it." The radio broke squelch then came on again.

"Oh, Ben, make sure they have those meat eaters under control before you get out of the car. They'll make a mess of you," Sam said.

"Have you ever had a dog before?" Ben asked.

Martha frowned at Ben as they let the radio play die.

"No. The super didn't allow us to have pets in our building. Besides, they kinda scare me."

They came to the driveway of the McCracken farm, between the two tall palm trees. The sheriff turned east toward the mountains. The travelers found themselves on the gravel driveway under the limbs of mature walnut trees whose branches met in the middle and lined the driveway to the McCracken home.

"I've been driving by this place my whole life and never turned down this road. Never thought about who owned this property. Always thought the guy across the road back there watched over it for some rich dude in San Francisco."

Martha rolled the window down and stuck her hand out. She enjoyed the cool breeze against her hot, sweaty hand.

"Wow. It's really big," she said.

"Wow, is right. This is a nicely guarded secret, for sure."

The squad car came to a stop in front of a beautifully maintained two-story, white clapboard home with black-shingled roof. A battleship-grey porch wrapped around the home and allowed for viewing the sun rising and setting. Comfortable, almost feminine, sitting areas awaited company and a cool beverage.

"You wait here. I'll see if anyone's home."

As Ben stepped from the sedan two beasts bounded from around the house.

"Holy shit!" Ben's immediate thought was that the animals charging were wild boar. He jumped back into the vehicle and slammed the door.

"Roll your window up!"

"What is that? What are they?"

"I don't know," Ben exclaimed, drawing deep breaths.

The growling, baritone barking, surrounded them. Ben and Martha watched the beasts from within the security of Ben's squad car. Three mastiffs continued barking and circling. Large front paws weighed down the front, right fender. One of the beasts, then the other, shook slobber over the hood and windshield and barked at the intruders.

"Oh, my goodness!" Martha exclaimed.

"They don't seem mean, just big!" the sheriff said. He frowned at the mess the dogs were making of his car. "And slobbery!"

"I'm not getting out!"

The dogs sniffed the passenger and driver side windows and left foam running down the glass.

"Yuck!" Martha exclaimed

"Out!" came the command. The dogs trotted over to the house and took up residence on the porch and watched the visitors to their farm.

Jack looked upon the sheriff's car awash in dog spit and mumbled under his breath, "Holy, shit. Now you've done it."

He approached the two visitors and beckoned the officer to come out, that it was safe.

"I hope you don't have bad news for us, officer." Jack moved closer to shake hands with Ben. "McCracken. Jack McCracken." He looked into Ben's eyes for the direction the conversation might take.

"Names Ben. Ben Parker, Fresno County Sheriff's Office." Jack and Ben shook hands. "Is that yours all the way down the road too?" Ben asked. "This is really somethin'. One of the nicest places I've ever seen."

"It's one of the oldest in the valley."

"Those are beautiful horses."

"Creams. American Creams. Working horses and damned scarce, I'd wager."

"I brought you a visitor, Mr. McCracken."

"Oh! That's right. Today's the day we finally get to meet!"

Jack waved Martha out of the car as Ben kept watch on the dogs.

"It's okay. You can come out. Don't mind them; just guard dogs.

"My name is Jack McCracken and you must be Martha Yeats! I'm sorry I didn't get down to the courthouse to meet ya'll, but I'm so old I hardly make it down the driveway and back anymore." Jack shook hands with Martha as he balanced himself on his cane.

Jack noticed Martha's apprehension about the dogs.

"That big one's Diesel. That one's Kanga. And that little monster is Axel. He's all play!"

"They must be what, a hundred pounds or more?" Ben asked.

"Diesel weighs in at about a hundred and forty pounds. The other two are still young. 'bout eighty to hundred or so, each," Jack said.

Ben took a minute to take the dogs' measure.

With her arms folded in front of her, Martha moved between Ben and the squad car, seeking protection.

"Well, it's sure a pleasure to make your acquaintance, young lady," Jack smiled.

"So, uh, Mr. McCracken, Sam says this is a nice fit for all concerned, huh?"

"Sam was here the other day, yes, sir. I think everything is set up and ready for this young lady's inspection." Jack answered. "Floe, uh, Florence, that is. Florence is overjoyed about Martha coming here."

"I'm sure Martha is excited to get settled into her own room."

"Well, now, you'll have to talk to the boss of the place. I only built it, with my pa. I'm mostly retired now." Jack leaned on his cane. "Been thrown one too many times. Tired of smelling oat farts all day. I'm more a liability now, I reckon."

Jack straightened to stand a little taller, thumbs in his blue suspenders now. "Florence, my daughter-in-law, is the boss now. Runs everything. Apples to zucchini! What a woman!" he bragged.

At the top of the porch, Martha saw the large woman in a cotton work dress and apron. As the no-nonsense woman watched what was taking place before her, Martha watched her untie, then wipe her hands on her apron. The woman then roughly folded the apron and set it in a chair next to the front door.

Florence descended the steps in a powdery huff and granny shoes.

She pushed her wire-rimmed glasses higher on her nose. "It's okay, now. You can come out, dear."

Florence's voice was smooth and inviting. Martha thought Florence looked like a grandmother. "Martha! Finally! Thank heaven you made it out here! I'm so excited to see you again!" Florence noticed the lipstick kiss on Martha's forehead and thought it adorable. "Just lovely!"

Ben approached with Martha and kept an eye on the beasts shadowing him. He kept his right hand on the butt of his revolver as a precaution.

"Hello, Mrs. McCracken. It's good to see you again. I believe the Madera Sheriff's Office contacted you about us coming out today? I'm sure you remember this young lady."

"Hello Martha. That's a beautiful dress you have on. Matches your beautiful eyes." Florence smiled and hugged Martha as might a bear.

Florence grabbed both of Martha's hands and stepped back to look her over. Her hands were strong and reminded Martha of the butcher's wife back home, before her mother became sick.

Turning to Ben, "Yes, I've been expecting you, sheriff." Florence pulled Martha to her and squeezed again. She stroked Martha's hair and kissed the top of her head. Florence told Martha how sorry she was for all the troubles she'd had lately.

Florence dabbed, with her thumb, the tears welling up in Martha's eyes and hugged her even harder.

"Yes, officer. We've been anxiously awaiting this one's arrival."

"Martha! It's such a beautiful name! And aren't you just the prettiest thing I've ever seen?" Martha looked to Ben who looked as though he might start crying.

"Come on you two! Come in and let's get to know each other."

Florence grabbed Martha around the shoulder and together they climbed the stairs to the porch and front door. Floe held the screen door for her visitors as Diesel rose from his place on the porch. The brindle mastiff's chin rose six inches above the porch rail.

"You're kidding!" Ben exclaimed. "My god! That's the biggest dog I've ever seen!"

Martha was speechless and put Floe between her and the mastiffs.

Floe looked at Diesel. "He's just the sweetest thing."

"The men are all out working, sheriff. Out clearing a field, getting ready for plowing, and planting next spring," Jack said. He wiped his palms on the back pockets of his overalls.

"They've been working on that field for two years. Maybe this year, now we got some help. But the work, it never ends."

"Anyway, let's see if we can get them up here to the house to meet you, Martha. It's about time to eat."

"Come have a look at this young lady," Jack said. The two walked back to the front porch. Jack depended on his cane. Martha looked back to Ben for reassurance.

"Diesel! Get the boys! Go on, now! Go get the boys!" Jack encouraged the mastiff.

Diesel leapt off the porch headed for the field where the men were working. Behind Diesel, the two adolescent mastiffs, Axel and Kanga, bounded off barking and playing on their way to retrieve the men. Axel pulled on Kanga's collar. They tumbled into a ball of tails and legs. Gaining their feet, they playfully bounced into the distance.

Martha giggled and enjoyed watching the big dogs bound off to retrieve the men.

"Have you two had anything to eat, sheriff?" Florence asked. I was just fixing food for the men. We have plenty."

"Well, let me get a snack anyway and . . . ." Florence looked at Martha. "Milk, or do you drink tea?"

"Would you like to come with me, dear?"

"Yes, ma'am," Martha replied.

"From now on, you may call me Floe. We're going to be best friends." Florence took Martha by the hand. "You're practically a young woman yourself and I need a friend like you with all these men to take care of; like herding kittens!"

Martha took an instant liking for the older woman who wanted to be her friend.

"Let's pick out some cookies for you and some for the sheriff to take home."

"Hey, now! That'd be swell!" the sheriff said.

Floe and Martha went to the kitchen and put together a tray with tea and cookies.

"I've only had time to bake a few types of cookies. I like these gingersnaps and let's put a few of these shortbread cookies on there too. Joseph likes those the most. Dashiell will eat anything that won't eat him first. Which do you like, Martha?"

"I like them all, but mostly the chocolate chip cookies," Martha said.

"You know, chocolate chips grow on trees here in California. Just kidding!" Floe joked. She was happy to have Martha in her home and it was apparent to Floe that Martha was enjoying her first few moments with her.

The kitchen was immaculate. Martha had never seen one so well-organized and stocked. "The large plate for the cookies is right over there." Martha already felt at home and useful.

The two younger mastiffs, far off on the other side of a young pomegranate orchard, barked excitedly that the men needed to come home.

The two pairs of Creams snorted their anxiousness to return to their paddock. They were not agitated by the barking dogs that ran up to them and in-and-out of their legs. Joseph and George loaded dynamite and fuses into one horse drawn buckboard.

Dashiell loaded the pulling chains, single and doubletrees into the other wagon. He then unharnessed one set of Creams, removing the tugs, collar, and hames and loaded them into the wagon. George loaded the tree chains in the back of the wagon with a weighty thump. Dashiell drove the wagon loaded with equipment.

George trailed Dashiell's wagon and had his hands full controlling the stud, trying to keep him from taking off for the barn.

Joseph drove his wagon with dynamite a good distance behind the others as a safety precaution.

The men and beasts would return later in the afternoon and load the morning's cuttings and, if time permitted, they would start loading large chunks of granite that had been blown out of the ground to make way for the plows.

Ben searched the living room for clues of the family while Florence and Martha prepared the cookie plate. The home was simple, but large. The furniture shined and the floors were highly polished. Ben appreciated the heightened level of cleanliness.

He recognized it for a man's home. Animal skins and trophy heads decorated the floors and walls. There were two walls of books on just about every subject. Ben noticed the hunting and safari books that Ivor and Jack collected. There was a smell of tobacco. Decanters were set on a table opposite the fireplace and were full with bourbon, scotch, and gin.

"It all seems really nice, Martha," Ben said. "That's quite a collection of books, Mr. McCracken."

"My father taught me an appreciation for hunting and books."

"It's really nice here. I like it," Martha said.

"Thank you so much! That's very kind of you." Floe was glowing and thought she might burst.

"Well, young lady, Florence is looking for a smart, strong girl just like yourself. We would be honored to have you stay with us and be that girl. It's clean and you'll be safe here, child. Plenty of food too." Jack and Floe smiled. "Think you might like to give 'er a go?"

Martha was nervous. "I think I would, if that's okay with you folks."

"Honey, come here and give me a hug. I want to show you your new room. Do you have luggage, dear?"

"I got that out in the trunk of my car. I'll be right back. I have some paperwork for you folks, from the court."

Ben took the sack containing Martha's possessions to the room off the kitchen.

"Hey! This setup is better than my place!" he teased. What do you think, Martha?"

"I like it! It's so nice! Thank you Mrs. McCracken."

"Floe, dear."

36

"Say Dash," Old man Saroyan, the owner of the Madera Market, said, "How are you and your family?"

"Hello, Mr. Saroyan. Good. Lots of work lately with the harvests and all. Mom says we're taking the day off next Saturday. George has been swell. He's a farmer too. He and Pa were in the army together."

"We're gonna get started on oranges next week. I'll bring those four boxes next trip, if that's okay."

"Good idea. That'll be just fine, Dashie." Mr. Saroyan said. "I'm glad your father has found some good help. How is that young lady working out?"

"She's great. Really nice kid. She and mother are inseparable."

Dashiell pulled a dozen more produce boxes from the flatbed and dollied the crates to the back of the market, four at a time. He completed his next to last delivery.

Mr. Saroyan went through the boxes slowly, squeezing and smelling. Finally, he was convinced McCracken had served him well.

"What you make of this war goin' on, young man?" Mr. Saroyan asked.

"I don't really know. Old Europe's problem, I guess. I've read a little about Hitler." Dashiell chuckled. "Even the communists and socialists hate him. He must be pretty bad." Dashiell wiped his brow and neck with his handkerchief and replaced his worn hat on his head.

"Wait and see, my friend. You've never been out of California, have you? No, of course not." Mr. Saroyan patted Dashiell on the back as they exited the market. "You farmers don't have time."

"Poland, Germany, Austria, Russia, England, France," Mr. Saroyan shook his head, "They've been fighting for hundreds of years. Yes?" The old man looked weary. "It gets worse from here. Trust me." He signed for the produce.

Dashiell threw the dolly onto the flatbed and secured the last load.

"I came here through Ellis Island, you know, Dashie? I know about those people. That's why I come to America. They can all go to hell!" Mr. Saroyan yelled.

"They killed my entire family! My poor mother and father, my little sister. What harm can an old woman and an old man do? My sister, she wasn't even ten years old yet, Dashie!" Old man Saroyan's eyes filled with tears.

"America is greatest country in the world! Stay out of Europe's business. That's what I say. I come to California to get as far away from Europe as possible!" Mr. Saroyan's fists were balled above his head. "Ah, what do I know? I may be just an old man, but I know this will not end well, my young friend."

The men shook hands and Dashiell fired up the flatbed. He wrote the order for Mr. Saroyan's produce in his order book then replaced it between the back cushion and the seat of the truck.

"I'll get the order to you as soon as harvest begins. You take care Mr. Saroyan."

Old man Saroyan approached the cab of the truck. "Dashie," Mr. Saroyan said, "You're a good boy. You're a big, strong American boy. Be a good boy to your momma and papa. Don't smoke and drink like dem other boys over at the fountain, eh? Okay, Dashie?"

Dashiell smiled, "I won't. Thanks, Mr. Saroyan! See you!"

"Hey! Hey, Dashie! When we gonna start gettin' the rabbits again. It's been a while. I have customers." Mr. Saroyan ducked his head, "I'm just sayin' I need rabbit and fowl."

"I mean if a young man wanted to start a little rabbit business that might be a way to go, eh?" Saroyan referenced the loss of rabbit sales attributed to Bert's murder.

"I'll give it some thought. I'm not sure how I'd run an operation like that. Ma keeps me pretty busy."

"Start small, Dashie. Build from there. You could do it," Mr. Saroyan said. "If I had a son, that's what I'd tell him. What's happened, happened. We move forward."

Mr. Saroyan patted Dashiell's arm that stuck out of the truck window. "Hey, hey, nice sweet veggies, okay Dashie? Aw. You're a good boy!"

Dashiell pulled to the curb in front of the five and dime and unloaded the last of his produce through the back door of Kenny and Diana's five and dime and malt shop.

After unloading the boxes and securing the dolly to the flatbed that sat in front of the diner, Dash entered the malt shop as a customer and tipped his hat to the young people gathered around the door as he passed. He searched for Jennie who was helping her mother stock buttons.

Dashiell was greeted by a few catcalls from the young people. He waved over his shoulder, then slapped his gloves into the palm of his left hand, before shoving them into his right hip pocket.

A few girls sat up and looked over their friend's shoulders at McCracken the younger. Martha leaned back on her stool at the counter and gave the girls a sour look.

Dashiell noticed Martha was not impressed with the girls. He basked in her protection.

"Hey, kid. How's the malted?" Dashiell asked. He grabbed her and knuckle-rubbed her scalp. He then bent over and gently kissed her on top of her head.

"Those kids annoying you?"

"Well, mostly the girls. They keep staring over here, Dash." Again, Martha leaned backwards to stare at the giggling girls at the end of the counter.

Dashiell shoved his hands into the pockets of his worn, leather jacket. "Am I late?"

"Don't you worry about this one, Dash," Diana said. "If we close, you know where you can find her. Jennie wouldn't mind a little sister, either."

"Ma said I'd have to keep an eye on you two or Martha might disappear." Dashiell smiled and winked at Mrs. Smith. He gathered up Martha's bags.

"She's aces, Dash. What a doll," Jennie added. She brushed Martha's hair with her hand then pulled it into a ponytail.

"What are you reading?" Dashiell asked Jennie. He took the book Jennie had set on the counter and thumbed through it.

"Stoics."

"Nice. More folks should read."

"You can borrow it when I'm finished with it."

"Thanks. What else have you been doing?"

"We walked over to the newspaper and put in an inquiry, to see if anyone knew of a Herold Yeats and to contact us here at the five and dime."

"Good idea."

"Maybe we'll hear something soon, huh runt? Ready to go?"

Martha gave a thumbs up while pulling air through the straw at the bottom of her malted. She leaned across the bar and hugged Kenny and then Diana. She waved at Jennie.

"Maybe we'll see you later, Miss Smith," Dashiell said and winked at Jennie.

"You know where to find me, Mr. McCracken."

"I do. The library."

"Mm, this girl!" Diana exclaimed. She hugged her daughter. Jennie called him *Dashiell the Distractor.*

Jennie Smith was three years and one hundred and eleven days older than Martha. This information was determined when Martha had her first sleepover at Jennie's home. They ate feely from the family's malt shop. Martha drank two malted milk shakes. During the sleepover, she learned Jennie's feelings for Dashiell and she relished the opportunity to be a part of the intrigue that made up their relationship.

Jennie had always been an enigma to Dashiell. She did not hang out at the malt shop like most of the gang, she worked there. It belonged to her family. Asked to be the mascot at the high school's sporting events, Jennie declined. She was more interested in cerebral pursuits, like reading, and participated in spelling bees and debate. She was always reading.

Martha walked out of the five and dime ahead of Dashiell and curled her nose up at the older girls watching. Dashiell smiled at a couple of the teenagers and punched one young man in the shoulder on his way out.

The sun sat fat on the edge of the western horizon and glowed orange through the rectangular, back window of the flatbed truck. Martha liked the sound of the gravel beneath the wheels of the truck as the asphalt ended and the two farm kids found themselves on the unnamed dirt and gravel road that led home.

37

Root crops such as garlic, onions, carrots, beets, and greens were continually harvested on the McCracken farm, interspersed with the harvest of tree fruit.

Another winter brought the beginning of another citrus season; oranges, lemons, mandarins, and grapefruits. Martha was enjoying her new family and the community to which Florence had been introducing her. Jennie was her new best friend.

Floe and Martha prepared food for the men before setting out to visit with Diana and Jennie at the five and dime. From there all four would then continue to the church where the women's sewing circle was finishing up quilts to be raffled at the '41 Christmas bazar.

"Are you sure you can't come along, Dashie?" Martha teased.

"I'd rather have my eyes plucked out!" Dashiell responded.

"Dashiell! Don't talk like that!" Florence shook her head.

"Father, here's the food for whenever you men get hungry. A nice casserole and salad. Vegetables are in the pot on the stove. Pie's on the pantry shelf. It's your favorite."

"What a woman!" Jack shouted. "Martha, angel, you can learn from this princess right here!"

"Stop!"

"Go on, now! You girls be careful out there. It's gonna rain."

"We will. Let's go, hon," Florence said to Martha.

"Nice and easy, now! The road will be slicker than . . . ," then thinking better of himself, "well, danged slick! So, careful!"

Florence started down the driveway with Martha waving through the glass of the passenger-side window. Jack waved at Martha.

The men finished preparations for the packing shed to receive the incoming fruit. They checked the brushes and waxers they had experimented with the last few seasons that allowed them to polish the citrus to a high sheen with the hope the cleaner looking and brighter fruit would be more attractive to their buyers. The men tightened nuts and bolts, greased gears, oiled chains, and checked the water supply that would be used to clean the fruit and aid in removing bugs.

Sunset brought with it a kind of rain particular to the San Joaquin Valley and was more like a heavy, continual mist that made it difficult to see.

"I'm goin' in where it's dry and warm. I'll kick the fire up," Jack hollered to Joseph and George.

He then headed toward the house to wash up and lay out the evening meal Floe and Martha had prepared for the men's supper.

Dashiell gently placed the hens' eggs in his fedora. He gave each of the horses a can of oats and listened to his father and George ruminate on the state of affairs of the world. The big Creams ate their evening meal.

Joseph scratched his whiskers.

"'Get big or get out.' Isn't that what caused so many problems for farmers that ended up out here picking our fruit?" he asked George.

"Those winds sure enough destroyed the soil, Joseph, but only after they opened up all that topsoil with plow and disc, as the government men instructed. At least that along with too little rain," George said. "Farmers wrongly suspected that some politician, who'd never farmed before, knew more than them."

"We use irrigation. We won't have that problem here as long as we can keep water on the soil," Joseph said.

Dashiell dumped the last coffee can, full of oats, into the horse feeders atop the alfalfa. The three men headed back to the lights of the kitchen where Jack was setting out the evening meal.

"Boy!" George said. "I'm so hungry, I could eat the south end out of a north bound mule."

A low, black sedan stopped and idled at the entrance to the McCracken farm. A man in a dark suit got out and quietly closed the rear passenger door. The car slowly continued down the driveway toward the McCracken home. The mastiffs barked a warning that visitors were approaching.

Joseph was the first to see the headlights of the vehicle and thinking it was the sheriff, waved.

"Dang! I forgot to lock up the tack room," George said. "I'll catch up."

George did an about face and headed back to the now dark barn.

"Come along, dogs," he said to the eager mastiffs.

Joseph and Dashiell were caught in the blinding headlights of the car as it approached. The headlights of the sedan were not turned off.

Dashiell shielded his eyes from the bright headlights with his right forearm as he continued with his hat full of eggs. The driver turned on the vehicle's high beam lights. Joseph lowered his head and shielded the light with his right hand.

"Hey! What are ya tryin' to do, blind us? Turn those damned lights down!" Joseph yelled.

The slow-moving car came to a stop. The two driver's side doors and the front passenger door opened simultaneously.

"You don't like the big lights, maybe you should mind your own bidness, stay in the country with the other animals, plowboy."

Joseph and Dashiell had not made it quite to the corner of the house when they stopped.

"You know them?" Dashiell asked.

"I don't think so, son."

"Hey, blue jeans! You want to go to San Francisco and stick your big nose in everyone's bidness? Well, I'm here with my compadres to stick our noses in your bidness, big shot. How you like dem apples?" The pimp turned to his men. "Get it? Apples." The three enjoyed their laugh.

"You're the pimp from San Francisco," Joseph said.

"Well, pimp? I don' t'ink I like that term. I'm an independent businessman. I own a diner and manage entertainment," the pimp said from behind his driver.

"Almeda, you remember her, blue jeans? She sends her regards. She would have come," he snickered. "Get it? But she's busy working for me." The pimp smirked and traced the brim of his white, broad-brimmed hat with his finger.

"Dat's right farm boy. She's working for me now, tuff guy. She has a little problem with the needle. I'm helping her with it though. Know what I mean?"

"Is that the guy from San Francisco?" Dashiell asked.

"'fraid so," Joseph said.

"You need to leave." Joseph and Dashiell continued to hold their arms in front of their eyes. Dashiell balanced his fedora that held the eggs. Joseph could not tell how many guns there were. Their feet made no noise on the gravel driveway.

"Who's that with you? That your boy?" Manny, the pimp, asked.

"Get on your knees, farm boy."

Dashiell did not move.

The gun from the front passenger seat shot a round into the gravel, between the two men in the headlights.

Manny and his hired guns chuckled. "I tol' you, boy. Down!"

"You plowboys don't hear so well, do you? Must be all the bullshit in your ears."

Dashiell stood his ground, his senses peaked. He looked right to his father.

Jack was prepping the evening meal when he heard the noise. He knew the shot was not from one of their guns. The caliber was too small. The lanterns in the living room had not been lit as Jack had only made it as far as the kitchen. He moved quietly to the living room and saw the headlights from the car idling in front of the house, no more than forty feet away. He saw the three short men standing on either side of the sedan with the high beams on. Raindrops were illuminated in silver as they fell before the sedan.

Jack moved to the mantle for the sawed-off shotgun that rested, upside down, in the rack above the fireplace. He broke the Lefever side-by-side in half and chambered two rounds of birdshot from the box on the bookshelf next to the fireplace.

Jack peered from the side of the window and saw the three men still standing beside the idling car. Gun smoke emanated from the passenger side. Jack could see the two men on the driver's side had revolvers. He quietly opened the screen door and stepped gently onto the darkened front porch.

The right barrel exploded. What shot did not hit the two men on the driver's side, skidded across the top of the sedan and pelted the face of the man on the passenger side of the car.

Dashiell dropped his hat full of eggs. He and Joseph quickly ducked behind the house. Once behind the first cover they could find, without a word, they moved along the side of the house to the back door.

Birdshot ripped through clothing and flesh.

The pimp and his driver lie crumpled on the ground, groaning. The birdshot blew out the windows of the vehicle and slammed the driver into the side of the sedan before he fell to the gravel driveway. His revolver lay beside his still body.

The pimp took most of his shot in the upper left shoulder and bottom part of his face and neck. His flesh was more pelted than shredded, but he bled. He rose to his feet, then fell into the backseat and moaned for his associates to come to his aid.

The face of the gunman on the passenger side of the car was blistered with stray pellets. He gathered himself up off the gravel.

From a crouched position he looked through the sedan toward where the shotgun blasts had come. All was dark.

From Jack's position on the darkened porch, grey smoke wafted into the night rain. He had already stepped back into the concealment of the porch, out of sight of the gunman on the far side of the sedan.

The gunman turned his attention to the two men who had been stranded in the headlights of the sedan. They were nowhere to be seen. The gunman moved behind the front, right tire of the sedan. The car's engine idled. The passenger's ears rang from the gun blasts. Blood ran down the side of his head and neck. He searched for his gun.

The gunman could not hear the dogs come from behind, encouraged by George, who had taken the dogs behind the home.

George loosed Kanga and Diesel on the lone threat then followed the dogs to the back of the vehicle.

Kanga tore into the gunman's arm while Diesel went for the gunman's flailing legs.

"Dios mio! Help! Get 'em off me!" He screamed for Manny, anyone to help him. He swung fruitlessly at the attacking dogs in a vain attempt to protect himself. Nearly three hundred pounds of angry mastiffs were too much for the screaming, little man to rise. The dogs latched on and shook their heads vigorously to tear and maul at the flesh of the threat. Axel whined for a part in the attack, but remained beside George.

Jack stepped out of the shadows on the porch and moved to better watch the dogs work at tearing the man apart. The man's legs flailed as he continued to scream and kick.

Dashiell and Joseph came through the kitchen. Joseph grabbed the pistol belt with two Colt revolvers from the bookcase that held the shotgun shells. Simultaneously, they opened the cylinders of the revolvers to check the rounds as they made their way to the porch where Jack had been standing.

"Coming out, Pa! Coming out!" Joseph yelled.

"Coming out!" Jack responded.

The pimp groaned. He held his neck with his left hand as he lay bleeding on the back seat of the sedan. His white hat, pocked by pellets lay in the yard. His revolver lay cool on the ground outside the vehicle. Rain drops beaded on the blue-black metal.

"Stay here, son."

Joseph approached Manny, the pimp, from behind his Colt revolver and secured the man's weapon.

George took the peashooter from the gunman who had been checked by the mastiffs. George palmed the .32-caliber Smith and Wesson and noted how feminine the pistol felt.

"Mr. Mac, can you take Ax for me? Thank you, sir."

The pimp attempted to rise from the backseat of the sedan while holding his neck with his left hand.

Even in the rain, the air smelled of black powder and cordite. George was in full-war mode as he walked around the back of the vehicle.

"I got this, Sergeant Mac." George patted Joseph on the shoulder and reached into the sedan to turn off the vehicle's headlights.

"Out!" The Civil War veteran commanded the dogs to disengage from the shooter on the passenger side of the vehicle as all went dark. He pointed the Lefever two inches from the man's nose.

George reached for the knife in his pocket.

The veteran grasped a handful of the pimp's trouser leg and pulled. George cared not a whit that the pimp's head slammed atop the gravel as he was pulled from the backseat of the sedan. Thinking of his recent exploits, George folded the knife and returned it to his pocket. He held the gunman's weapon in his right hand.

"You can't come in here and threaten this man's family."

Tightening his fingers around the gunman's revolver, he grabbed the pimp by the front of his shirt and raised the man's head off the gravel driveway. George was bent over the man and it appeared as though the veteran reached for something high up and behind himself. George brought the side of the .32 down with all the strength he had on the left side of the man's head, sending him back into the wet, crushed rock.

Joseph winced at George's cruelty and moved to gather up the pimp who lay crumbled in the driveway.

"George?"

George stopped and quite softly spoke to Joseph.

"Joseph, I mean to take care of this situation for you and yours. Now please. I have work here that I need to attend to."

George could not see the man's face well, but could tell from the dark sheen that the man was covered in his own blood.

"Get up!"

The pimp was not cognizant of what had happened and pain had not yet entered his consciousness.

"Get up, or I'm gonna shoot you in your face!"

Dashiell stood, unable to move, shocked as he witnessed his friend, George, the good, the veteran, at work.

"Dios mio! Don't shoot!" the bloody pimp begged as he slowly rose to his feet.

"Dash, grab me that pistol over there." George said and pointed to the driver's revolver. George stuffed the gunman's small revolver into the waistband of his trousers.

"George?" Joseph cautioned.

"We're good here, right?"

Dashiell handed the driver's .32-caliber to George.

"All good, Sergeant Mac. All good. There's only three of them," George said.

The hired gun slowly rose from the passenger side of the sedan, clothes torn to shreds by the mauling mastiffs. The thug held onto the car door to steady himself. He looked over the roof of the sedan at the farmers that surrounded him.

A shot rang out against the sound of the idling engine. The gunman, who had raised his head just above the roof of the sedan, was driven back by the force of the round from the driver's revolver piercing his skull. He fell, in a heap as his legs gave out.

"Why Joseph, in all the confusion, I believe the driver, tragically, has shot his friend. Quite by accident. Same fellow that first shot at your very own father who then shot back in self-defense." George shot another round into the night sky. "Tragic."

George walked over to the driver and replaced his revolver in his right hand. He then walked around the vehicle and squeezed the man's hand around the pistol grip of the .38, then shook it from the man's hand.

Dashiell continued to take in the action before him.

With the driver and passenger dead in the driveway, Joseph said, "This piece of shit looks like he might make it though."

Joseph inspected the broken face of the pimp. "He's gonna need to get to the doc's soon."

"I would venture to say, Joseph, he's gonna need a lot more than a doctor. Probably ought not make any long-range plans, either. May I have that peashooter, Joseph?"

George grabbed the pimp by his nappy hair and turned him towards the driveway entrance.

"What are we doing here, George?" Jack asked. Dashiell and Joseph stood by, idling at a high rpm for what might come next.

George grabbed tightly at the oily hair on the back of the pimp's head.

"We're making sure this never happens again, sir." Then looking back at the pimp, "Aren't we, you shit stain?"

"George, we don't need this, it's over. Let the sheriff take care of it," Joseph suggested.

"No trouble at all, Joseph. Happy to help, old friend. My life should have been over years ago. You saved me, Joseph. I will use my borrowed time to do good deeds."

"Dash, could you kill the engine for me?" George asked as if they had been working under the hood of the sedan on a Sunday afternoon. He checked the rounds in the pimp's revolver and locked the cylinder in place.

"They came prepared to deliver lead, it seems," George observed.

Dashiell looked to Joseph then reached into the sedan to pull out the throttle and turn the ignition key on the dashboard off.

"Start walking. Say one word and I'm going to shoot you. Is that clear my friend? One word and you're done. Believe it. You don't want to test me."

The veteran shoved the pimp toward the rear of the car. "Walk." he commanded.

"There's nothing down there," Manny whined.

"Ah!" George knocked the pimp on the back of his head with the butt of the revolver. "I said not one word. Last time you'll be told that. Walk, very carefully so we don't have a mishap." George poked the pimp's revolver into the back of the man's head and pushed the pimp down the gravel driveway toward the road.

"Not one word, now," George whispered melodically.

The veteran and the pimp left the three men at the house and walked slowly into the night's rain. The dark walnut trees dripped with fat rain drops. Within a moment the two men were enveloped in darkness.

"Who's that?" George said aloud. "Who's out there?" he said louder.

"All your compadre's are dead," He tightened his grip on the pimp's hair. "You're gonna be dead too if you don't come out with your hands up!"

George poked the pimp in the back.

"Not one word now. Shush. I mean it," he whispered.

He matched the pimp step-for-step. George then held up and let the pimp continue limping down the driveway on his own. Silently, George ducked into the walnut trees and continued to pace the pimp from the back side of the trees. The pimp hobbled down the driveway.

All was silent except for the pimp's footsteps on the gravel driveway.

George saw the flash from the muzzle of the handgun. He took quick aim where the flash had come from and returned fire.

The men waited. A shot rang out in the darkness immediately followed by three others.

Joseph and Dashiell took up a position behind the engine block of the car, Colts at the ready. Jack returned to the living room. As a precaution he reloaded the Lefever and moved through the kitchen and around the north side of the house to catch the shooter with a flanking shot once Joseph and Dashiell distracted the lone gunman that might approach.

George found the fourth gunman across the driveway, dead at the base of a walnut tree. The pimp was dead in the middle of the driveway. George squeezed the .32 caliber into the pimp's hand.

The men continued to quietly wait. The rain came down harder. The pimp's car sat ticking in the driveway, doors opened and dripping with blood and rain. The mastiffs remained agitated on the front porch, whining for a part in the kill.

"All clear!" Came the voice of assurance the men were waiting for.

"Coming in!" Jack hollered back.

"All clear!" Joseph and Dashiell shouted simultaneously and looked at each other. The two rose together and looked at each other again.

The men gathered between the pimp's vehicle and the front porch.

All eyes were on George.

"Those two desperados shot one another, I believe," George said coolly. "However, it is raining and hard to see tonight. I'd like to think they would be better shots in the light of day. The poor dears. They just weren't used to hunting at night. We'll have to forgive them. It's all so confusing at night. And scary."

"How'd you know?" Dashiell asked.

"Well, seeing what terrible shots they are, and with their horrible hunting skills, why bring only two guns?" George asked rhetorically. "There was an extra window seat for the lucky soul that wanted to come along for the ride."

"They must have shot each other by mistake in the dark when the pimp turned and ran, after being shot by Mr. McCracken, here, in self-defense, of course, sir." George said.

"Imagine that," Jack said.

"Tragic, is what that is, sir."

38

It was late in the evening when Florence and Martha were returning to the farm after attending the church sewing circle and dropping Diana and Jennie at home. Martha had fallen asleep about a mile out of Madera.

Up ahead, Florence could just make out a number of red flares that cautioned all vehicles to slow down. Flares were dropped perpendicular to the road. Behind the flares a sheriff's vehicle sat with the red emergency light flashing, headlights on.

Florence came to a stop and was met on the road in front of Bert and Ethel's place by one of the Madera County Sheriff's deputies.

"Yes, ma'am. There's been some gunplay at your place. The sheriff is there now with the investigators."

"Oh, no!" Florence exclaimed. "What's happened?"

"It looks like an attempted robbery. Mr. McCracken said we should stop you from going up there."

"How is my family?" she asked anxiously.

"The McCrackens are all fine." The deputy looked away. "Looks like the robbers were shot. They didn't make it. We'll go up and tell them you're here."

The vehicles coming and going from the farm were in no hurry. The four bodies were loaded into the coroner's wagon and taken to Fresno.

The men were questioned one by one. All agreed the rain and darkness made it difficult to see and therefore none of the men were sure what exactly had taken place.

"It was just good fortune for us they were all bad shots and knew not how to maneuver in the darkness," our veteran reported. "Just plain lucky none of these fine people were injured once those gangsters started firing in all directions."

"Is that the best you got?" Sam asked George. "You know, death and mayhem seem to have visited California about the same time you arrived."

"Those men came here with guns to do great harm to our friend's family, sheriff. We are all fortunate the women were gone for the evening."

"Yes, sir. That's the best I've got."

"It was, plainly, too dark for anyone to see for sure what was happening with all those men firing their pistols in all directions. And it was raining. Write that down. It was raining real hard and must have been difficult for them to see. I'm sure you can imagine, sheriff. I kept my head down the whole time so as not to get shot myself. I will confess, I'm a bit of a coward."

Sam's face was flat and showed no signs of emotion. He closed the notebook in which he wrote his scarce notes.

"Joseph?"

"It was dark, Sam."

"Do any of you have anything of substance to add to this?" Sam questioned the men in frustration.

"I think they were gangsters looking to rob us and who knows what else they might have done," Jack opined.

"Really, Jack? You too?"

The sheriff and the team from Fresno went over the crime scene for weapons, shell casings, and other evidence of the attack on the McCracken farm.

The sun began its ascent from behind the Sierra Nevada Mountains. The tow truck drove past Bert and Ethel's place headed to the McCracken's farm to retrieve the pimp's sedan and passed the coroner's wagon going in the opposite direction.

It was a full day before the sheriff and coroner's office had finished their preliminary investigation.

When the investigation was finally concluded it was determined that the two men at the end of the driveway must have shot each other by mistake in the dark and confusion. The slugs taken from the bodies were from the other's weapon.

The sheriff's report concluded the gunman on the passenger side of the sedan was shot by accident when the driver attempted to shoot the dogs that were mauling his accomplice.

Jack had shot, in self-defense, when the passenger pulled his gun on the Civil War veteran, just before the pimp turned and ran back down the driveway, after being shot.

After the Madera sheriff's investigation team had completed their investigation of the crime scene, Floe and Martha were allowed to return to the farm. It appeared as it had when they left for Madera the previous evening.

Dark coal-colored clouds drifted overhead throughout the cold and wet morning. Rain continued to fall and washed the blood from the gravel driveway in front of the McCracken home. The mastiffs sniffed around in the driveway for remnants of the previous evening's kill, tails wagging.

39

Dashiell pulled the flatbed, loaded with fresh farm produce to the curb along Madera's Yosemite Avenue. Martha hopped out of the truck to do some small Christmas shopping with the money earned working with Floe and to visit with Jennie. Martha pulled her collar up and tucked her head into her winter coat to warm her face. She pushed open the door of the diner as Dashiell crossed the street to the park. He surveyed the congregation as he walked.

Lonely and drunken men napped under old grey blankets and newspapers, or Hoover blankets as they were called. Men talked in small groups. Dashiell pulled down old postings of past harvests, then tacked up his flyer notifying men of the need for pickers during the upcoming citrus harvest. Men gathered around to read, some to be read to.

Dashiell noticed the large crowd gathered across the street at the five and dime. Young men waved him over. Dashiell waved back, pointed at the fliers he held high in his hand and continued up the street, posting his handbills.

A loud whistle got Dashiell's attention. "Hey! Dash! Get in here!" a buddy yelled from down the street. "It's War! The Japs bombed Pearl Harbor, Hawaii! They're attacking, right now!"

Silence greeted Dashiell upon entering the restaurant. Only the small bell chimed his entrance. People sat, petrified. The clerk from the feed store sat motionless at the counter; a cup of coffee inches from his lips. A lawyer, sleeves rolled just below the elbows, sat two stools down, hat pushed back on the crown of his head. A cigarette poked out from his lips. Smoke spiraled above his head uninterrupted. Customers leaned from their booths to hear the radio.

"Hey! Turn that up will you, Kenny?"

With her right hand, Diana clutched a rag under her chin. She had stopped in the middle of the fountain surrounded by the stiff patrons. She looked to the radio high on the wall for a clearer understanding of what she was hearing. Jennie stood, motionless, behind the counter with the box of napkins retrieved from the back storage room.

The speeding, anxious voice, ". . . Again, we interrupt this program to bring you this news bulletin! FLASH! Pearl Harbor, Honolulu, Guam, and Manila are now reporting attacks by the Empire of Japan!" The radio announcer continued, "I'm sitting up in the mountains and watching the aerial attack on Honolulu as it's taking place! It's a horrific site! Black clouds of smoke cover Honolulu as the Army and Navy return anti-aircraft fire. My God! Those brave men! Japanese dive-bombers, too many to count, weave in and out of the strafe. The Japanese are losing some airplanes. I can see them explode in the sky! My God!"

"Folks, this was a complete surprise attack! This is not a drill! I repeat; this is not a drill! Now, back to news central for further updates!"

No one moved. A spoon hit the floor in the quiet diner.

"Jesus Christ! I never saw that comin'," a patron said to his wife.

"I figured Germany, Europe, you know? Holy shit!" another man said to no one.

"By God, if it's war they want, then it's war they'll get!" a blind veteran from the Great War said to no one in particular. "You cain't lay down for these sonsofbitches or they'll eat you alive."

"Hey! Ladies about, sir."

"Huh? Oh, sorry, Kenny."

"Come on! This is nonsense! One of them Orson Welles stories, like he did a couple of years ago." The insurance man snapped his fingers and tried to remember, "What was it?" he asked aloud. "Yeah. That's it. *The War of the Worlds!* They're just trying to scare people. It's a gag, I tell ya!" the man said. He laughed nervously hoping he was right.

"A gag? Are you kiddin' me? Hitler just ran over Poland, Czechoslovakia, and France. And now they're looking at England! For Christ's sake, man, wake up!" a mechanic admonished. "Germany and Japan signed a pact over a year ago!"

"That Neville Chamberlain is a damned fool, I tell ya!"

"This ain't good," a fat, bald man grunted and looked into his plate of half-eaten food. Kenny frowned at the man's double entendre.

"It's *War of the Worlds*, not *The War of the Worlds,*" a teacher from the high school said with clear disdain for the uneducated insurance salesman.

"If we had just torn down our war industry, like Bertrand Russell said, other nations wouldn't have a reason to dislike us so much. If they no longer disliked us they wouldn't have a need to attack us. It's so simple. Why can't you understand that?" the teacher condescended.

"The Germans are simply taking back the Rhineland, it's . . . it's like their garden that was taken away during the Great War," she lectured.

"There ought 'o be a law,'" a plumber said. Kenny could not conceal his amusement. While pumping his thumb at the teacher, the workingman tossed a quarter on the counter.

"Oh, and you have the enlightened position?" she challenged, as if scolding one of her students, or perhaps her husband. She had an education and would not be talked to in such a common manner.

"Lady, have ya ever seen them war paintings from before guns were invented? They was killin' each other with pikes and hammers." The plumber turned to Kenny.

"Think how screwed up the kids are gonna be in eighty, a hundred years from now. My God! The year 2000! What's that gonna look like? The poor bastards."

"What do you mean by that?" The teacher was obviously offended.

"What I mean, lady, is that the Rhineland ain't no garden. It's their industrial area. It's where they make machines for war. Get it? It was taken away during the Great War to keep them from building up another war machine!"

"I was there, teacher. Maybe you should indulge more beyond those ivy-covered walls of your campus."

Turning to Kenny, "I gotta go dig a sewer line. See ya," the plumber said.

Dashiell and Jennie shared glances.

"Come on kid," Dashiell said to Martha. "We better get going. Dad and the others will want to hear about this."

The two shuffled to the door amongst all the rising conversations and clatter in the restaurant. Dashiell looked at Jennie who was looking at her father, Kenny, for answers.

Young men talked, boldly bracing their fears with big talk and speculation of what America's military response should be.

"Which branch of the military are you gonna join?"

"We bring you this news bulletin! Flash!" the radio continued.

Mr. Hashimoto, who grew nuts and grapes sat at the counter and looked around the diner for the patrons' response. He quickly glanced to Kenny and then to his plate of cooling food in disbelief.

"Hash, I don't blame you," Kenny said.

Mr. Hashimoto had been born in Madera. He went to high school with the other young men and women at Madera High School. His grandparents had migrated from Japan to San Francisco and were eventually drawn to the Valley because of the climate and growing conditions. There they scratched out what would become a successful family farm west of the McCracken's farm. The neighbors shared equipment, the latest technologies, and muscle to assure the other's success.

Mr. Hashimoto's parents had participated in the 4H club, the school's booster program, the Boy Scouts of America where Hash, as he was called by his friends, earned his Eagle Scout rank.

He had always felt like an American. The fact he was of Japanese ancestry never distracted from his patriotism or his friendship with the other multi-cultural citizenry of the county. He played baseball, went swimming, and participated in the school dances with his friends.

Initially, no one questioned Japanese loyalty to America. However, within three months Roosevelt would issue Executive Order 9066, interning Japanese Americans in camps.

The Japanese community in the Valley was shattered. They would pay the price for others', foreigners' mistakes, their loyalty and patriotism thrown into question and expressed through judgmental eyes.

Mr. Hashimoto paid for his meal and quietly left the diner without making eye contact with his friends and neighbors.

40

December 8, the United States declared war on Japan. December 11, 1941 was a grey day. The temperature was a cool fifty-five degrees with a slight five-mile-per-hour breeze. Joseph and George were cutting lettuce to fill orders in Madera and Fresno when Floe and Martha returned from Madera with the most recent news.

Germany and Italy had just declared war on America. For miles around all eligible men, most everyone Dashiell knew, were signing up for the war. Young, freshly graduated high school boys, men from Madera, Fresno, and other small agricultural towns like Clovis, Easton, and Selma. Even fruit tramps, hoboes, and walking men stood in line to enlist. Men of all ages stood together in long lines, like the soup and bread lines, but with a different and much more lethal intent.

They talked of farming, sports. Some stood silently reading the latest edition of the news on the war.

Recruiters instructed the men and boys in the procedure of signing on with one of the branches and when to report to the Tulare Street train depot in Fresno for departure.

Within days of hearing about the bombing at Pearl Harbor, Dashiell told his father of his intention to join the Army.

"Your great grandfather, your grandfather, and I all fought. We all did our part so we could have this farm. War's no place for you."

"There are plenty of migrants around that need the work, Pa."

"We need you here," Joseph said. "Can't you see, if anything happens to you all we've worked for these three generations ends with me? Your mother can't bear any more children. Besides, there are exemptions for farmers. The war effort requires us to grow the food. That's our job now, son."

"I'm no hero, but I'm not a cripple, nor a coward. I just couldn't look anyone in the eye again if I didn't do my part. Besides, all the other guys are joining up."

Joseph stopped forking manure into a two-wheeled cart. "This is your part," he said.

A few short days later, Joseph sat on a wooden bench in the bay area between the horse stalls and his barn. The afternoon's slight breeze was cool as he worked the leather on one of the horse harnesses.

Dashiell pulled the pickup truck into the gravel driveway between the house and the barn. He gently closed the truck door then released the handle, not wanting to draw attention to himself. Joseph called out from the bay area.

"Hey Dash! You sound like some poor soul sneaked in after being out too late. What's up?"

Dashiell stood at the entrance to the horse bay.

"Hey Pa. Where's grandfather and George?" Dashiell asked to prolong having to tell his father the news.

"Pa, it's what I had to do. I have to go." Dashiell looked into his father's green eyes and saw an emptiness and a hurt he'd never seen before.

Joseph slowly stood and turned away. He hung the mended horse halter on an old, rusty hook fashioned and welded from two horseshoes.

Dashiell stood motionless and after some time, Joe turned and walked back into the light of day and gave Dashiell a hug and patted him on the back. Joe then kissed his only son on the cheek and put both his hands on Dashiell's neck.

"I knew you would. I've been regretting this day." Joseph said. "I did the same thing to your grandfather. I was just hoping something would come up that would keep you here, you know, like Jennie, maybe."

"Why don't you feed the animals? I'll go tell your mother."

"Thanks, Pa, but I'll tell her when I go in, if you don't mind."

Joseph examined his son who seemed to grow into a man before his eyes. "Okay, then. Good idea."

Dashiell hugged his father and watched a much older man trudge toward the home in which they had both been born.

Tears welled up in his eyes as he divided the alfalfa amongst the Creams. Dashiell dumped oats into the horse feeders from the old coffee can. He checked the water in the trough.

Joseph watched James and Floe talking with Martha from the corner of the house. "What a difference that young lady has made on Floe," he thought. "God, I love that."

Martha learned much from Florence her first months living with the McCrackens. She went to town with Florence to learn the retail shops where she conducted business.

Martha was introduced to Floe's friends at the hair salon, then Mr. and Mrs. Smith, who owned the fountain and five and dime, their daughter Jennie, Mr. Saroyan at the market, Gigio and Milly at their diner.

They drove to the post office and inquired with Mr. Highsmith, the postmaster, about Martha's father. They scoured the motels and flophouses in Fresno and Madera looking for Martha's father.

The two planned and enlarged their garden. Floe taught Martha to keep track of the canned vegetables and the money collected from their business venture.

Together they prepared meals and took the men food while they worked at clearing a far-off field. They ate in the shade of the giant live oak trees. Floe taught Martha how to feed and water the hens and to gather the eggs. Floe schooled Martha in all the subjects of which time on the road had deprived her.

Martha quickly became settled and comfortable with her new family. Florence had just begun teaching Martha how to crochet.

She even rode shotgun regularly with Dashiell on his deliveries and met the customers to whom they sold their produce and meat.

As Joseph approached, he watched Floe and Martha peel potatoes into a slop bucket on the back porch.

Joseph felt tired and rubbed the sore muscles and arthritic joints of his hands.

His father sat in the rocking chair made by his father, Ivor, almost a hundred years earlier. He sipped coffee made by Martha under Floe's guidance and listened to the women talk.

George prepared and lit the evening's fire in the main house and checked the blackout curtains. He brought in enough wood to see the family through the night.

Martha began her story as George rounded the corner of the house and started pulling a dark green tarp over one of the many windows.

"Getting chilly out here folks," George said. "Everything looks good, Joseph."

"Agree. This party will continue in the kitchen," Floe commanded.

"Don't be long, George. I'll have a drink waiting for you when you come in." Jack said.

"I like the way you think, sir." George slightly bowed.

George pulled his jacket closed as he walked to his cottage. The winter night air was brisk and bit at George's nose and cheeks. The three mastiffs followed close by.

George kicked up the smoldering fire. He pulled the blackout curtains of the cottage windows so no light would escape.

Along with Diesel, Kanga, and Axel, George headed back to the main house for the evening meal with his new family. The dogs stretched out on the back porch while George entered the kitchen from the back door.

Dashiell gathered the last of the day's eggs into his hat and slowly walked to the back door of his home. His father had not said anything, so he thought he might postpone telling his mother about his enlistment for another day.

The talk from the back porch continued in a huddle around the kitchen table. Joseph poured old number 7 as Jack spoke of his father, Ivor and his mother, Ti. Martha checked the potatoes boiling on the stove. Floe checked the boar sausage.

"Dashiell would you get a jar of green beans out of the pantry? That's the one. Thank you!"

"George! Come! Sit here," Floe said as she and Martha laid on the evening meal.

George took his assigned seat and Floe patted him on the shoulders.

"Isn't there anything I can help with?" George asked.

"No. Just sit, but thank you for asking, dear."

"Here ya go, George." Jack handed George two fingers of Jack Daniel's.

Floe cut the bread and was as happy as she thought she had a right to be.

"Martha, you were just beginning to tell us of your family, back home, how you came to California. You've had quite a life for one so young," Jack said. "Talk to us, child. Tell us about your adventures."

Her soft voice was like a melody, her story the lyrics; so clear and gentle in tone. Martha was at peace and happy living with the McCracken family and George.

She confessed, finally, to having an aunt and uncle. Martha told of her mother's cancer, and how her always-angry aunt turned on her and her brother. She spoke of the trials and hardships that she and her brother, Frankie, had endured while catching out on freight trains and meat trains in the dark. She told of working their way to the San Joaquin Valley, one meal at a time, and the long days that were sometimes between those meals as they traveled in search of their father.

"Where was it you say you were when you met that one-eyed fellow?" George asked. He had a vague recollection of having met one-eyed Jack while he traveled across the country to California.

"You rode on the coupling between two boxcars? For hours?" Dashiell asked.

"Well, that's just incredible! You poor child!" Floe was stupefied. "No one should ever have to live like that! It's just horrible. I'm so sorry for the difficulties you've had to endure." Floe hugged Martha.

Dashiell cleared the table while Martha and Floe started cleaning dishes in the large tubs that had been set on the stove.

"Well, I'm glad you made it this far, squirt," Dashiell said.

"Aw. Someone has to keep an eye on you in town," Martha joked with Dashiell.

"There's a story for you to write, George. Write about Martha."

Joseph and Jack agreed. "Add that story to your collection," Joseph said.

"Well, that certainly was incredible."

George turned to Florence and Joseph. "And thank you for a wonderful dinner, folks. I'm going to get the dogs in and get the fire cranked up."

George turned to Martha. "Thank you. I'm glad I've had a chance to hear your story." George turned to the family, "Nite folks! Thank you, again."

The chorus of "goodnights" rang from the family as George and the dogs descended the porch steps.

Kanga and Axel bounced and pulled at the other's neck. Diesel stayed close by George's side. The beasts enjoyed spending the cold, winter evenings sleeping before the small fire in the gardener's cottage with their friend.

George pulled his boots off, then poured himself another drink. He sat at a small writing table by the fire, warming his feet. He slowly sharpened a pencil with his knife and listened to the dogs' heavy breathing. He thought of Martha and her brother's odyssey on their journey west. George pulled his new, wire-framed glasses over his ears. Not a scratch on them.

The two skinny road kids, sixteen and thirteen, had hitched rides on fast-moving trains. They worked and walked their way across America during the Great Depression. They chased the setting sun in search of their father, now lost in the migratory masses that have descended upon the San Joaquin Valley.

"The little gypsies!" George thought.